APOCALIPSTICK

HELL IN A HANDBAG

LISA ACERBO

Enjoy the read!

Lisa Acerbo

TG Publishing Partners, LLC

ALSO BY LISA ACERBO

HELL IN A HANDBAG SERIES

Apocalipstick

COMING SOON:

Blush of Death

Liquid Foundation

Life is bad after the apocalypse . . . the undead just made it worse.

"My dreams pre-pandemic included a high school graduation party before attending college and marrying an attractive future lawyer. Instead, I'm praying for a long, sharp knife and a big gun to survive the undead." —Jenna

Jenna Martin lives in a world gone insane after a mysterious pandemic kills much of the population. Being alive after an apocalypse is bad, but it is made worse when the multitudes killed by the disease return ravenous for human flesh. Jenna, in serious trouble and pursued by undead, heads to the safest place available, a cemetery.

Ready to give up, she finds the strength to persevere for one more night and meets a group of survivors willing to take her in. The group caravans to Virginia, where they plan to inhabit an isolated inn called High Point, but the undead are always close behind. Packs of zombies, known as Streakers, attack, leaving Jenna and the other survivors battling for their lives and racing toward safety.

Once safely isolated at the inn, the group rebuilds society and Jenna begins a relationship with Caleb. Although he withstood the virus, he has not come out unscathed. He and some others now labeled the New Rave have changed into what many would call zombie kin—vampires.

Jenna's falls hard and fast for Caleb, which causes more problems than she ever expected in the fledgling society. But there are worse things than vampires and zombies searching for her, and *they* arrive at the inn's door ready for destruction.

To my daughter, Dominique.

Thanks to everyone on the DLG Publishing Partners team who helped me so much. Special thanks to Michelle, the ever patient editor and the amazing cover designer, Wren Taylor.

PROLOGUE

THE WORLD WAS UPSIDE DOWN and this boneyard a sanctuary —a flimsy metal barrier protection. Evil roamed the streets.

When the world had been normal, a cemetery was a place to avoid, Jenna thought as she scaled the fence, *Now it's my haven thanks to this locked gate. I'll take the small pleasure these days,* she reminded herself.

The oversized, mud-encrusted camouflage jacket she wore—fouled by stains of death—caught in the spokes and she teetered for a moment on top.

Her body seesawed before the crash, ground reverberating upon her hard landing.

A groan exited chapped lips. She bent and traced her already swelling ankle with dirt-stained fingers. Rolling it back and forth, the sad realization formed that survival had become a little more complicated.

With the first step, a sharp inhale stung her lungs before she huffed out the breath and limped into the hushed graveyard.

Pain be damned.

The overgrown, bleached-by-the-sun grass crunched

under each footfall. She'd never been so thankful the residents here died well before the coming of the pandemic.

Fallen headstones separated her from the crypt. A blinding sun against the horizon made it swim in her vision. Her ratty backpack itched aching shoulders and caused drops of sweat to roll down her back. She tugged the backpack close feeling for the container nestled within. That box was her motivation to lurch forward.

She studied the graves stretching before her in every direction.

"By the pricking of my thumbs, Something wicked this way comes . . ." Shakespeare unit in English class. A remnant of a life full of family, friends, and school long ago.

Gone. All gone. But they would come. Always did.

Three days searching for a safer place. Little sleep and less food. Sanctuaries few and far between.

The angels adorning the dead called to her.

Would she join their ranks, or would her fate be that of so many unfortunates?

Her scarred hand embraced the rough stone. Fingers roamed over the carved name.

"James Smith."

Was he really dead? Why not join him? *Lie down, Give up. End it. Time to die.* Words bounced like cannon balls and demanded reaction.

A scream formed, but Jenna swallowed it, jerking lank and greasy hair off her neck. The mocha brown tresses had once been a source of joy and pride. Now they were one more problem without a band to keep them out of her eyes. Finding an elastic, locating anything useful these days had become damn near impossible.

Don't despair. A promise to her mom when she was a teen. *That was three years ago but seemed like a lifetime.*

Wanting to live, Jenna hobbled onward.

A mass exodus of birds flying overhead and a flurry of leaves behind her, had her picking up the pace. Heavy heart ramming against her ribs, fear made instinct erupt and Jenna ran. And she didn't stop until stomach cramping, bile filled her throat.

Able to finally see past the mausoleum she'd first spotted, a small shack nestled behind it. Although a mishmash of stone and wood, it was enough, and she wouldn't have to bed with the dead as she would in the tomb. Jenna approached, tugging on the door, but it remained locked and sturdy even though the metal roof was pocked and rusted.

Skulking towards the side of the building, her hand shimmied across the wooden casing of a window. She reached to push it open only to have shards of broken glass decorate her coat sleeve. With the thrust of an elbow, Jenna knocked out the remaining glass.

She cleared the remaining slivers with her backpack before launching it through the empty frame and into the murky interior. Biceps screaming, she hauled herself up, belly pressing tight against the wood before she flopped inside like a dying fish.

Once nestled on the floor, tempted to rest, she focused on finding anything useful. It was the practical thing to do to keep the fear at bay.

A rusted wrench, hoe, and shovel sat propped in a corner along with discarded can of beans and a forlorn granola bar wrapper. The tools would make good weapons but were too bulky to haul all together. A salvage job. The wrench would work. The handle of the shovel could be dislodged from the base.

In addition to the tools, Jenna found a few matches near the charred remains of a fire littering the back wall. She hunkered down, shovel in hand, and began to ply the handle apart from the base. There was no telling how soon evil would arrive. Once her task was complete, she curled herself into a corner and fell asleep.

When she woke her vision filled with red. There was no time to scream.

1

8 MONTHS LATER . . .

Jenna propped herself against the ledge of the roof and huffed a breath. She'd completed her daily regime of jumping jacks, push-ups, squats, as well as some hand-to-hand practice.

A girl could never let her guard down.

She studied the landscape from the red brick, two-story building that had been home for the last two weeks. A large field and playground dominated the side, grass overgrown, a battered swing set in pieces on the ground. One main street in front of the building led into Johnstown, Pennsylvania, a former manufacturing community. Across the lane, empty homes with cracked windows, peeling paint, and boarded doors. The elevated roof of the two-story building on which she stood provided a clear view of the area and the small city would hopefully provide supplies and resources desperately needed.

She yawned with boredom and scanned the street. Her

eyes narrowed and her hand rose to shield them from the early morning glare of sun.

Like the trickling of a slow, muddy sewer on the side of a ditch, movement caught her eye.

"Streakers!" The scream scorched her throat.

The undead limped from the shadows. Bodies shuffled in and out of the heavy air, numbers hidden by the haze of heat. A corpse turned the corner of a nearby building, stepping into sight. Arm missing, the monster lurched forward. Mottled with decay, the dead woman wore a rash of pale gray skin. A few clumps of rot sprouted like mushrooms along its scalp.

The Streakers were broken and twisted, catatonic, but staggering along the road. One had all his limbs attached, but its face seeped off the skull like pus. An eye dangled by its nose.

"Streakers." Jenna's scream clanked and pinged around the roof like a pinball machine.

Ford, an agile middle-aged man who somehow managed to maintain a small paunch belly despite the end of the world, ran over and put a hand on her back, scooting close. "They found us?"

The teen twins, Eric and Billy, skidded to a halt at the ledge next to Jenna, leaning over to observe.

"They're an ugly lot," said Billy. He turned to his twin, playfully punching his rail-thin brother on the shoulder.

"You're an ugly lot, and the two of you need to take this more seriously." Jenna smiled at the tall, tow-headed boy to take the sting out of her remark.

Eric shifted position to protect his arm from further brotherly abuse and turned his blue eyes on Ford. "Can we fight today?"

The older man tilted his bald head and squinted. "They just came into sight. We don't have a strategy yet, but I wouldn't get your hopes up. We might pick up and go."

6

Billy pushed long, unruly bangs out of his eyes. "Sucks that." He peered at Jenna. "Put in a good word for us."

"Maybe. No promises. What do I get if I do? I'm not nice for nothing."

Billy and Eric exchanged glances.

Jenna chuckled, pushing away their awkwardness and surveyed the sidewalks and roadways, watching the zombie parade for a minute before pointing a gun at a desiccated corpse that had separated itself from the herd like a lost cow. The blast pounded. One of the monsters exploded, remnants flying into the air.

It was a callous joke by the survivors, calling the undead Streakers after the people who used to get naked and run through public spaces for protest or prank, especially because these creatures hobbled, shambled, and trod. The world no longer made sense, so why should their name.

"It's been nice to have the quiet. Guess that's over." Ford frowned into the horizon. "I was beginning to hope they wouldn't find us but here they are."

"Never hope." Jenna didn't take her eyes off the Streakers in the street.

Ford raised a hand to the sky like an actor on stage. "The sweet morning silence and quiet bird songs rang like symphonies. And yet you call the mumbling evil masses to us by shooting one."

"You are a poet, Ford. You should write that down." Jenna's green eyes turned hard. "Don't lecture me on using the gun. If they are this close, they've detected us already. I helped establish how many are around by taking one out and drawing them here. No lectures from you, old man."

The twins pushed away from the building ledge in unison, and one of them muttered from behind her. "The undead always find us. It doesn't matter what we do to keep them away or how quiet we try to be."

She couldn't tell who said it, they sounded so similar.

Jenna cocked her shotgun, aimed, but didn't fire. "We try our best but what will be will be."

More Streakers stumbled into sight, hugging the building, clawing at the windows and exterior walls. They'd find a way in, always did even if it took weeks.

She hoisted the gun resting on the roof ledge. "I'm going to get a plan in motion." Nodding at Ford and the twins, Jenna departed, heading downstairs.

Streakers threw humans into panicked action. Caleb's response would be different.

As if reading her mind, he met her in a dark pocket of the corridor.

"You don't need to warn anyone. The New Racers heard you shout from the roof and filled in the humans."

Jenna, as always when she saw him, squinted to ensure he was real.

A member of the New Race, he was an anomaly caused by the pandemic—strong in a time when humanity scurried like dirty vermin on a dying planet. And beautiful. He was so damn lovely. While the New Race were intoxicating, Jenna had serious concerns about their disposition, having stepped closer to the Streakers in nature if not in appearance.

With midnight black, shoulder length hair and unblemished, pale skin, Caleb radiated a movie-star persona, but those eyes.

Who has red eyes? What else has changed with the New Race? They can't read minds, can they? You've lived with them for four month so no. You'd know by now. Shouldn't be contemplating this just in case. Think about anything else. 1, 2, 3, 4, 5, 6.

She began to list the weapons needed to fight the undead. "I'll get ready." Jenna hurried away.

Exchanging the shotgun for a semi-automatic pistol from a stash of weapons, she checked to ensure it was ready and full of ammo.

Caleb inched close. "Good?"

A shiver itched her back. "Yes." The grumbled word escaped her lips, then she turned. "As good as a girl can get with Streakers beating down her door asking for a dinner date."

"You might want a bigger gun." The smile made him no less intimidating or more human.

"Not if we're inside. This one is accurate in small spaces."

He watched her, unblinking. His eyes spiraled into liquid pools of blood.

Creepy. Hate when that happens. Is he full of a dark hunger like the other humans say? How can there be an understanding between the races? Stop thinking about this.

He signaled them forward with a wave of his hand. Without the aid of lights, the darkened corridors of the former school were labyrinths.

She rounded the corner, and the crunch of glass bloomed loud underfoot.

"Keep it down," he joked.

It didn't matter if the Streakers heard them downstairs. The monsters would make their way inside no matter what, but her pride was injured.

Who was he to chastise her even jokingly? She shook her escalating emotions away. Fighting the undead did that. She needed to focus before the battle. *Can't blame him for the differences. I'm sure the freaking New Racers lost their social skills along with their humanity. They can't be all bad, right?*

Memories of the day in the graveyard when Caleb found her surfaced.

After long, fear-filled hours waiting for Streakers to attack, sleep had inched in and formed a cocoon around her.

Dead to the world, the fire burned to embers. In the smoky darkness, those intense, red eyes had been her awakening. A demon, she believed, had risen to claim her soul. When other voices encircled her, she'd brandished the knife nestled in the coat pocket.

Ford had knelt next to her, a gentle hand on her arm. He told her he was part of a group of sixteen people trying to find a place to settle. Water and food were offered. She'd joined them and they'd become her family, coexisting with the New Race, although at times tenuously. The pandemic that run amuck, bound humans and the New Race together for a chance at survival.

Faint footfall whispered from behind her and brought her back to the present. Turning, Jenna peered up at Quentin's sincere smile. Large and scruffy, his arrival reminded her of an endearing Golden Lab ready to show some love.

"Emma wanted me to give you this." He handed Jenna army dog tags and shrugged. "She said it was for good luck." Emma, who took care of the sick and the wounded, liked to play mom, but she was tough as nails and serious about her science and medicine.

Jenna accepted the gift, shoving it into the pocket of her jeans. "You know those healers and how they're into all that voodoo and mysticism."

Quentin smiled at her joke and Jenna felt a wave of nostalgia. He should be catching a wave not sending her off to battle with good luck chachkas. In another world, she'd be happy to join an attractive mid-twenties surfer with an I-don't-care attitude in doing exactly that.

What were they all doing here? How did this happen?

"Good luck." He merged back into the darkness.

"Thanks," she called after him before taking a step in the opposite direction. Another crunch of glass detonated under foot. "Damn it."

Caleb's smirk left her with an overwhelming desire to smack it away. How was he able to sidestep every obstacle while she flailed about, clumsy? All thanks to those gifts he never earned. Envy made the silence simmer between them.

Not a liability. The thoughts bounced through her mind. *Can't sell myself short.*

With the aid of a watery light seeping through boarded-up windows, his back her guide, they treaded forward.

A laugh tickled her dry throat, and she bit hard on her lip to stop it from escaping.

The march toward possible death continued.

If the Streakers weren't enough for the humans to deal with, the New Race had a liking for human blood. She couldn't understand them and their need to feed or their fate, one so different from the other survivors.

Those freakish red eyes. That's the least of the changes.

Biting harder on her lip, she attempted to clear her mind of the stress-induced gibberish running through it but couldn't.

Good news for her and the other survivors, the New Race in her group avoided leaving trails of lifeless, chewed up bodies. Yet, while she lived with the New Race, Jenna still clung to the belief they were kin to the Streakers. Mythology and lore had come to fruition. Vampires and zombies running amuck, and with them, death in heavy doses for humans.

The gun barrel slid down in her moist hand. The dog tags from Emma scratched against her thigh. As she trudged onward, only Caleb's back continued to guide her.

Where were Gus, Jackie, and Victor hiding?

At this point she'd even be happy to see George.

Maybe not George.

No one approached. Jenna had a sinking suspicion she was on her own with Caleb.

This is it. My fate is sealed. Pausing a beat, she listened for the thump of footsteps. *No one follows except death.*

She threaded her way from one dreary corridor to the next, Caleb in the lead.

The light grew brighter through slits in the wood nailed over broken windows, and Jenna stopped. She needed numbers. It would be imperative to their survival to know how many Streakers waited. Heaving back the end of a splintered board, the world outside came into view. An eyeful of roaming, bloated, sunken-cheeked zombies greeted her. Two already clamored close to the entry. Three shuffled listlessly, heads bent, mouths open as if lobotomized.

Sensing dinner, their disfigured, swollen faces and cataracted eyes swiveled in her direction.

The undead first spotted from the roof had multiplied. Seven stumbling masses of excrement, rot, and death waited.

"Not good." Fear knotted her voice.

Control it. Ask why it's only the two of us. Does he want me dead?

More Streakers would arrive, numbers multiplying, but they were stuck outside for the present. The group had learned a lot even since Jenna had joined. Lives lost early on because of attacks like this taught some hard lessons. Now, every place the faction settled had to be secured. There were protocols and rules. Lots of rules for survival. Fighting with only one other person was not on the list. Yet, here she was alone with Caleb.

She gazed into the street for a last look and sucked in morning air only to inhale the rancid smell of death.

Zombies scraped and clawed. Time to kill the living dead.

2

STREAKERS OUTSIDE SOUNDED like rats digging through a wall.

She'd heard the sound often enough and hated it.

Jenna didn't need to look through the window to see the undead clawing against the building, peeling their fingers, layer by layer, to the bone trying to dig through the brick. They were pressed together against the building like a stack of pancakes and shooting them with any accuracy would be near impossible while using up large quantities of scarce ammunition.

Inside, standing next to Caleb, it was gray and damp.

"Where's everyone else?" Jenna worried her lip.

"We don't need them."

"The two of us alone?" She double-checked the ammunition in the gun, fiddling with the weapon as she spoke. "You don't want more people here to help?"

"The Streakers are wedged against the building. Can't shoot them often enough in brain to bring them down. The group's ready upstairs and on the steps. They'll deal with them if they make it by me. They won't get past me." He brandished a machete.

"I'm part of this little entourage."

"They won't get by *us*." He emphasized the last word of the sentence. "I'll kill most of them as soon as they enter the main hall. I'm much more accurate than a gun."

"And with a much bigger ego. If you can take them, why am I here?"

"You're going to cover my back. Don't let Streakers make it to the stairs. We'll take them down together. In the unlikely case there's a straggler, the twins can practice their hunting skills on the leftovers."

"Be serious, "Jenna huffed. "I counted seven of them and two of us." She stepped into the expansive, main hallway of the school where a few steps away, mutilated faces and distended bodies waited.

"I don't want to risk anyone else down here."

"Except me." Her ponytail whipped when she shook her head to clear it. "I'm confused. Am I'm going outside? I could go out the back and catch them unaware."

They should've prepared before coming down. How'd she end up with one wall between her and the horde and no plan? She'd thrown survival lesson number one out the window all because it was Caleb in the dark corner of the hallway. Anyone else, she'd have been more rational, organized this whole little adventure out in detail before hitting the steps and standing before the double doors at the school's entrance.

"Not right now. You're better as my back up here. The entrance to the school is large enough that streakers can't back us into the corners. It makes sense to invite them in here where we're prepared and can spread out. There's only one staircase that hasn't been fortified and people are at the top waiting just in case."

"Outside we have even more room."

"There could be more undead around the corner." He shrugged as if discussing a raccoon tipping over a garbage can. "No one wants to send you outside alone and risk your life."

Jenna found the shrug irritating. "There are always more monsters." Her words turned clipped. "Clarify this brilliant plan for me, *please*."

"Letting them inside isn't optimal, but Streakers won't get beyond this room. Once they hit the shadows in here, they're body parts."

"They're already body parts. Nothing more."

"But they won't be walking, reanimated body parts."

She studied the entrance to the high school, considering the best tactical location. No corners. No stairs. Her foot planted on a torn, plastic banner proclaiming "Special Things Happen Here." She'd see if it held true after putting down some Streakers.

Those corpses wanted to wipe out the world by lunching on it. From all indications, they were doing a good job. Her mission since being rescued from the cemetery had become destroying every stinking, rotted moving undead bag of bones she could before they took her down.

A stacked jumble of long-toppled desks had decayed into rusted metal and splinters. They'd make a terrible shield. She turned to find some other form of cover, but Caleb blocked her view.

Peering into his eyes, she asked, "Am I worth losing? Is that why you made me come downstairs with you?"

He stepped back and studied her. "I'm not putting you in harm's way. Nothing bad will happen to you. There's only two of us so others don't get hurt. I don't want to accidentally slash one of the human with this. They won't heal like the New Race." The machete glinted in the little light.

"What could go wrong?"

"Not a single, damn thing." His chin angled toward the door. "Ready to start this little party?"

"I'll hang by the security office, but there's no cover or protection."

"After you open the door, bring as many down as possible from your position in the back. Anything gets by me that you can't shoot, run upstairs for help. Don't be a hero. What you don't slow down when the Streakers first enter the hallway are mine to deal with. I told the group to be waiting, but we won't call on them. You're the best shot."

She huffed and bit back a thank you.

He began to walk away but turned back. "If this goes awry, call for Ford."

"One minute ago, you said you had it under control."

"Please, Jenna."

"Fine." Jenna peered over her shoulder at the empty steps. "Don't miss."

"I won't miss the shot"—the words were clipped—"If I hit you, it will be on purpose."

"Kidding. I trust you."

She pursed her lips. *Sure, he does,* she thought. *He just brought me down to dazzle me with his almighty fighting skills. It's always a competition. Why can't he pick someone else to spar with?*

Caleb pulled her close and his frost-bitten breath made her dizzy. Their eyes met. "Nothing is getting into the gym behind us." He pointed at the door. "Good?"

"As ready as I'll ever be." She stalled, gathering the strength to do what she needed to. "Wouldn't you rather wait until after breakfast?"

"More will show if we don't dispatch them now. I have no idea how they communicate, if they do, but when one arrives, others follow unless we take them out."

He didn't get the joke. Always so serious.

Swallowing the fear, she drew away from him. No matter how many times she dined with death, the rot and decay were always unnerving. Only fools felt different. Pre-game jitters. She shook them away.

Images of the cliché female character running into or out of harm's way scampered through her mind. She'd loved scary movies growing up, especially when they'd been part of family nights with her terror-loving parents. The more gore the better for Mom and Dad. Then they became the evil, and this wasn't a movie. She'd never run even when the fight lasted until death.

A laugh climbed her throat like a spider on the wall. She squashed it.

Striding to the entrance, she tore away the wood. When the last board came free with a snap, the door reverberated from the weight of the Streakers pushing against it.

The undead shrieked and clawed and chomped. She hated the chomping teeth the most. The endless gnawing and masticating unnerved her.

From the shadows, Caleb said, "Get by the stairs and cover me. I got this. Don't put yourself in danger."

"It's not safe for you. It's daytime. I'll move after I open the door." She braced her shaking hand on the knob.

After a second of hesitation, Jenna pawed at the lock.

She jumped when Caleb's hand covered hers, stopping the turn of the knob clasped between her fingers.

Damn, he was stealthy.

"I worry about you."

Her lips became a dash and she refused to meet his gaze though she could imagine his intense, red-eyed stare. "I'm fine." Words erupted like a geyser. "If you're so worried, get more people down here."

"I don't want you to get hurt, but others will just be in the way. Haven't you heard the saying, *'too many cooks spoil the meal.'* All I'm asking is you don't put yourself in unnecessary danger like I've seen you do. I've got this covered."

Tipping her head, she processed the words, but fell back into the habit of ignoring him. She peeked through a crack in a close by, boarded-up window, focus shifting to the Streakers writhing like a mass of maggots outside.

The undead scratched and tore at the wood, trying to get closer. Their malfunctioning brains unable to grasp the idea of using the doorknob.

Jenna squirmed herself, coming to terms with the fact she had to let them inside to destroy them.

Caleb whispered her name, but she disregarded him. He caught her shoulder, pulling her close.

"Listen to me." They fit together like pieces of a puzzle. "Open the door and run. Be safe."

"Stop playing my dad." She tried to shrug away, but his tight grip refused to lessen.

Back off, she thought. *I scorn you, scurvy companion. Thrice-double ass.*

Damn, danger brought out the snark and the Shakespeare. "I'll be careful, open the door, and lead them to you. That's it. Then you do your thing, all right?"

"My thing?"

"Dispatching Streakers. Acting lordly. Our savior. Being the superhero."

"What do you mean? I'm none of those things."

"Whatever. I'll stay in the shadows and cover your ass from the rear. And, yes, I'll stick to your plan, whether I agree or not. My opinion obviously doesn't matter." She raised her eyes to his. "We good?"

"Yes."

His grin irritated her. Anger drove her to want to open the door and fight the undead. Still, she recognized that at the worst time ever, he aroused some deeper emotions. Obviously, the end of the world had left her without much time or opportunity for sex even when others in the group didn't seem to struggle with the same dilemma. It didn't mean she had stopped wondering about the carnal act. In fact, recollections of life and love crept in most when she could be dead in the next few minutes.

Reign it in. This is crazy. An apocalypse can do that to a person.

"Did you say something?" Caleb asked.

"No." *Shut down the stupid one-sided conversation. Talking to yourself makes you look insane. You don't want to appear that way in front of Caleb. Stop it. Focus.*

With Streakers trying to kill them, she couldn't go into a fight flustered. This little game of words was her mind's attempt to stop her from obsessing about what was going to happen in a few minutes.

"Focus, damn it." Jenna couldn't banish the ridiculous notions.

His eyes met hers and his words turned soft. "You are talking to yourself. Don't worry, I've seen you kick Streaker ass. You're a superhero too, but superheroes still need to take care. Someone has laundry duty tonight if I remember the schedule."

She watched Caleb's lips form words and considered what it might be like to nibble on them, hearing little of what he had said.

"Right." Heat rose the length of Jenna's neck.

Did he discern the recent moment of weakness about him? That's all it was, a stupid moment before she faced possible death. It was a normal reaction.

She filled her head with Rachel Platten's Fight *Song*. Remembering the lyrics, a damn miracle, but one that kept the focus on staying alive and ignoring Caleb.

"Ready?" Stepping around him, she fiddled with the lock.

The double doors cleaved open. Sunlight spread throughout nearly half the huge foyer. Sprinting into the gloom, Jenna found her place at the bottom of the stairs. The smell of rotten meat wafted inside with the shambling monsters.

Hoisting her weapon, she focused on the entrance. Her first shot went wide. She huffed a breath and steadied the gun in shaking hands.

A streaker, flesh ravaged and shredded, advanced.

Caleb attacked the living dead, a hawk ambushing a mouse. The lethal machete caught the sun with each downward stroke. The long blade was sharp and longing for blood. The fight blurred, a photo out of focus.

Violence seemed easy and effortless for Caleb and he did it well. The head of a Streaker flew across the room. Another monster entered, putrid and skeletal. The Streaker was held together by little more than muscle and mucus, dirt, and dried blood. It jerked closer even with a dangling, stump for a foot.

Two more creatures stumbled across the threshold after it, their clothing in tattered remnants. Breasts careened sideways like green and gray pendulums.

Jenna dropped to her knees and gagged at the appalling stench the long-dead brought with them. Wiping tears from her eyes and spit from her lips, she rose.

Three. They had to fight three at once. One down. Seven total to kill.

Another shot. She stepped back with the recoil. The Streaker didn't react. She let bullets fly as they shambled at Caleb.

She aimed and disposed of a zombie at the door, keeping it from passing the entryway. Body parts and blood sprayed the walls and littered the floor.

The clack of metal on the floor drew Jenna's attention. Caleb had dropped the machete. He wrestled with a Streaker in the middle of the room, ripping it limb from limb.

Jenna fired at another, cursed how resilient they were. The bullets like bee stings for the undead. She dropped the ammo-depleted gun.

"Watch out." Primal moans soaked the air. Another

Streaker crushed the remains of its kind, demanding entrance.

How many were still out there? Had seven been the wrong count. That kind of a mistake could lead to death—hers and his.

She grabbed a lengthy. solid block of wood.

Jenna ran to Caleb. Darkness and rage had overtaken his face.

Not so beautiful now.

"Call for help." She huffed.

A Streaker wobbled close.

"We need backup." She wanted him to shout for reinforcements, but Caleb's pride would keep it from happening. That, she was sure of.

"Stay out of the way." His eyes focused on the decayed target.

"F- you." Two-by-four secure in her hands, she sidestepped Caleb and moved into the sunlight the open doors let in.

Thwack. She enjoyed the suck of flesh coming loose and crunch of breaking bone. The creature dropped in front of her, stymied by the blow.

At the same time another Streaker wobbled through the open door, glass sprayed from the window. Pinpricks of pain embedded in her cheek. Her jacket had protected most of her upper body, but the harsh lash of fragments whipped her face.

The Streaker thrust through the broken glass in the window. Bits of flesh sliced away as it tumbled onto the tiled floor.

The undead stood and then in a macabre dance, the monster advanced. It sniffed Jenna out through rotted nostrils. Exposed bones had started to chip away while the remaining muscle oozed yellow pus. Jack-o'-lantern lips revealed a skeletal smile.

The makeshift staff carved the air. *Thump. Thump. Thump.*

Her arms ached as she hoisted the weapon once again. The Streaker was undeterred. Teeth gnash inches from her face.

With a wolf-like snarl, Caleb grabbed the machete off the ground and then twerked the arm of the offending Streaker.

Jenna heard the blade whip through the air before the undead fell. A quick pivot, and Caleb's fist drilled into the remnants a lumbering Streaker's skull. When Caleb drew back, the monster froze and then dropped.

They both turned towards the open doors, but only a breeze entered. With the last zombie disposed of, the bird songs erupted outside like a Disney movie.

Cadavers littered the floors, most headless. An arm twitched in the corner.

The street was clear of the undead for now, and her group would be safe for a while.

Jenna sank into a crouch, adrenaline leeching from her body.

Caleb offered a hand. "Your face is cut. I'd get Emma to doctor you. Don't let it get infected." He brushed a few stray hairs out of the bleeding scratches.

She lifted herself after a moment, face aligning with his broad shoulders and studied him. Caleb appeared rested, possibly revitalized by the fight for survival. He looked like he'd spent the first part of the day training for a triathlon and the afternoon at the spa.

"Yes, sir." Jenna replied, but he'd turned his back to her.

She heard footsteps on the stairs.

Victor, a tall, broad-shouldered man, clomped down the dark steps. "Quentin," he called. "Can you get people to take the bodies outside and burn them. After, we need to shutter the window again?"

"On it." Quentin nodded and sent the other man a thumbs up. "Come on mates. Let's get to today's dirty work."

Billy, Eric, Jody, and George hustled down the steps and into the light. They carried hammers, pliers, and canisters of nails, which they set down at the entrance. George handed Caleb a hammer before grabbing a severed arm and leg and hauling them outside.

The joy of living like roaches, she thought as people performed various tasks in a choreographed ballet. *Scurrying from dark corner to dark corner in empty buildings and abandoned houses.*

Jenna found the strength to move and the search for Emma began.

She reached the top of the stairs and spotted the other woman.

"I need some assistance." Jenna touched her face. Sappy blood blotted her fingers.

"I see. What caused those scratches? They don't look like they came from Streakers." A physician's assistant in her past life, Emma had taken over caring for the crew.

A shadow streaked across the floor, catching the corner of her vision.

"Jenna got scratched when a Streaker crashed the party through a window," said Caleb. "All the damage was caused by flying glass, but she might need antibiotics, so she doesn't get an infection."

Where'd he come from?

"No shit, Sherlock." She dusted the glass from her jacket, pricking her fingers in the process. "I can tell my own story." Jenna used a cloth Emma handed her to wipe brain fragments off her face. "I'm sure our industrious physician's assistant can determine a treatment plan."

"Hello to you too, Caleb." Emma pulled Jenna towards the gym, where she washed and dried her hands before forcing Jenna down in a chair. "I'll do my best to take care of Miss Jenna here. Thank you for following up on her medical care so promptly."

"Glad to help." Caleb shot Emma a smile but didn't leave. His squinted, a scowl replacing the smile when he addressed

Jenna. "Later, you and I need to chat. You risked your life. I told you stay back, but, as usual, you didn't listen. I had it handled."

"I can handle myself."

He ignored her and stalked off.

Jenna sank into a chair and dug into her pocket to return the Army dog tags.

At least she wasn't dead. That's something.

"They were my husband's. He survived four tours in Iraq but couldn't defeat the zombie hordes."

Emma grabbed iodine and dabbed the burning liquid on her cuts.

More pain. Yup. That's how life is. Suck it up buttercup.

"Ouch." She pushed away, avoiding contact with the medication-infused cloth. "You're supposed to be a caring medical professional."

"What a baby." Emma handed over some hard-to-obtain antibiotics. "Swallow these."

3

Oppressive air swirled. The night was similar to a thousand others that had preceded it and yet the intensity of the dream was like nothing she'd experienced. Jenna squirmed in her sleep, on the verge of waking. A moon in bloom cast an ominous glow.

"Jenna."

Darkness wriggled like a worm from the corners of the room. Sprawled on her makeshift bed comprised of a ratty, patched sleeping bag, mismatched blankets, and a torn pillow in a flowered case, she tossed, voices all around.

"Please save me."

Shooting up, the smell of rotting flesh met her. A Streaker lumbered into view.

"Too late. Evil is coming for you."

She bolted from knotted blankets, shifting into consciousness.

A dream. The same one had plagued her for months.

Wiping at the sweat stinging her eyes and dripping between her breasts, she flicked back the hair obscuring her view.

A gunshot fired through her sleep-muddled brain. The

noise erased the nightmare lurking seconds before. Awareness washed over. She smoothed the disheveled bedding.

What's wrong? Why the nightmares? Isn't reality bad enough?

Body rigid with fear, the questions refused to leave until another gun blast shook the stillness and Jenna out of her malaise.

A moment of silence. Another bang echoed off the concrete walls.

She rolled on her side, her face to the wall, not ready to embrace the morning.

It had been a few days since the attack. She conceded panic had lodged in her mind since.

Whatever's happening outside isn't my problem. Practice? Wolves? Bears? Stop worrying. Let other people deal with it. No use.

She was awake and staying that way.

Jenna swung into a sitting position, feet anchored against the wooden floor. The scuffed surface held rusted soda bottles and plastic bags. Mildewed textbooks had been chewed through by mice, some still using the tomes as a place to reside. A large plastic banner held the school motto, "A family of learners." Much of the debris had been pushed against the walls, but it felt like a fashion statement for the new world.

Though the survivors had hauled and lugged, dumped and discarded to make the large room habitable, the loud scurry of rats collided against the quiet steps of the inhabitants.

Vermin thrive while humans barely survive. New school motto right there, Jenna thought.

On autopilot, her hand searched under her bedroll for the flashlight. Flicking the switch, the dim beam provided enough light for her to locate the rough leather boots perched at the edge of her sleeping bag and slip them on. The beat-up camouflage jacket came next. Torn and stained, it was still protection and comfort, even in the heat. Knife and gun waited by her bedside, both never far. She secured the smaller weapon in her jacket pocket.

Dirty little beasts. She kicked out at a rat. It scampered away unconcerned. She hated vermin almost as much as she hated Streakers.

She put her hand to her mouth to cover a yawn. Pinpricks of pain exploded from the lacerations. Schooling her lips into a straight line, she stretched and threaded through the maze of personal belongings and sleeping survivors. A few souls, roused like she by the noise, sat and listened, curious.

Jenna scouted the other early risers. Ford, Gus, Emma, and Jenna had taken to calling themselves the breakfast club and tried to meet each day— for what she wasn't really sure. While she considered all sixteen members of this tribe family, Emma, Ford, and Gus had made her feel like she was home.

"How's your face?" The dim light of Emma's flashlight did little to illuminate the area.

In her late thirties, dressed in clothes the group scavenged along the way, Emma somehow managed to look fashionable. Long, golden curls piled into a bun at the nape of her neck, hanging like a heroine in a romance novel. Her husband's army tags, the ones she'd loaned Jenna for luck, dangled from her neck.

Jeans, tattered and sitting tight on her hips, amplified a curvaceous figure. The oversized work shirt tied in a knot at her waist showed off a hint of flat stomach. Work boots, muddy and scuffed, looked less like a necessity and more like a fashion statement.

"Fine." She peered down at her filthy jeans stained shiny by wearing them one too many days in a row. The green and brown pattern on her jacket had morphed into a dull gray.

I should try harder and be more like Emma, but there's no need to care these days.

"There's a little hot water by the portable stove if you

need it." The blonde thumbed over a shoulder, punctuating her comment. "Hurry. You know how quick people use it. I'm already behind. Let's sit and chat tomorrow."

"Thanks." The final remnants of sleep fled.

Emma ventured into the sleeping commune, her hand-held light source sent beams to lick over and around those who continued to slumber.

Jenna shuffled to the makeshift stove, poured tepid water to wash her face, then filled a cup.

She paused to make a mental note of the day ahead: join in the watch and the scavenging party, find wood, help Emma catalogue the remaining food, do laundry, and make a meal of whatever remained in the pantry. Of course, there was always the chance she'd have to kill something.

At one time, she might have mourned for those destined to receive the bullets, if they had not already been dead. Now emptiness filled her.

Mounting the stairs toward the roof, her neck tingled, goose bumps chilling her flesh,

A quick glance behind. *Nothing.*

The roof door opened to the morning air. She clicked the flashlight off to conserve batteries. They were harder and harder to find these days.

At the ledge, Jenna peered into the lingering shadows. She traced the remaining darkness from the sidewalk to the road and into a deep patch of woods surrounding the school.

She was thankful not to be outside at street level before the sun came up. Anything could be out there.

Safe now with the group. Anything evil, lurking close, will be taken care of. Why the shots? Find someone who knows.

At the corners of the building, stood a sentry with a shot gun. He stared, intent on locating anything dead moving below.

Gus, a stocky, bearded man, greeted her with a smile. He

raised one hand for a high-five. His brown skin blended into the shadows.

She smacked her hand against his. "Morning."

Jenna could never guess the elder's age, but his grey whiskers, bald spot, and wrinkles suggested mid-fifties. What she did know was Gus was ex-military, and his training had saved the group many times over the last year.

"How are you?" His sincere, sweet manner opposed his military dress.

"I'm here." Her hands reached out to capture the air.

"Doing okay, today?"

"Who was shooting?" She changed the subject.

"The twins. Billy and Eric are always up to trouble, but you got to love those two. Reminds me of my own boys. God, I miss my family more every day. Let's hope I can share some of the good lessons I was saving up with those two scoundrels."

The man is a saint, she thought.

Jenna chuckled before saying, "My world makes sense again. Who should I relieve?"

"No time to chat today? I can fill you in on the joys of deep-sea fishing."

"Maybe tomorrow."

Maybe never. Love that man, but deep-sea fishing, not so much. When would any of them have a chance to take out the yacht for a joy ride?

She couldn't deal with excessive sympathy today, and Gus always had a kind word for her even when she was in dark moods, more often than not of late.

Stay tough.

Gus pointed at Caleb.

Of course, just the person to talk to at the crack of dawn.

She'd done so well to avoid him since the disposal of the Streakers.

"Should've known." Jenna gave Gus's arm a gentle squeeze, then moved on.

The moon drained out of an expansive sky. Morning would erupt momentarily.

How could something so beautiful occur in the middle of so much death and chaos?

The laughing and joking on the roof appeared unnatural, but Billy and Eric squabbled, play-fighting.

Forget that former life. College, friends, family, laughter and love no longer exist. Squelch those emotions. It's all about killing another Streaker. Taking as many of them out before your time comes. That's the focus of existence now.

Jenna marched over to the twins and put on a scowl. "You woke me up. Gus told me you're the ones shooting things, and I got to say, I'm not surprised."

The twins' heads bobbed. Some of the youngest in the group, the teens were just learning how to shave, but for the most part, ignored the grooming ritual. Unkempt stubble and whiskers protruded on their faces.

While young, they were becoming skilled shooters and killers, both necessities these days. Still, for having tragedies equal to the rest of the survivors, the brothers made it to this point relatively unscathed, able to laugh and joke, to recognize some joy remained in the world.

"Sorry, Jenna," their singsong reply harmonized.

"Be stealthy and quiet. You don't know what's around."

"Something caught our attention in the woods, and we shot at it. But it must have been an animal." Billy shrugged away Jenna's chastisement.

"Nothing's around anymore." Eric pouted, not at all contrite. "Look over there." He pointed to a dead, dangling branch.

"What about it?" Jenna could not see anything remotely interesting about the limb.

Eric grabbed a pebble off the roof top, then pitched it at

the branch. "We noticed the branch and wanted to see who could dislodge it first. We were trying to make it fall, but we're not allowed to have any fun." As if to emphasize his point, Eric slammed his foot on the concrete. "Gus was right on us. Told us to stop fooling around."

"And yet the branch remains part of the tree. I guess you need a few more lessons with me after all."

"It's at a weird angle." The shorter of the two boys, Billy had a cowlick Jenna always had the urge to smooth it away. "We learned our lesson. It's not our job to save the group from dead branches unless they turn into zombie trees." A lopsided smile detracted from his attempt of rebellion.

Eric leaned close, confiding in a conspiratorial whisper. "Gus tries to act like our father, you know?"

"Really?" Jenna, at 21, was closest to their age, yet felt like she came from a different generation. She widened her eyes as if in on the boy's hustle and held back a laugh when both the their heads bounced in unison.

The twins looked like they ought to be anywhere but in the middle of the apocalyptic pandemic.

An image of them driving a tractor on a farm in the midwest with their freckled, homegrown, innocent faces, flashed through her mind. The overalls Eric enjoyed wearing almost every day added to the cliché.

"You wouldn't want to announce our location, would you?" Jenna tried to be stern, but she could not help but show a rare gap-tooth smile.

She reached out and brushed Billy's shoulder, working hard to keep her fingers from his cowlick.

"There's nothing around." Eric shuffled from foot to foot. "It's been so boring the last couple days."

"Then you have time to hear Gus's deep-sea fishing stories."

Eric opened his mouth to protest.

Jenna held up a finger. "Not a word. You love how Gus

looks out for you both. Someone's got to keep the two of you in line, and I'm too young to mother you."

Billy blushed in response and shrugged her off.

Jenna was well aware he'd developed a crush on her over the last couple of months. There were few women in camp under thirty and other people in her group had developed relationships. Jenna never dreamed of realizing love anymore, not in this world. Sure, there were fantasies, but dreaming about sex and the reality of her situation were two different things.

Billy opened his mouth. "I, uhm—"

"I need to relieve Caleb"—it was too early to discuss anything serious—"but maybe I'll whip you guys at poker tonight."

"I doubt it, but you're welcome to try." A grin tugged at the corners of Eric's mouth.

The boys' smiles appeared so similar, Jenna did a double take, then waved goodbye. "See ya."

A pang of envy for the ease they lived in this new world overtook her.

Stationed by a crumbling chimney, Caleb stood immobile in dark jeans and a black hoodie from which a hint of a profile peaked. His black hair obscured his face and the rest of him was inked in the shadow. He was a loner like her, and Jenna had made it her goal to avoid him since the attack. Now, thanks to guard duty, she marched over.

Does there need to be a further discussion? No.

He nodded. She returned the greeting, and the two stood side by side silently, watching the sky. Minutes ticked away.

"My friends." Emma's arrival and voice made her jump.

"What?" She didn't bother to filter out the annoyance in her tone.

"Someone's on edge." The older woman put a hand on Jenna's back.

"So, it seems." The words followed Caleb's restrained chuckle.

Jenna scowled, wishing she was anywhere else.

"Peace offering." Emma handed the younger woman a bowl of something lumpy and lukewarm, then turned to face Caleb. "Doesn't look so wonderful out today. I was hoping for sunny and a high of seventy-five."

Jenna peered over the edge, the final cloak of darkness being slowly pulled away. "Not much like Alaska?"

"Not much like anywhere." Emma had been vacationing on the Jersey shore with relatives, a long way from her home in Alaska, when the pandemic hit. She'd never made it back to find out about her former life.

Losing family is devastating, but not knowing must be much worse.

"Alaska was cold so I guess I shouldn't complain about the weather, but it's too hot here for me." Emma drew in a breath of air as if it provided nourishment. "Like the weather is our biggest problem these days."

"I miss the sun." A hint of longing etched Caleb's voice. "What I wouldn't do to stand in it again."

"I'd help you with that if I could, but my medical knowledge only goes so far." Emma gave him a pat on the shoulder, then continued her rounds, leaving Jenna holding a bowl of breakfast but having no desire to eat.

Jenna bit into her bottom lip with her top teeth. The food balanced on the four-foot wood roof railing, and she pushed her spoon around in it for a few minutes. "Will we make it to Virginia soon?"

"We're already in Pennsylvania. Maryland's pretty small. We should be there in a couple days if all goes well, and we find fuel for the trucks."

"Will things be normal there?"

"Nothing will ever be as expected again." His face lifted. "I should go inside." He turned, then took a few steps toward the door. "Find me later."

She nodded but wouldn't. Being alone with Caleb was disconcerting. For now, the New Race and humans were allies, all fighting the common threat from the undead, but Jenna knew peace wouldn't last. Why would *they* need humans once the Streakers were gone?

Jenna shook her head clear.

Lucky to live until tomorrow or next week. Don't need to obsess over a future.

Focusing on the morning watch, scanning the ground below, her mind wandered as minutes ticked away and tedium set in.

Sick of always being on the move, the group wanted a permanent base. They were heading south to the High Point Inn in rural Virginia after almost a year of wandering, everyone desiring some permanency. With supplies dwindling, and the little band of survivors growing, the group had hoped to move away from over-populated cities and suburbs where the Streakers ran rampant. Even this small town in Pennsylvania, it would seem, had its share of undead.

The day the Streakers attacked, Jenna realized, was the beginning of worse things, and by things, she meant hordes of zombies to come.

Emma had been the person who recommended the move to the inn. She'd stayed there on vacation a couple times and said it had everything the group needed to survive. Plus, it was well away from any major city.

With nothing interesting or undead in sight, Jenna pondered what Emma had told everyone. There was a reservoir for fresh water and accommodation for everyone. Jenna was hopeful they'd make it there soon, without any losses, and be able to plan and prepare for the winter.

The last year on the road had drained life and vitality for all. And the year before had almost killed Jenna.

Her stomach clenched. She traced the scar there. Her hand slid to her hip bone, now prominent against the waistline of her jeans.

Footsteps brought her back to reality.

"Supply run today. You available?" Gus put two fingers to his temple. "George decided he wanted to stay behind."

"Should I ask why?"

"No. You want in?"

"To traipse into a deserted town and face the maggoty dead to find a left-behind can of soup? What could be more fun? Sign me up."

4

AFTER HER TWO-HOUR shift on watch, Jenna, snuggled in her camo jacket on her cot and retrieved the journal she wrote in hopes of capturing the details of the pandemic unfolding. The journal helped pass the long hours. Rereading it made her sad, but she couldn't help skimming the pages, scanning random entries. How immature she sounded, though she'd been eighteen and a senior in high school. A lifetime had passed since she wrote them.

She thumbed through the frayed paper and stopped at an entry.

March 27, 2020

The year started like any other. Everyone came back from winter break and school went on like normal. It was weird when we started hearing about this virus spreading throughout the world. I arrived at my 7th period chemistry class and sat in the same seat I had been in all year. Word of the illness spread throughout the hall-ways. No one was too worried when they spoke of sick aunts or cousins. I remember sitting in class one day and hearing people remark that schools around us were closing. "This can't be that serious," had been my initial reaction. March 13. Happy day of destruction. I'm sitting in class and an announcement from the principal plays on the intercom. "Please gather everything from your locker and all personal possessions. School will be closed until further notice." We all celebrated. My friends and I were out of class and that's all we cared about. A few weeks to relax and party down by the lake. Little did we know things would never be the same. I never returned to school.

May 19, 2020

Mom and Dad have it, whatever it is. They're both in bed with a fever, and I don't know what to do. We canceled my graduation party. I'm not going to see friends. No presents. This could only happen to me. Since the quarantine, life's been so lonely and sad.

It's not just my parents who are sick. I'm one of the few people on the block free of the virus. Haven't caught it yet. The old man at the end of the street is okay, too. I see him wandering around in his garden. He kind of looks weird though, but he's always been mean and salty. I would love to speak with him and find out more about what's going on, but I'm scared.

Mom and Dad want me to stay in the house, but they won't let me visit with them, and every time I go into my parent's room, they make me leave. They're even wearing those stupid masks in bed. It's not like they'll contaminate each other.

I want to see my friends. I'd enjoy anyone's company. I'm so alone. Maybe I'll sneak out and attend one of those virus parties they're throwing. My parents would never believe I'd do it.

The news says it's just a stupid flu bug, but Mom and Dad are sick, sweating and coughing. Their skin has this awful purple tint to it. They don't eat the food I bring them. I make sure they at least have some water. I want to call 911, but they keep telling me "no."

All the television programs say the same thing, which isn't much. Why can't I leave the house?

Texting and Facetime don't cut it. Online schooling sucks. I hate seeing my parents sick, and I want to visit my friends, at least *the few of them who don't have this stupid disease. Maybe I'll text Kate or go run.*

I must get ready to play soccer. I'm so excited to start Massachusetts College in the fall and can't wait to see Aunt Jill. She's coming to help out tomorrow. I haven't seen her since Christmas.

Jenna flipped a few pages and jumped ahead to a time that still haunts her waking dreams.

July 21, 2020

I never got to say goodbye to Mom and Dad. I miss them so much, but I can't cry. With so many dead, they don't conduct funerals, but bury people in mass graves. Aunt Jill made us join the others in a safe house, more like a prison.

We were going to go to her house in Massachusetts, but she got sick. They moved Jill out of our make-shift room and wouldn't let me see her. I don't know what's happening. No one talks to me because they believe I'm a kid, but I'll handle it. I wish it was all a dream. I don't know if I'm alive or dead.

I should be dead. I'm so gross because they're conserving water and won't let us shower. My body odor is terrible even, though I try to rinse it off every day. But I only have a couple changes of clothes and the box with my parents' stuff. No one is taking that away from me.

They don't have anything here except some disgusting soap.

No shampoo, no deodorant, little toothpaste, and everyone smells.

The safe house is at a local elementary school. But I don't see any of my friends from high school, just a couple kids I recognize from the halls. We're all kind of numb. The adults don't explain much to the people they consider young.

Stupid grown-ups, but all of us just do what the grown-ups tell us. I'm getting kind of sick of it and want to find my aunt. Maybe when I do, we'll steal a car and get out. Go to her house. I can't stand this.

She rustled the pages until she found an entry near the end.

October 31, 2020

It's Halloween!

A fitting day to write with so few left. About one hundred survivors live in the school. The adults keep telling us to wait, it will get better, and someone's coming to rescue us.

Who will rescue us? There's no one around anymore, and it's so disgusting in here. I wonder if there are others outside who are better off?

Recently, the heat stopped, and now, we also must collect water and boil it. Luckily, there's a park with a lake nearby.

We never regained power after losing it at the end of September. The school had a generator, but that's not working anymore. Wood for the fire is getting low, and the weather's turning colder. We have a lot of canned food and bottled water, but I sure miss home-cooked meals. What I would do for a hamburger now.

The cases of the sickness are diminishing, but the adults keep whispering weird stuff. All I hear are scary rumors. They say there are dead people on the streets, some of them all rotted, some with red eyes. Not just the corpses of the dead littering the sidewalks, but dead people staggering around.

That's crazy, but I don't know what to believe anymore. The kids, I'm included though I'm a legal adult, having turned eighteen in May, are detained inside the school. I'm sick of it. I want some fresh air. Smells like old people and bathrooms in here. The so-called adults discuss leaving and finding others.

At least Joe is teaching me how to shoot a gun. The only person taking me seriously. He's not bad for an old guy. This is probably one of my last journal entries. My pens have run out of ink, and this damn pencil is nothing but a stub.

Inching forward, she came to another entry.

November 30, 2020

Vivid dreams haunt me. Maybe they'll go away now that we're moving.

Things keep attacking the school, but how? How can they be alive again? How do they know we're in here?

The journal slapped closed. Not long after the final entry, everyone was dead, well, almost.

Thump. The leather-bound book hit against the other items in the ratty shoebox. A few personal and important mementos sloshed together. These extended hours would drag on with chores unless something worse showed up and needed disposing of.

How had those creatures been human once?

She scratched the scabs on her face—one more scar to add to the collection.

While the group had moved many miles away from her home, she questioned if one of those creatures could be a former friend or relation? It was likely school mates and family had died by her hand, so she could stay alive.

While intelligence eluded the undead, they still resembled the humans they'd been. What if she came across her mother, her aunt? Could she kill them?

They're empty shells, decaying, or so she told herself. *You can't reason, rationalize, or apologize. You kill them, or they eat you.*

It was every horror story told; every menacing thought of doom, every nightmare turned real thanks to a pandemic out of China.

Her eyes drifted upward.

Decay had lined the ceiling. Chunks fell away and revealed stained and damaged pipes—a great analogy for life. When no longer able to ponder the metaphysical importance of the ceiling, she headed to the stove, surrounded by random chairs scavenged from the building.

She waved to Jackie and George who chatted. Victor sat in what was once a comfortable office desk chair, staring at the camp-fire stove. Next to it, another fire simmered in a tall metal barrel, and water in a container boiled, rolling continuously.

Jenna grabbed a drink of cooled liquid and scanned the

room. She found Emma and waved her over. "What time is the supply trip leaving?"

"Soon." Emma checked the temperature of the boiling pot —158 degrees Fahrenheit. "Quentin is getting the weapons organized."

Billy, without his twin, strolled over to join them. "I'm coming with you on the hunt for supplies."

"Big day for you." She punched his shoulder. "Emma, you sharing those army tags with this one for luck?"

"You read my mind." Emma reached in her pocket and handed the tags to Billy. "Keep it safe, or you'll owe me."

He pocketed them.

"What? Not going to wear it?" Jenna asked.

"Kid." Quentin's arrival was anything but subtle. At six-plus feet with long arms and legs, the man couldn't hide. He didn't need to. No one was more of an asset in a brawl with the undead, except the New Racers. "Did you drop some pounds?" A playful jab and cross hit Billy's midsection. "You're skinny as a stick."

"Shut it." Billy stared at his sneakers, once bright colors muted.

"Concerned for your health and welfare." Quentin smothered his guffaw, then handed the boy a long plank of wood with protruding nails. "For you today. I'm here to keep you safe. I'll be in the back if needed."

Jenna noted how Billy turned red, then glared at the older man.

The duo ambled toward the exit of the building, Quentin trailing behind.

"Hey." Jackie came running, closing the space between her and the search party. "Don't forget about me."

Outside, Emma didn't let the conversation drop. "Billy, you get we all just want you and your brother Eric around for the big sweet sixteen party everyone's planning. Quentin's looking out for you, and we're trying to keep you safe until you're eighteen. Then you can fight whoever or whatever you want as often as you desire. For today, going into town will have to be enough excitement to satisfy you."

"Yes, Mom." Billy rolled his eyes.

"The sass on you." Emma's words didn't relay a scolding. At any other time in history, she would have been the epitome of a stay-at-home soccer mom. Now, in combat boots, ripped jeans, and a KISS band T-shirt, she looked more warrior princess.

Jackie's words could be heard even as she lagged behind. The opposite of Emma, Jackie was a fiery Brazilian. Today, her long hair flew out at all angles from behind a bandana, framing intense brown eyes. While not so handy with a gun or knife, her cooking skills were unsurpassed.

You could bring Jackie any odd combination of canned goods, and she'd create a gourmet feast with a little flour and a couple cans of condensed milk. She was the reason the group was alive and not suffering from malnutrition.

Jackie and Emma might be opposites, but they both managed to remain presentable and, more importantly, sane. Jenna wasn't sure she'd accomplish either to a degree people would believe.

Her eyes moved down to her stained shirt, and she ticked off items on her personal inventory.

Camouflage jacket filthy and covered with muck. Check. Jeans stained with God knows what. Check. Unkempt, unwashed hair pulled into a severe ponytail. Check. Uniform complete. Doesn't matter what the weather. Yep, a mess in more ways than one.

At least she'd managed a quick wash this morning and didn't smell like the rotting flesh of the undead. A common perfume on many a days.

Kicking away a rusted soda can brought on reflection from pre-pandemic days. A friend had warned her to start dropping pounds, or she'd end life an overweight middle-class homemaker who spent most of her time transporting school-age children to boring events and fondly reminiscing about her few thin, high school years with the rest of the suburban parents.

What bullshit.

Now, one healthy meal a day had become a luxury and the strength to fight a necessity. Living in abandoned buildings, sleeping when possible, and sustained by hunting or scavenging was wearisome.

Her life had become a series of encounters with Streakers punctuated by periods of drudgery and boredom. She faced days of standing and staring into an empty horizon for hours, cooking for the group, hauling water, and washing and drying load after load of soiled clothes, forever stained with the remains of the undead. In these times, the survivors were always on the go, attempting to avoid Streakers following their every move.

No one could figure out what attracted zombies to the living, but they never ceased to emerge from the shadows or around the corner of a building. Being ready to jump ship at a moment's notice produced constant packing and unpacking, sorting and resorting items, including the canned foods the group survived on, the bedding, and the makeshift stove for cooking. It also meant being anxious and forever looking over one's shoulder.

Today would be no different. The small posse headed along the abandoned road. Billy engaged phantom Streakers with his nail-studded bat.

She wished he'd stayed back at the school. The teen was young and everyone wanted to keep him safe, but scavenging parties offered good training. It was unlikely the group would come across more Streakers after getting rid of so many.

Jenna shifted her baseball bat between hands and noticed Quentin carried a similar one, along with a gun. Emma and Jackie gripped long knives. The blonde also had a shotgun strapped to her back. While firearms were more useful for killing Streakers from a distance, the loud noise often summoned other undead. Baseball bats and knives were most peoples' weapons of choice when not high on top of a building. Cars would have been faster, but the engines also attracted Streakers, and why waste gas for the short trip deeper into town to search the stores?

Emma carried a lifeline, a walkie-talkie.

Better safe than sorry, but let's hope there's no need to contact the base camp.

If they were quiet and remained on guard, the small group could get in and out of the center of town without a problem.

"How are you, Miss Jenna?" Emma nudged her, breaking into Jenna's reverie.

"Are you probing for information? Do you want to know if I'm okay after the attack?"

"Maybe."

Jenna nibbled her bottom lip with her teeth before answering. "A little tired but otherwise just dandy. Stop looking at the cuts on my face. They're scratches. They're fine. I don't know why everyone is concerned. It was just one more Streaker attack. We've lived through plenty, remember?"

"You never know what will kill you these days." Emma matched her pace, step for step. "But you sound like your old, cranky self, so you must be good." The older woman placed a hand on her shoulder. "I have to warn you"—her smile full of compassion—"George started a ruckus about women—I take that back. It was about you—fighting. He wanted to be the one battling alongside Caleb to prove his prowess to Jackie." She leaned close and whispered in Jenna's ear. "He's afraid Jackie will leave him for a New Racer. George was mad as the dickens you beat him to the party." Her shoulder brushed Jenna's. "A little secret, Caleb requested you join him and

44

specifically asked not to have George go down. There's no doubt George is a good shot, but not much of a team player."

"If George wants to engage Streakers, he can take my place any time." The words leapt from her lips.

No one liked to risk his or her life, but everyone had always fought side by side—equals in every way.

Billy joined the two women, kicking at the dust-covered litter infiltrating the otherwise empty streets. Discarded bottles and cans shared space with rusted appliances, tools, and rancid trash. After the first year, the worst of the malignant odors had evaporated, but the group avoided any place one could smell before seeing.

"Is it always this way? Quiet?" The teen sent an empty, chewed can of shampoo into the bushes with a strong kick.

"Yeah, when kids don't talk." Jenna nudged him, then sent a wink his way.

"I miss real shampoo and getting my hair done." Emma turned. A sheer look of longing masked her face. "What do you miss?"

"Pizza." The word rolled off Jenna's tongue without hesitation.

"Baseball." Billy swung the nail-laden board at an empty shotgun shell casing, sending it flying into the air. "Home run." He sprinted off, following the impromptu ball.

Contemplating the days when pizza was plentiful, questions resurfaced. "What do you remember about the first days of the pandemic?" Jenna squinted her eyes as the group turned the corner, walking into the sun. "Most of it's starting to blur, except the important stuff."

"Like what?"

"My parents. Their faces remain vivid even now. Images of my school and friends are always dancing in my brain. And I couldn't shut out my new reality even with my dying breath. Try as I might, the days of the pandemic are foggy. And the memories blur more and more every passing hour."

Jenna didn't want to dwell on what had happened to her. Even Emma didn't know that piece of her story.

Maybe Emma has information that explains why no one stopped what occurred that night.

She stared at the ground. "Does anyone understand its origin, Emma??"

"Sweetie, I remember the horrors of the disease. It left people dying in the streets. Families, neighbors, and strangers running, never to be heard of again." A deep-seated sadness etched Emma's voice as she grabbed the younger woman's elbow, marching her onward. "Some people, after seeing the aftermath, committed suicide rather than face the new world. I was on vacation when things started to fall apart. Thank God I found you and the rest of this crazy group." She gave Jenna's arm a quick squeeze.

"Will we find more people? We can't be it." These days, the group was lucky to come across new survivors. Humans dwindled, heading for extinction.

"You never know. I remember from back when news stations still existed, a reporter said when the pandemic first hit the United States, it killed most of the population. Close to eighty percent of people gone. Just like that."

"Do you think more groups like us exist out there?"

"If wishes were horses, then beggars would ride."

Jenna scowled. "There has to be."

"Don't get your hopes up. When the virus first hit, mass graves overflowed with bodies."

"Do you recall all the rumors at first?"

"Sure, people believed the dead coming back to life was an urban legend, a scare tactic by the government or a sick joke, but the dead returned."

"I can't remember much after my parent's death, and my aunt got sick."

"I doubt many could survive both the virus and what came after. You're strong because you were able to do that."

"We both did." Jenna pressed herself next to Emma for an awkward side hug.

As humans died across the globe, Streakers proliferated.

Bodies clawed their way out of the graves and attacked anything living and breathing.

In those first months, some people stayed buried, but many who died in the pandemic returned with a taste for human flesh. Survivors had no idea how to combat them and succumbed under the creature's violent, decaying hands, only to add to the undead's growing population.

Another mutation emerged from the virus: The New Race. Ostracized at first, believed to be kin to Streakers, most thought the New Race ready to destroy those humans who remained. Both groups realized together, they had a better chance for survival. Now, humanity would most likely be extinct without the aid of the New Race.

"Why did this happen?" Jenna let the question slip from her chapped lips.

"I don't know. I can't reflect on it anymore. It is what it is. You got to stop driving yourself crazy. Be thankful you're alive."

"It's all I wonder about."

Silence fell between them until a few minutes later, the large grocery store came into view.

Quentin jogged from behind and pushed in between the two women. "I still picture the store full of people wearing masks getting groceries for the week. Remember the smell of rotisserie chicken? My favorite to go meal. I wasn't much of a cook then."

"Some things haven't changed." Jenna met his blue eyes. "Should we ask Jackie what she plans to feed you later?" She turned towards the woman still following behind, engaged in a loud conversation with Billy about the merits of spices.

"Don't start you too." Emma said. "I'll tell you what I miss the most: fresh fruit. And God knows who I'd kill for a bag of potato chips." Emma grabbed her elbows and held on tight in a self-hug.

The insignificant action reminded Jenna of her mom, who would have been one of the people getting groceries on a busy Saturday. Back in her room at home, she'd have refused to help with such a menial, tedious task as the stubborn selfish teen she'd been then. If only there was a time machine.

She missed her mom so much and wanted the chance to offer thanks for all the wonderful things her family had provided. If Jenna could return to pre-pandemic times, she'd join her mother on every trip to the grocery store and do every boring chore ever.

The group closed in on the dilapidated store, the last in town they hadn't checked.

No indication of life or Streakers crept out of the shadows.

Looking through the broken window at the empty shelves, Jenna was quite sure other survivors had ransacked the place numerous times.

After the initial outbreak, looting became common. When things spiraled out of control, people did unmentionable acts to stay alive. She considered herself one of the lucky ones, even if the slithering scars across her stomach said otherwise.

Emma nudged her forward.

They approached the open door.

The interior had fallen into an expected state of disrepair. And the sign hung crookedly—graffiti decorated the walls. Broken glass, plastic gloves, a face shield, a human bone, and the remains of mildewed, blighted boxes lay next to overturned shopping carts.

"Emma and I will go first." Jackie took charge. "I need some goodies to make you all a good dinner tonight. The cupboard is bare, so to speak."

Quentin rubbed his stomach. "What I wouldn't do for another round of the empanadas, rice, and beans you made."

"That was months ago." Jackie shook her head, but a smile lit her face.

"I will never forget them." Quentin brightened at the memory. "That's how we should eat all the time."

Jackie stared up at him. "Maybe once settled at the inn, we can find all the ingredients, and I will make it for you again. Sound like a plan, *el compadre?*"

He held out a pinky. "Promise?"

"Swear." She hooked their fingers together.

"Let's get going." Billy shuffled his feet at the waiting.

"Are we ready?" asked Emma. "Billy, you're in the middle where it's safer. Quentin and Jenna, bring up the rear."

Nodding in agreement, Jenna and the small band entered the ravaged interior.

Without electricity, flashlights sprayed little enough light to catch what was inside, dead or alive.

5

REMNANTS OF TOPPLED CASH REGISTERS, broken carts, cardboard boxes, and plastic bags littered the floor.

"Paper or plastic," Quentin kicked a white bag. It flew across the room like a specter.

Brazen vermin squealed and scurried in front of Jenna's feet. Most of the shelves were not only empty but badly deteriorated. Still, Emma and Jackie were able to gather a few cans that had hidden in dark corners or under filth.

She stepped over a long-dried puddle. It was hard and black.

"Clean up in isle four." Quentin's voice rang out behind her.

They wandered through the maze of aisles—skirting empty. molding containers, broken shelving, and avoiding the darkest of places.

A noise caught her attention and that of the group, signaling for everyone to stop.

Jackie motioned for Jenna and Quentin to fan out. Quentin gave her a thumbs-up before he prowled ahead. A broken sign dangled. The words *cereal* and *bread* still attached by thin chains.

Quentin pulled out a wallet and handed Billy a one-hundred-dollar bill. "Go crazy. Buy whatever you need."

"Gee, thanks." Billy took the money, but a moment later let it slip through his fingers. It sailed to the floor, landing gently.

They could be dead soon. Why had she never tried to get to know Quentin? Everyone loved him and his off-beat sense of humor. Something she didn't understand and shied away from.

He'd been part of the group for more than two months. One of the last human survivors she and the rest of them had run across. It was their first scavenging party together.

Always friendly since day one.

Did his antics make her feel protected? She couldn't remember how that worked. Why had she remained aloof?

"Attention shoppers." His hands cupped his mouth, so the words echoed in the emptiness. "Today's specials include dented cans of long-expired veggies. Don't forget those condiments. A bottle of ketchup can spice up any type of zombie brains."

"We don't eat zombie brains," Jenna blurted.

He smiled at her. "I know."

Exactly the reason staying quiet is best.

She studied him. He stood at least five inches taller than Jenna, and when he turned back, hoisted his bat, and winked at her, the tight, long-sleeved T-shirt highlighted muscled arms. Tousled brown hair fell into his blue eyes. She'd seen it all before, but it was as if today she took it in and etched his features in her mind.

He waved her forward and she joined him.

"The town's been quiet since you and Caleb vanquished the last batch of Streakers." Mice, frightened of his voice, surged forward, leaping over Quentin's steel-toed boots. "Free of the undead types and humans."

Jenna jumped back before huffing out a breath. "Yup."

So much for practicing those social skills.

51

"Looters cleaned this place out long ago." He ran a long, straight index finger along a shelf, picking up a layer of dust mixed with animal hair. "Nothing's here but the stench."

"And the rodents." Jenna pointed to the boots the vermin had just run over.

"Those too." He held her gaze.

"We should have searched houses. You know how people stockpiled at the end."

"Staking out each house, ensuring there are no Streakers, and then searching takes so much longer. Grocery stores are a one and done deal."

"Does it make sense to split up?" Emma peeked around a corner.

"It will make the search go faster. I doubt we'll find much in here." Jackie smoothed a lock of hair behind an ear.

"Not too far apart." Emma headed away from the group and Jenna. "We can see each other from the ends of the rows. Let's stay in sight when possible."

"Come on." Emma grabbed Billy and followed Jackie. "You two take the rows at the other end of the store. We can meet in the middle. Yell if you need us."

Quentin bumped shoulders with Jenna. "Partner."

She ignored him. He repeated the contact. This time more forcefully.

"Stop." The growl emerged from deep in her throat. She strode away until she found an interesting store aisle and then meandered through it; Quentin followed a few steps behind.

His breath hit the back of her neck and she stopped short. "Do I need to yell over to Jackie for a rescue, or are you going to behave? I like my personal space."

What does he mean by all the close contact?

Quentin didn't take the prior hint and started a drumbeat on the back of her jacket.

"Stop," she protested.

"What are you going to do about it?"

"Are you ten years old?" Posture rigid, exasperation leaked out. "We're on a mission here."

"I'm old enough." Quentin's blue eyes twinkled.

"Good to know you're so seasoned and battle ready."

"Look at these arms." Muscles bulged under his shirt. "Do they look like the arms of a pre-teen? I'm ready for battle… and other things."

"All I see are the lovely and appealing stains on your shirt." She did a double take. "Actually, I recant my statement."

His smile was wicked. "I knew you would."

"They look like the arms of a small child. Someone needs to be hitting the gym a little more often."

"Ouch." He shoved her.

Catching her off guard, she stumbled.

He reached out and drew her in. "Sorry." His whispered word tickled her ear.

He didn't let her go and she stood cocooned in his warmth. He might be flirting, but she could be reading too much into this encounter.

Maybe he needs someone to smack him to make him understand boundaries?

The heat of his body, close and warm, was confusing.

Where's the snark? Must remain protected. Don't envision his arms around you. It's been such a long time since physical closeness with anyone was normal.

"There's a pharmacy at the end of the next row we should check out." She tried to break the spell of the moment.

"Really?" He didn't take the hint and relinquish her. "There's a lot going on right here I want to examine."

"I take it back." She wiggled out of Quentin's grasp, then punched his arm.

"What?" His arms went limp at his side.

"You're acting like a toddler." She inched closer to the

pharmacy, placing more distance between Quentin, the confusing emotions, and herself.

"Everyone okay?" Emma's voice echoed from the next row.

"We're good. At least Quentin is good. I'm suffering through his antics." Jenna wasn't sure what was going on or why, and she didn't want to begin to address the sensations careening through her.

It must be sleep deprivation.

"Try your best not to judge him too harshly." Muffled laughter filtered through the ramshackle shelving.

"I'm trying my darndest."

To be over there with the rest of them. Why am I stuck in a teen dating movie?

She chalked her bewilderment and awkwardness up to the recent near-death experience with Streakers and nightmares. After some quality sleep, everything would be fine and dandy.

Like anyone slept well these days.

"Come on." Jenna tugged the arm of his T-shirt.

He remained planted like a tree.

"We have a job to do and not a lot of time to do it." Jenna edged back. "Let's get moving."

He groaned but followed, kicking at the discarded face masks littering the floor, some flaked with dried blood.

She checked the nook of a shelf on the way to the pharmacy.

Vermin squeaked, scurried, then scattered, sending dust bunnies flying as well as the edge of something aluminum.

"What do we have here?" Jenna stooped, then dislodged a dented can of beans under the shelf.

"Nice find." He opened the sack he carried.

Jenna tossed the can overhanded, and it fell into the bag. "Score."

"If only."

She tilted her head. "If only what?"

The wink was comical. "If only I could score a beautiful babe in this less than lovely world."

"And where would you find one?"

"There's one close by."

"At camp? Who are you interested in?"

"Never mind." Quentin exhaled.

"I want to know."

"You already do."

"I don't. Really. Tell me."

"Let's drop this conversation." He called to Billy.

"All good here." Billy's voice sounded far away.

At the pharmacy, long-ago hair dye and serums had bled upon and decorated the shelves.

Please let there be toothpaste. The baking soda the group used is less than lovely.

"Look here." She licked her lips. "Chapstick. I miss it so much." The tube dropped into the bag.

Quentin salvaged a half bled out bottle of shampoo and a rat chewed, dried wedge of soap. He stopped in front of a torn and ransacked makeup display.

"Can I buy something to pretty you up?"

"Funny. Ha. Ha." Her voice remained deadpan.

He plucked the cap off a tube of bright red lipstick. "I was going to ask you to the prom next week and thought you needed a new lipstick shade to match the color of your dress."

She studied the color. Something looked familiar, but she couldn't dredge up the memory. "Red? You'd dress me in red?"

"I would have enjoyed taking you to the prom and the after-party. Couldn't care less about the color of your dress."

"Stop." The word came out petulant.

"Maybe we would have skipped the party and went straight to the hotel room." He waggled his eyebrows.

She stepped back. "You're being an ass."

A thump from the back of the store silenced a longer retort.

"Time to go." There was an edge to his words. "We don't know what the noise was, but It's probably Billy or the rest of the group. Let's grab the pharmacy stuff and skedaddle."

"Who says skedaddle?" She stuffed the lipstick in her pocket without thought.

"Grab whatever, and let's go." He pilfered random items, not looking at what they were.

She sneered at the sight of her partner holding a box of condoms and opened her mouth to say something but sucked in decay and death.

A Streaker lurched out of the shadows.

"Damn"—the word came out as a whisper, then she found her voice—"We're screwed."

How could she have forgotten? *Always be careful—more than careful.*

The lackadaisical attitude she and Quentin had shared could now bring death.

"Damn." The beat of her heart accelerated.

We just killed a bunch of these shits. Can't there be a few Streaker free weeks? We normally don't get new hordes for weeks. Nope. Not this time.

"Let's get out of here." The words were ripped from between Jenna's clenched teeth. The deformed corpse lunged with unexpected athleticism.

She ran, blinking away the fear. The fetid, decomposing monster following her as she skidded around the edge of the bakery kiosk was close enough that it blurred into a Picasso painting, face rearranged, a pallet of murky brown, green, and gray.

Her sprint intensified.

Outside, she spun in a full circle hoping to catch a glimpse of Emma or Billy.

"They're not here."

"I didn't see them inside either." Quentin huffed the words.

She prayed they hadn't been trapped by other Streakers inside.

The rest of the group had vanished, except for Quentin who'd remained in step with her.

"Next door." He dragged her along. "Inside."

"What if we get trapped?"

Ducking inside a Quick Mart, he grabbed an empty magazine rack, hauling it in front of the door. "Have to hide somewhere. Outside we're too unprotected, and noise from a fight will bring more of them.

There wasn't a lot of room in the small store. She kicked away empty cigarette packs, plastic bottles, and discarded remnants of lotto tickets. There was a kiosk where coffee had once been prepared. Remnants of shattered pots melted together with brown stains, but at least no high shelving.

A flimsy barrier wouldn't stop the Streaker for long, but it might allow for a few extra seconds for them to prepare or find another way out—the difference between life and death.

She sprinted to the rear, Quentin on her heels, his breath blowing down on the back of her head in short puffs.

The creature crashed against the door.

My fault, Jenna replayed the conversation in her head. *Goofing around in the grocery store was a rookie mistake.*

Bantering with him had been enjoyable, something that hadn't happened since high school pre-pandemic. She should have stayed serious and remained with the rest of the group.

Discipline would be a priority if she got out of this mess, but the situation could turn problematic if more Streakers arrived. Too many people died this way.

Quentin thrust her into a corner and signaled for silence.

He inched back toward the front door, the baseball bat high overhead, ready to swing.

Another boom echoed, and the door slammed open an inch. The barricade between safety and the Streaker weakened.

Jenna watched from a crouch, realizing she'd soon be in serious trouble.

No longer did a single dead thing ram the barricaded door, but two.

Quentin readied his bat, but unlike the New Race, he couldn't kill two Streakers on his own. She searched for another way out. No windows. There was an exit sign in the back, but someone had barricaded it with a coin exchange machine. She couldn't push that aside on her own, and Quentin was otherwise engaged.

She moved to join him in the fight, hoisting her bat.

The undead rammed the barricade again and shambled through the door. Missing his tie and most of what might have been a designer suit, his engorged, distended belly exposed bowels through the tattered remains of a button-down shirt.

A second Streaker stumbled through the opening, an elderly female corpse, composed of little more than muscle and bone, wearing remnants of a long dress. What little remained of the creature tangled itself into the tumbled magazine racks and fell to the ground.

Its wormy body continued to slither across the floor, pus oozing, teeth snapping maniacally, skeletal hands clawing the tile. It inched closer.

Spokes of the magazine rack held the creature back, but by the squeal of metal against the tile, the undead would not be long delayed. The resounding slam of the front door trapped them inside.

Jenna slid behind Quentin, who hit the man's skull dead center, producing a cracking echo.

The wooden weapon popped back, glistening with blood and gray matter.

He slammed it in short, measured strokes. Upon the bat's final release, the pucker and slurp of brains competed with his heaving breaths. The body collapsed to the floor.

The old woman remained tangled, slowed by a mess of fabric trapped in a metal magazine rack, but that no longer stopped her from gaining ground. Like nails on a chalkboard, the screeching rack scraped as the creature gained inches.

Jenna sidestepped in front of Quentin, bat at the ready. A third corpse dove against the door. Bloody fingers shoved through a gap, forcing the way open. Another of the evil dead had arrived.

This one will be the end of us.

A horn honked. The monster in the door disappeared, spurred on by the loud noise. The tangled Streaker on the floor eyed Jenna with menace, but the repeated bleating created a beckoning cacophony outside.

The commotion caused the creature to heave itself out the door, leaving behind only the discarded magazine rack.

Gunshots rang in quick succession.

She made the sign of the cross even though she no longer believed in a God.

Someone took the Streakers down. We'll be okay.

The hum of a motor idled in the street. With Quentin at her side, the two ran for the entrance.

Whatever waited for them outside was better than what they had just faced. She hoped it turned out to be her friends.

Billy, Jackie, and Emma greeted them from the back of a Ford 350 flatbed truck. Gus was at the wheel. They hopped in, and the truck roared to life, heading along the road.

"We were overrun. Had to call for back-up." Jackie patted her walkie-talkie like a beloved pet. "Gus to the rescue. He drove in from camp to save our asses."

"How'd you find us?" Jenna focused on slowing the ragged breaths escaping her mouth.

"We searched for the Streakers. Duh." Billy's eyes glazed

59

with excitement. His speech sounded like machine gunfire. "Better than any video game I ever played. I can't even remember the names of them, but this was real. So intense. When I lost sight of you two." He pointed at Jenna and Quentin. "I vowed to stay and fight every last one of them to get you out."

Emma crossed her arms. "We're moving out tonight. It's too crowded around here for us."

6

THE CAMP at the school was in disarray by the time the group returned. Quentin wandered off to get his belongings. Jenna ran into Caleb and Aiko.

Aiko displayed her curves as often as her kukri knives. Today the tight T-shirt appeared a few sizes too small.

Did she grab a child size?

With the world at an end, Jenna could hope Aiko would have the decency to throw on a baggy sweatshirt like the rest of them now and again, but no. Her long, plaited hair accented her heart-shaped face and ample cleavage. She somehow managed to look feminine and Disney princess pretty in the middle of the apocalypse.

Why is she the only one who didn't give a rat's ass about appearance at a time like this? Or is she jealous?

Had she turned on the emotions she'd buried and believed they'd never surface?

Caleb and Aiko were making short work of their project, deconstructing the camp stove and communal area. As if he had a premonition she was back, Caleb turned, a smile flickering across his lips before Aiko asked a question, diverting his attention.

She closed the gap between them. "Need any help?" Exhaustion trickled from every pore, but she was nothing if not a team player.

"No. You'd better work on organizing your own stuff." Aiko's words dismissed her.

Leaving them, she followed the smell of venison stewing. The growl her stomach released was louder than a Streaker.

When had she last eaten? She couldn't remember the last real meal, inedible morning mush not counting. Deer meat was a favorite and a staple these days.

She scarfed a bowl of grub, reminding herself where it came from. The New Race were experts at hunting and killing big game. With improved vision, they were adapted for the chase.

As if sensing her fatigue, Caleb appeared at her side with a cup of instant coffee, one of the few luxuries sometimes available. She inhaled the bitter scent. Her stomach growled in response.

"I thought you could use it before I put everything away."

"Thanks." The words stuck to dry lips.

He was considerate, not only to her but to everyone, but she needed to keep her distance. The scars on her stomach itched, confirming her decision was correct. She avoided investing emotionally in any of her companions.

This week was a miserable fail.

She chugged the bitter brew before moving to her sleeping area, where the goal was to pack her meager belongings for the next part of the journey through Maryland. Along with a bedroll, her life easily stuffed itself into a couple of canvas backpacks. Other than the clothes on her back, Jenna kept little. Her journal, though she refused to write in it these days and a shoebox containing the memories of Mom and Dad, were the only non-essentials.

She'd cram the remainder of the space with changes in clothing and shoes, mostly rugged T-shirts, sweaters, sweatshirts, and jeans though. Jenna made room for a few nicer items for celebrations. The group tried hard to recognize birthdays and commemorate the passing of time with special meals. Sometimes these festivities worked better than others, but Emma had taken on the chore of counting the days and remembering everyone's birthday.

Caleb left her side and she believed he'd glide back to Aiko, but instead grabbed a dilapidated chair and brought it close. He made himself at ease, stretching his legs into the gloom.

"It's going to be dark in a couple hours, and the group wants to make the most of the night for travel. We're heading out ASAP. Do you need me to do anything for you?"

"Help me? Absolutely not. All my stuff will be packed in five."

"Ready for some nighttime travels?"

"Night or day, what does it matter?"

"With the New Race driving, we haven't lost a member to a Streaker attack for close to a year."

"I'm not sure driving ability correlated."

"Will you sleep?"

"I'd rather volunteer for the watch. Even the scavenging parties are better than sleeping."

Better rethink that one after today's adventure, but sleep means nightmares. The creatures, real or imagined, are always lurking one step away.

"Are you sure about not needing the help?" He didn't move from the chair. "I'm ready, willing, and able to be at your service."

"I'm good." But in truth, the earlier conversation with Emma ran rabid around her mind. Images of the Streakers from the store would haunt her for many nights. Her past must somehow connect with the present, and Caleb, being of the New Race, had insight.

Would understanding the past help her survive, or if not

63

survive, find some semblance of peace. *Caleb must know more than she did about the New Race.*

"Last chance." Chorded muscles popped from his arms. He pushed from the seat.

Without realizing she was going to speak, she said. "Can you answer a question? I'm missing a piece of the puzzle. What do you remember about the start of the New Race?" She jammed her clothes into a beat-up duffle bag, trying to hide shaking hands. The information was important to her, even if she couldn't figure out why.

Fingers threaded through his thick hair. "All I know is instead of dying some survivors like me, mutated into the New Race. The scientists couldn't figure us out. Called us vampires, monsters, others. Those were some of the names given to the people who survived the disease and changed but not into Streakers. I'm not a monster."

"You're not."

"More of a modified human." Vivid red eyes radiated sadness. "There are things I like about the new me, but other things I can't stand. It's who I am, and I can't change it. Just like I can't alter the aftermath when the disease hit."

"Why'd the pandemic happen?" The question persisted, though no one had an answer.

"You have to focus on the future. We can't change the past."

"I need information. It's like a puzzle I have to solve."

"I don't have the answers."

"Did you get that novel vaccine they were trying to sell everyone at the end?"

"Yes. Did you?"

"No. My parents were dead by the time it was released. I wasn't in the mood to comply with the authorities."

"When the government realized there was a link between the vaccine and the New Race, they started rounding up people like me who were changing. I hid, but the military came in. He shrugged. "I guess I was easy to find. They put us in camps to see if we'd turn into Streakers." Caleb bowed his head. "Conditions were horrible. We were all crammed in cells, no clothes other than what we wore in. Maybe two beds for twenty people. They must have already decided we were evil or dead, or both."

"They believed they were helping."

"I doubt it." His fist tapped his thigh. "Everyone worked in panic mode. Act first, think later. At the camps, we learned about Stephen's Flu, named for patient zero.

Jenna nodded. "Everything happened so fast."

"After the virus started mutating, they shortened the name to S1, S2, S3. The government got to S11 before the whole thing imploded and Streakers arrived."

"What happened to the people you were with?"

"I was separated from my friends. It's worse when you're alone. I'm sure you relate. The round-up was supposedly for our safety, and they said we could leave, but it was a lie. We were prisoners, but my family had all died, and I had no one else and didn't have an option."

She stopped packing, placing a hand on his arm. "What happened in the camp?"

She'd never asked about his story. She was a shit.

"They moved me to a laboratory in a military base where scientists worked to find a cure. Everyone there'd begun to mutate, but not into Streakers. The New Race had been born, and the scientists tested, poked, and prodded us. I was essentially a lab rat."

She didn't want to believe it, but history told her people would do anything to survive. "I'm sorry."

"The New Race can't abide the light because our skin developed a severe sensitivity to it, like an allergy. Hives, blisters, and dangerous burns when forced into direct sunlight, something Streakers don't care about in the slightest. One of the first tests the lab conducted after I got there was to make us sit in the sun and see how long before we fried."

Jenna furrowed her brow. "It can't be true."

"Painful and true, but we heal if not out for too long. We tend to be stronger and healthier. This was helpful, especially when the disease started to consume the military base. One night, all the captives decided to escape."

"How'd you do it?"

"We could outrun the guards, and if they tried to stop us, well . . ." The words to his story fell apart. "We did what we had to do."

Jenna tried to lighten the mood. "You don't fall into a coma in the day?"

Caleb's mouth opened and closed. "What? Like a vampire?"

"Joking."

He remained stoic. "No, but our senses are sharper at night. It's easier to hunt. We eat food like everyone else, but hunting . . . I can't explain it. The warm blood of prey you've vanquished is a rush of energy like you've never experienced."

Jenna's head tilted. *Too much information.*

She took a deep breath to control the shudder that attempted to escape. "Like a high?"

"It's hard to explain. You know we mostly hunt deer and animals in the woods. Their blood keeps us healthy and alive, more so than any other food. There's a thirst for it."

Worrisome. What did he mean by a thirst for it?

She was about to ask when a whistle blew, informing the group time was running short to get packed and leave.

The puzzle remained unsolved for now. Rumors existed about clans of the New Race who were worse than Streakers. Stories of attacks and feeding off humans emerged from the shadows like urban legends around the campfire.

"Do you believe the gossip about the New Race collecting humans and enslaving them for a source of food?"

"It's possible," Caleb replied. "Anything is possible these days." His hand topped hers. A cold shiver cascaded along her arm.

Having finished packing, they went to the water barrel for a quick drink and then separated to help load all the gear into the vehicles. Their caravan, a random assortment of ten trucks and cars, lined the road by the entrance, ready to move. While ragtag in appearance, all bore armor or improvements. What the vehicles lacked in looks, they made up for in strength. The group's trip would last five to six hours using the back roads, which usually had fewer car wrecks to maneuver around.

Jenna found it hard to hide her desire to leave this shit-hole of a Streaker infested town.

7

DARKNESS HAD CONQUERED the landscape by the time Jenna jumped into the passenger side of the last vehicle in line, a Jeep Grand Cherokee. Someone of the New Race would drive, and humans would sit shotgun. She needed peace and wanted time to contemplate.

Victor, a happy, chatty New Racer in his mid-forties, usually drove the Jeep. Despite moody Italian looks, he always found something positive to say, and she'd have to do little more than murmur approval.

Jenna's mouth dropped open. The thud of her heart and her palms turning hot and damp, indicated Caleb's arrival instead. She wiped her hands against her pants, hoping he wouldn't notice.

He saw everything.

A lopsided smirk greeted her before he settled into the vehicle and adjusted the mirrors. Long, lean legs stretched under the dash. The seat moved backward to accommodate his bulk.

"Is it okay if I drive the Jeep tonight? Victor wanted something a little roomier."

"Whatever."

This is going to be a long night. She tugged the end of her ponytail.

Quentin emerged from the darkness. "Any extra room in the jeep?"

"Yes," she said.

"The back's full of supplies," Caleb contradicted.

"We could probably move them." Her brows dropped into a V.

"No time." Caleb glanced at the line of car headlights. "Aiko needs a copilot."

"Cool, man." Quentin gave a wave before strolling through the line of cars in search of an empty seat.

This sounds like a set-up.

Jenna eyed the half-empty seat behind her. "We could fit him in the back."

"True, but Aiko needs company too." He winked before the Jeep sputtered to life and put it in gear, sliding into the line of cars. Streetlights, uncommon in the area anyway, hadn't been functional in years. Caleb focused on the road ahead, his strong jaw set.

The hum of the engine against the midnight black landscape created an eerie void. Time passed in a slow drip. She slid away to stare out the side window, hands resting in her lap.

"I heard all the gory details about what happened at the store." Loud words filled the car. You doing okay after this afternoon?"

"Sure." She shifted to relieve cramped legs, his profile in view.

"I worry."

"About me?"

He frowned at the road. "Of course. Who else does all the stupid shit you do?"

"Hey. I don't do more stupid shit than anyone else."

"There are people in the group who would disagree with

your statement."

Why does he care? Most likely because the group becomes weaker every time a person falls ill or is lost to a Streaker attack.

While the New Race were humans, intuition warned her to stay away from the handsome man driving the Jeep.

He's possibly dangerous. There could be some darkness caused by the virus inside him. Since her parents had died, it was hard to separate the New Race from the Streakers sometimes. They were offspring of the same virus. Rationally, the idea was ridiculous, but after losing everything, blame had to fall somewhere.

It didn't help Caleb was quiet and reserved, even for someone of the New Race. Much like her.

He hardly ever sought out the company of humans, preferring his few New Race friends. Except for her.

She didn't understand the change in him the last few days and wondered about this more congenial, more communicative side.

"I look out for my own."

She bit her bottom lip before speaking. "No one owns me." The darkness outside the window beckoned.

"I don't own anyone, but I also don't want something to happen to you. With a strong swing and killer reaction time, the troops are desperate for Jenna clones."

Was he joking or sincerely concerned her death would hurt the group? Not sure, she bit her tongue.

"You're a good fighter. I trust you by my side."

"Remember the fight the other day, you did all the work. I made more of a mess."

"Don't underestimate your skills." Caleb reached over and gave her hand a quick squeeze.

A shock shivered through her system.

She must be getting sick. Or is something else possibly going on between them? God, she needed therapy. What was happening to her? When did it go from survival to getting the shivers when a boy

70

touched her? Keep those defenses up. Don't let anyone in. It's the only way to live these days.

"Here's a scenario. Since I'm so amazing, I get to stay in bed all day. You can bring me breakfast and do the laundry. You can also have all my latrine duties if you like."

"I'll take the bed part. The rest is negotiable."

The Jeep skidded to a sideways halt, squelching the witty retort on her tongue. "What the . . ."

Without a seat belt to shield her, she slammed into Caleb's shoulder. His hands pushed her back to the passenger seat before he hopped out the door. He was on his knees in the darkness, crooning and making kissing sounds into bushes on the side of the road. Like a mad man, he clucked.

Jenna cracked her back, wondering if she had whiplash. Even with the Streakers' craziness, this came off unbalanced in a world where nothing was normal.

Outside the car, sweet words gentled the night.

But who were they for? Maybe insanity was setting in. It was bound to happen to someone, and she was a likely candidate.

Curiosity won out. Jenna needed answers. She scooted across the seat and jumped out next to him, bat in hand.

"Don't need that. Unless you plan to bludgeon a cat," he said, without looking at her.

"A cat? You stopped for an F-ing feline?" She wondered how he saw the animal. The sky lacked a single shining light or glowing star in the immense and haze filled horizon. While she was an animal lover, stopping in the middle of the night, put everyone in danger. Their current situation called for caution, something he lacked.

"It's hurt."

"Now you're a veterinarian too?" On cue, the animal meowed. A small grey and white feline with yellow eyes emerged and twined around Jenna's feet, limping slightly, ignoring her companion and his attempted rescue.

"It likes you." He scooped the cat up.

She huffed. "We'd better get going. I don't want to fall too far behind. They'll turn around and come back for us. We shouldn't have stopped in the first place. What if the cat has rabies?"

"Seriously?" He loaded the unresisting cat into the car with one hand and grabbed her with the other. When she was close, he shoved her toward the passenger side. "We battle Streakers daily, and you're worried about rabies. Get in."

The moment she settled into the passenger seat, the feline settled in her lap. Loud purrs filled the lonesome quiet. She patted the cat's head with a single finger. "This is your fault."

"It looks like you're the proud owner of a cat. What are you going to name it? How about Smudge or Ozzy?"

"He needs a dangerous name. It must be something appropriate and memorable. We should name him Killer Cat."

"That's not a name."

"I'm practical. We'll call him 'Cat' for short."

"Whatever you want. He likes you, and he's safe now." He reached over to pet the cat, but the feline hissed at him.

"He's got good taste."

"You don't know for sure it's a boy."

"Killer Cat works for any gender."

"You can come with us to Virginia, little guy. I'll protect you from Jenna when she gets grumpy."

"All this for a cat. I wonder what you would do for a pony?"

His laugh battled with purring, and Jenna relaxed to the point she could enjoy his company.

What was happening to her?

A companionable silence filled the vehicle while it bumped along. Caleb steered with one hand, having no problem avoiding potholes and wrecked and abandoned cars scattered in the road.

"The group's lucky to have met you and the other members of the New Race. I feel like traveling, finding supplies and gas for the cars, even surviving day to day, would have been a hundred times more difficult without your company."

"Naw. You give us too much credit for something we don't want but can't change. This New Race thing is more a curse than a blessing."

"It's a blessing for our group."

Even so, she had a hard time coming to terms with the genetic changes all too obvious in them but needed to get over the prejudice and fear. To believe the words she said to him. It had been a long time since her parents died and months since she got the scars lacing her stomach, the ones that left her wary. Months were as long as years with Streakers roaming.

When he reached out to pet the cat a few moments later, she didn't notice. His hand slipped to her knee and stayed there. A row of stalled, flashing headlights distracted her.

"This can't be good." He parked and exited the car. Jenna gently placed the cat in the back seat and followed.

"What could go wrong now?" The words sounded strangled.

8

THEY JOINED Victor in surveying the unsettled landscape.

The older man ran a large hand through his short, salt and pepper colored hair and frowned in obvious displeasure.

"What happened?" she asked.

His dark eyes radiated unhappiness, unusual for a man who was jovial and eternally optimistic post-pandemic. When he couldn't find a positive spin to put on the situation, it was serious. "There's a huge pile-up of cars," he said. "It looks man-made. People might have been trying to create a barrier against the Streakers at one time."

"What can we do?" Jenna asked.

"We're scouting around to see how far it goes, but it's at least a couple hours of clean-up, or we try another route."

Caleb's lips pinched into a frown. "Will it give us time to get to our destination?"

"We're considering our options, but I don't know." Victor scowled at the scene. "We might have to stay a day in a town close by. It's called Pittsfield. A perfect name or what?"

The rest of the group had dispersed throughout the wreckage, and Jenna wanted to be of use. "What can I do?"

She hauled debris and moved rusty car parts while the New Race patrolled, watching for Streakers, ensuring everyone's safety. Hours later, Jenna's muscles burned. They'd hauled car fenders, tires, and barbed wire fencing. She prodded an old, broken Dodge Durango into a ditch. As Jenna deposited the last car battery in a pile that felt thousands of miles away, each foot became a burden to lift. Exhaustion swayed her.

Even with the concerted effort, the cleanup had taken almost three hours of hauling, jostling, and sweating. She caught her breath, watching Caleb trek close through the receding night sky. With the moon hidden behind murky clouds, it was hard to tell when morning would arrive.

"I'm exhausted." She bent at the waist.

"We're heading to Pittsfield. We'll have to spend the day there and then make it to the High Point Inn tomorrow night."

He put out an arm to steady her.

"I'm fine." She grumped and moved away.

"You're dead on your feet. Let me help you for once."

"I'm no more tired than anyone else. I can do this." She stalked back to the car and into her seat, checking the cat was still there before promptly falling asleep.

"Wake up."

Fear shot through her with those words. "What time is it? Where are we? Did we make it to Pittsfield?"

"We found an abandoned movie theater. There's a scouting party coming out now. The sun's about to come out too. We're all trying to hurry inside."

She shook herself awake. "What can I do?"

"Help unpack." He pointed to the back seat. People unloaded cars around her. Exiting the vehicle, she readied the equipment and placed them on the curb, waiting for the signal to move into the theater.

She surveyed the barren streets, mentally preparing an escape route if needed. Deserted. She didn't expect to find any survivors loping along. The group hadn't come across anyone for months, but maybe . . . there was always hope they would find more people before getting to the High Point Inn.

Jenna peered into the soon-to-be morning sky, unable to ignore the glorious sunrise about to bloom. Colors seeped across the horizon, clouds mixing gray and blue until they merged with the rising sun to blaze red and yellow.

How could the sun continue to rise every day when all the people she loved were dead? She couldn't wait to get to the inn and hoped life could be relatively normal once again. Her grandest dream was to start a garden like her father had when he was alive.

Remembering fresh vegetables made her mouth water. How she missed her mother's fresh-made marinara sauce from the tomatoes they grew and her secret-recipe vegetable stew. Not only could the garden feed them, but it would offer some independence. She didn't want to rely on the New Race for her own survival.

"We got the okay." Holding a heavy box, he nudged her forward. While the sun forced Caleb and the New Race inside the building, she finished unloading, carrying the cat inside last. An empty box would make a temporary bed for him.

"Be good. Stay here." She doubted he'd listen, but she wanted to find Emma.

The older woman was in the middle of organizing breakfast with Jackie and Ford.

Jenna joined in, helping to mix a large bowl of flour, baking powder, sugar, and cinnamon with a little oil and a lot of water, forming a lumpy batter for pancakes.

"Can we afford to waste all these supplies for breakfast?"

This would be a feast, celebrating the group nearing Virginia, but supplies were low.

"Got to enjoy life sometimes," Emma said.

They used a propane-powered griddle to heat the food. The pancakes were not like her mother's homemade recipe, but they'd supply people with the needed energy for the day ahead. The group had been lucky to find some canned peaches, and she hoped Emma, being in such a good mood, might break them out. People picked up the food and wandered off, breaking into smaller groups. Conversations turned into background noise when only the two women remained by the griddle.

She could always beg for the fruit, but that wouldn't be fair to all the others. Still, begging usually did the trick with the older woman, who wanted everyone to be happy.

When Cat wandered over, Emma screeched. "Rat. A huge rat. Get it away from the food. Get a gun!"

"It's a cat. Caleb found him last night. We adopted him."

"We?" An eyebrow arched.

"I decided to adopt him, okay?" The words slipped quickly out of her mouth.

"*We* wouldn't be so bad." The grin on the other woman's lips was pure smut. "You need someone in your life, and he's a good choice. So nice and helpful. I've seen you checking him out on a couple occasions when you believed no one would notice."

"I have not!"

"Plus, he has a nice butt."

"His butt? This is what end-of-the-world discussions have regressed to? We're trapped in a movie theater in an unknown town, likely surrounded by undead, and you're talking about Caleb's ass. Are we serious right now? Do I need to check your temperature? You're probably running a fever and hallucinating."

"There are so many body parts exposed on the Streakers,

but usually nothing good to look at." Her smile remained wicked. "But then there's Caleb. Along with a great butt, he has some fine-looking muscles. Did you see him last week when he was helping George hoist the Ford to fix the tire? Yummy."

"Wipe that smirk off your face. Please stop. You're acting crazy and making me uncomfortable. I cannot have this conversation with you."

"Who else are you planning to have it with?"

"I'm going." She grabbed a pancake and skedaddled, perching on a windowsill in a lonely corner.

The conversation wouldn't fade. Images of a certain someone entertained her.

When the group wasn't planning on staying at a place for long, there was little to do. No need to begin a project that couldn't be completed. Gear remained unpacked and clothes left unsorted. Laundry went undone. They would all go another day or five wearing the same clothes. The lucky people would have books to read or a pack of cards to play with to squander time. A day on the road included patrolling, rereading the worn copy of *Wuthering Heights* stored in her duffel, staring at the walls, or reminiscing about the past. A time when she found Heathcliff's crazy passion romantic. She didn't quite see it the same way now that Streakers were relentless in their pursuit and the New Racers often reminded her of the anti-hero.

Not in the mood to read, she lay by her stuff on the dirty rug, not bothering to unroll her sleeping bag. Cat nestled on her lap, and she stroked his fur, purr vibrating through the air. Too wired to nap, her mind wandered.

The room smelled of funk with decay evident in every direction. The dirt under her nails was a constant reminder of the conditions. Grimy, she wished for hot water, a loofah, and body scrubs. While everyone tried to stay clean, toweling off with soap and a bucket of water when available. Real baths meant hauling bucket after bucket of water to the stove, heating it, and bringing it to the big tub the group bathed in. Half the time, she'd rather take a quick, cold rinse than exert energy to heat the water.

The group strung a clothesline and curtain around the tub, but otherwise, privacy was minimal. They slept crowded next to each other in sleeping bags, ate in the folding chairs around the fire, and spent most of their days cooped in the abandoned houses or buildings. They knew each other too well, and yet some of the people remained strangers.

She missed washing machines and clothes shopping, but most of all, she missed her friends and family. One more day hanging out at the mall with Brooke and sharing her playlist with Caitlyn would be a blessing. School sounded fun.

"What's on your mind?" Caleb sat on her still-rolled sleeping bag.

Of course, it's him. Of all the people who could arrive to talk to me. Is there some kind of weird kismet forcing us together, or is he turning into something dangerous? Why would he be dangerous. He's been nothing but nice.

Jenna opened her eyes, squinting, and propped herself up. "Nothing important."

"I doubt that's the truth, but you don't have to tell me."

"Stupid stuff."

"I'm listening. Go ahead. I want to hear."

She fiddled with a hole in the sleeve of the oversized men's flannel shirt she wore.

"I wondered about the popular songs from before the virus. I'm trying to remember them all along with picturing my friends from high school. It's true we can't live in the past because it only makes all this worse, but I can't give it up." Her shoulders shrugged up. "I'm weird that way."

"It's not weird. I remember my family all the time. Instead of brooding about it, you should talk about them. Even better, let's do something we'd normally do in high school."

"What?"

"Well, we're at a movie theater. Let's pretend to watch a movie."

"Seriously?"

"Sure. Why not?" Grabbing her hand, he dragged her through a hallway into one of the deserted theaters.

"Tell me what your typical movie date would include?" A mischievous glimmer lit his eyes. "Romantic comedy or an action film? Popcorn or candy?"

"Comedy." She looked at him soulfully. "I have to choose candy or popcorn?"

Images of buttered popcorn and chocolate-covered raisins made her mouth water. She would happily settle for microwavable popcorn if still available, but it wasn't. She'd pop the corn herself if they could find any growing.

"I'll splurge for both. I want to impress you on our first date."

What was this man saying? Date? Joking for sure. He had to be.

"Front, middle, or back?" she asked while roaming the theater, carefully avoiding the chunks of fallen plaster from the ceilings and toppled the seats.

"What?"

"Where do you normally like to sit? The front, middle, or the back of the theater?"

He squeezed her hand. "That all depends on what I want to do on the date."

"What do you mean?"

"Am I getting any action? Am I more interested in the movie or the person?"

She swung at him. Caleb dropped her hand and easily avoided the fist aimed at his stomach.

"Rude."

"You pick. If I went on a date with you, I'd do anything you wanted." Truth rang in his words. "We could canoodle in the back." A lopsided smile spread across his lips.

"Who says canoodle? You have the weirdest vocabulary."

"I'm glad you're paying enough attention to notice." He closed the distance between them.

Their bodies touched. He leaned his head toward hers.

A screech disrupted the moment, and curses and shouting erupted in the hallway. They sprinted for the door. Once back in the main lobby, Jenna spotted Gus, Quentin, and George arguing. George's lined, pock-marked face was the color of ripened plums, hidden only by a grey-brown, ill-shaped beard. He clenched and unclenched his fists, dirty T-shirt revealing sculpted muscles he worked to enhance nightly.

Jenna's frazzled nerves intensified. Looking at the men causing the hullabaloo reminded her of the old Three Stooges comedies. They argued in the middle of the main entryway of the movie multiplex. Morning light bathed the large windows in the entrance. The theater, once a happy place for families enjoying Disney movies and couples on first dates, stood barren except for the remnants of old movie posters and a few fallen benches. The shattered concession stand glass littered the floor with pinpricks of light while the remainder of the theaters sat in a dusty gloom.

George plunged his oversized belly into Quentin. The younger man's hair, disheveled from the previous night of moving debris and car parts, stood on end like electricity had executed him. George's lips set in a snarl. His good-old-boys' attitude put her off, made worse by his lack of hygiene and his penchant for sleeveless T-shirts. Jackie had an on-again, off-again, relationship going with him, but Jenna tried to avoid his stocky, well-muscled, and overly tattooed frame when possible.

Gus sported his usual camouflage T-shirt with shined black boots. "Let's be rational, George."

"I'm on watch this morning." George pointed a finger in the younger man's face.

"I'm not saying otherwise. We need to figure out a plan providing everyone equal time." Aggravation competed with exhaustion in Quentin's eyes. His hand wiped at the dirt and sweat covering his face, only to leaves traces of more. The once popular, now shredded Abercrombie T-shirt displayed a rash of grime and wrinkles from working all night.

"We also need to make sure we utilize each person's strengths," Gus added, remaining composed.

A crowd grew beside Jenna. The men exerted their masculine dominance. There were many reasons to hate these arguments, which often ended in fistfights and blood-shed. It would be wise to stay out of the way, but she couldn't. Gus was like a second father, and she wanted to do everything possible to help. Nothing came to mind that would resolve the bickering.

What could she say to diffuse the situation?

"Stop with all the *machismos*."

The three men stared at Jenna for a few long moments before Quentin guffawed.

"We're busy here, missy," George dismissed her.

"Jenna realizes how irrational we're being, George," Gus offered in an attempt to placate him. "We need to work together."

"She wants to work together, does she? Go ahead and tell her to grab me a big drink of water," George mocked.

"Jerk off." Anger replaced any desire to help.

George, approaching in three steps, twisted her arm painfully. He spun her into his chest.

Rancid breath cocooned her.

Peering with squinty eyes, he spit words. "You believe you're better than the rest of us because you like to kill Streakers. You better watch yourself and that high-flying attitude, little girl. It'll come back to bite you real soon. You might just be the next one to go. Women better start learning their place in this camp."

"Get your hands off her." Quentin shoved George's arm.

The older man focused his attention on Quentin. His bright eyes showcased his wanton desire to fight. "You plan to make me?"

Gus interrupted. "We have work to do. Put your petty grievances on hold until we get to the Inn. Then I'm out of it, but right now, we have to set watch." A large group has formed behind Gus, ready to step in if needed.

George held his hands high in mock surrender, and people edged away, returning to their work.

She wasn't going to let George scare her off. "I'll do the first watch shift. I'll be on the roof until you need me somewhere else." Jenna grabbed a gun and a flashlight before anyone could tell her otherwise. She sauntered away and found a route to the roof. The interior passages of the theater were desolate. Dust, grime, and blood littered the floors like candy after a movie. Pushing against a door with an exit sign, she faced a set of stairs veiled in sinister obscurity. The flashlight flicked on but before the door could even shut behind her, shattering glass had her running back to the front lobby.

9

SPRINTING THROUGH THE HALLWAY, Jenna surveyed the dusty entrances to individual theaters in the huge complex.

In the distance, someone bellowed, "To the right."

Rounding the corner into the lobby, a Streaker burst through the large glass window, stumble to a halt, and focused cataract eyes on the twins.

Beth and Ford, husband, and wife duo in their forties, had been survivalists before the outbreak of the virus and joined many months ago with two young boys, the only members of the group younger than the twins, Billy, and Eric. All four had survived in the wilderness until they joined. The twins had attached themselves to the family. The survivalists hurried their two young boys into one of the empty theaters. They'd be safer locked inside until this was over.

"Get inside with the boys," Beth's panicked scream erupted.

"No," Eric latched like a weed to the spot where he stood.

"We're staying and fighting this time." Billy retrieved a dangerous-looking blade.

"We want to fight."

"Stay safe." Ford's words held the resignation of a father who no longer had control.

The Streaker shambled forward. With a guttural scream, Victor emerged from the shadows and swung a bat in a giant arc. With a speed and accuracy defying human ability, the bat lodged itself into the creature's wormy head, the skull spewing bone and oozing globs of tissue. The undead collapsed to the floor, and the enraged New Racer yanked on the wooden handle, bringing the bat back to his side. He took a step, another, but slowly sank to his knees.

In his fury, he'd failed to notice how far out into the light he had stepped, and the smell of burning flesh filled the room. The twin sped over, dragging Victor into the shadows behind a bench. The smell of the scorched skin turned into a beacon. Undead pressed against the large glass panes that encircled the lobby.

Jenna watched in horror.

The windows became a mural of writhing, creeping, ramshackle creatures in various states of decay.

Jenna lifting her gun.

The glass shattered, followed by the arrival of several stumbling creatures, crushing each other, shouldering forward. The twins dragged Victor's body from the darkness into the theater where Beth and Ford had gone. The two ran back out, brandishing their blades. Emma joined the twins. The remainder of the group, having grabbed weapons, stood united.

More of the New Racers emerged from the recesses of the building, but they didn't step into the sun-kissed, main entryway. Once again, they would only be helpful if the Streakers made it past most of the main hall and all the people in it.

Jenna planned not to let that happen.

"Shit, there's a lot of 'em," Quentin boomed from behind her. He examined a rifle, and satisfied the weapon was ready, braced the large gun, aiming at the creatures coming through the shattered glass.

"We need to barricade the window," Aiko's voice boomed above the moaning undead. "Let's pray the others hold."

Gus sent a bullet into what brains remained of the nearest Streaker. It went limp for a minute, but with a low moan, raised its head and met Jenna's gaze. Dark blood poured from both the new head wound and from the mouth of the creature, marking it a more recent creation. While some of its brain was torn away, it rose and shambled forward. Stumbling over the wreckage in its path, it limped toward her with disjointed arms and dead, unblinking eyes. She readied herself to fight, a large knife clasped in her sweaty palm.

"Get down."

She dropped.

Caleb pinched the trigger of his rifle from far behind. The weapon roared, a bullet tore through the remnants of flesh and bone that encompassed the creature's skull. He fired again before the monster flailed and dropped.

"There's too many. Theater One. Let's get in there now!" George yelled from its entrance.

Billy grabbed Jenna's arm, and they retreated along with the rest of the group.

"Where's Eric?" Caleb asked.

"I . . . I . . . I don't know. Wasn't he with Gus or you? Oh God . . ." Billy turned back to find his brother.

"Go inside." Caleb stopped them before he pivoted toward the main hall.

Jenna pushed Billy into the smaller theater and then followed Caleb back into the lobby.

Shots rang through the air.

A bullet from his gun clipped through a Streaker's skull, spraying muck.

The other half of the head and torso dropped to the

ground. But the Streaker's body continued to squirm, inching closer, leaving a trail of intestines on the carpet.

A zombie charged. Green ooze dripping from its nostrils and black patches of mold devouring the skin on its face. She hoisted her heavy-duty hunting machete and swung with all her might. The head of the creature flew off its decrepit shoulders and onto the carpet moments before its claw-like hands raked at Jenna's camouflage jacket. The body stood at attention and then pitched itself forward, slamming her to the ground with it.

Jenna refused to scream, even smothered under the corpse. She knocked it over, her hands sinking through the shallow layer of skin. Shuddering, she could not get out from under the headless, lifeless remains fast enough. Kicking it away, she stood and waited for what would come at her next.

"I got you. Where is Caleb?" Quentin asked from behind her.

"He's looking for Eric."

The deformed, hunched remains of an undead creature stumbled into her line of sight. Her blade sliced the air at the ready, but the figure fell to the ground with a thud, a bullet tearing apart its skull.

"I told you, I got your back," Quentin pointed at the nearby window. "They're getting in there. We need to board it up."

Nodded in agreement, she scanned the lobby for any signs of Eric.

It was Caleb who reemerged from the shadows of the theater. Head bowed and shaking. "I tried. I couldn't get to him. He didn't make it."

"What?" Tears pooled in her eyes.

Eric. Dead.

She sank to her knees.

"Too many Streakers. I couldn't get close to the body. It gives us a reprieve. Let's go back to the group," Caleb said in a monotone. "Get up."

Quentin dragged a sobbing Jenna into Theater One. Caleb stood sentry at the open door until they were inside. Gus closed the door and wedged old seating against it.

Jenna collapsed to her knees.

News of Eric's death spread in whispers only interrupted by Billy's sobs.

The teen huddled against Emma. Jenna wiped her tears away and joined them.

"Now is the time for action, not grief." Ford cleared his throat. "We have to barricade the damn window so nothing else will get in, and then find a way out of here." His voice faltered. He brushed Beth's arm.

Josh and Kyle hugged his legs.

"It's so early in the day," said Aiko. Her shredded clothes and long black braid flailed as she paced. "We have to wait at least five or six hours before we leave. We're trapped right now, and those things out there will keep coming. By night, this place will reek of Streakers. I'm not sitting in here waiting to die."

"We sure don't want to get trapped in this theater. We'll never make it out tonight if the creatures are all waiting for us to leave." George puffed out his pocked cheeks.

"We could try to move to another place close," Emma said.

Two large kukris formed delicate circles in the air when Aiko spoke. "The Streakers would just follow." Her rigid posture made her tall despite her petite five-foot-two frame. "This is the best place to finish our attack."

"We barricade the windows first," Ford said. "Did anyone see what we could use out there?"

"Then we kill anything inside." Aiko's knives refused to be silenced.

Jenna watched Ford and refocused on the conversation.

Imitate Ford. Lock emotions away. Grieve later.

"We'll get the window boarded and survive until the night. We have to." Aiko flicked her knives from side to side.

"Now I understand why all the trucks were in the road back there blocking the way to the city," Emma said. "They didn't want to keep the Streakers out. They were meant to keep the people away. We strolled right into death central."

"How many are there out there?" Jackie wanted to know.

"I counted at least seven." Quentin brushed remnants of Streaker and sweat from his forehead.

"We've killed a few already," Caleb paced. "Let's get back out there and avenge Eric's death."

"We've got to do this correct the first time. There are no second chances." Quentin indicated to the humans nearby. "The windows are so big, letting in both sunlight and Streakers. I can't believe we didn't board them earlier. Stupid, but we were all rushing, and the windows appeared strong. None of them were broken."

"They are now," George said.

Quentin pointed at Aiko and Caleb. "You can't get close the windows without burning yourselves. You saw what happened to Victor before."

"I'll do it," volunteered Jenna.

"You will not, missy." George's lips twisted into an ugly sneer. "Don't you ever stop causing problems? You've caused enough trouble."

"What does that mean," she asked.

"This is a man's job, not for a silly, little girl."

"George, relax. You both go, and I'll come with you," Quentin said.

George's eyes remained full of malice.

"Are you three enough?" Gus asked. "If you want more support, I'm in."

"We need you here in case Jenna screws it all up."

George's smile crawled like a spider. "I'm sure she will."

Jenna clenched her fist. "You're being an ass."

"Stop wasting time. This bickering has to end." Gus's voice cut through the tension. "Can anyone tell me what's in the lobby big enough to block the hole in the window?"

"The concession stand." Aiko stepped forward, sheaved her knives. "The glass is broken, but it's pretty big and bulky. Looked well made too. Caleb and I will push it forward, but the humans will have to move it the final few feet to the window and brace it there."

"There needs to be more than the three of us," Jenna said.

"I'll help," Billy said, "for Eric."

Silence met his words.

"I'll go too." Gus placed a comforting hand on the teen's shoulder.

"The rest of us will make sure to cover you from the rear." Peter emerged from the shadows. The sullen, exotic, New Racer held the nickname "Godfather" around camp. Sedate and older, his dark, slicked-back, oiled hair and intense brown eyes on a six-foot, four-inch frame only added to the mystery of his background, which he never shared.

He scared people almost as much as the Streakers.

Jenna nibbled her bottom lip. When Peter called for someone, they damn well better go and be quick about it.

Focus on the present. Must stop Streakers from eating us all.

An image of Eric roared into her mind, and she fought back the threat of tears.

"Sounds like a plan," Quentin said. "Let's move now before more Streakers get in."

"Jenna, you with us?" Gus asked.

"Ready and willing," she replied.

She stomped to the door, separating them from the lobby and the horde of undead.

Quentin's breath tickled her shoulder. Jenna accepted the machete Aiko offered.

The rest of the group fanned out behind them.

She paused at the entrance, noting the flaking gray plaster. Nothing scratched or thumped. It was too quiet.

They pushed the seating out of the way. The handle creaked, and the door cracked open. She peered into the darkness beyond. A pale white hand shot out, slapping the door before anchoring to the camouflage jacket. More hands reached and grabbed at her clothing. The relentless tug on the jacket jerked her step by step toward the mass of Streakers that rammed themselves into the theater entrance. Feet braced, hands behind held her in place. Until they didn't.

Undead tugged her closer, teeth-gnashing, hoping for a taste of flesh. Even as the machete slashed and her legs kicked out, the horde invaded. The machete hacked at the Streaker's arm. Each cut drenched the room with a retched stench of death. Even when weapon met with bone, the limb refused to separate from its master. Two dull, lifeless eyes stared at her, so decayed she could no longer tell a color.

From close behind, two gunshots exploded.

Ears ringing, she staggered back. Another Streaker stepped over the silenced body of the first and shouldered its way through the door.

Caleb slammed a bat against its skull, which popped and exploded on to the carpet.

Would this ever stop?

A third monster struggled over the fallen bodies.

"At least six more out there," Aiko yelled.

Emma caught the Streaker's attention and drew it into the theater.

Jenna followed the others into the lobby, ears full of chiming bells. The door to Theater One slammed shut, sealing her fate. Hiding in the shadows and avoiding the undead, they reached the bulky concession stand made of panels of pressed plywood.

The concession stand squealed when thrust forward.

Streakers turned and stumbled in their direction.

Shots rang out. Jenna's machete was at the ready. The undead staggered nearby. The gunfire dispatched three before they could get too close. Caleb and Aiko made quick work of the bulky concession stand, prying away bolts that locked it into the floor and moving it toward the broken window. When they could go no farther, they lifted the concession making it look like it weighed no more than a few pounds and heaved it at the front. The stand held. Caleb and Aiko returned to the shadows.

Her turn now.

Jenna grunted, sweating. She and Quentin labored side-by-side to wrangle the heavy concession stand the last few feet to form a barricade in front of the broken glass. Muscles protesting, she shoved.

Movement slithered around her. Jenna spotted two grotesque figures lurching along the street outside, stumbling over the debris littering the otherwise empty sidewalk.

Billy shifted position and tugged the corner of the heavy wood concession.

They're so close. Jenna glanced over her shoulder to make sure nothing inside wanted to eat her. *Trust Caleb and Aiko. As long as they engaged the living dead inside, she'd be okay to finish this.*

She thrust with all her might, and the hulking concession stand shot forward a few inches. The movement forced another look outside. Numerous swaying undead, drenched in gangrene, converged on the theater. The mass of undead joined together to form a sea of rotting flesh.

"More coming," Jenna shouted. "We need this done."

With a final surge of strength and panic, they angled the concession stand against the window.

"It's too low. They'll just climb over it." Fear laced Billy's words.

Outside, death moved closer.

Without warning, Caleb approached from the shadows, holding another tall, heavy counter. "Move."

Stumbling out of the way, Jenna watched in horror.

He stormed into the sunlight, placing the counter atop the concession, barricading the window against Streakers.

Caleb's burning flesh filled her nose, but she ran forward and dragged him back into the darkness.

Charred flesh triggered the three remaining Streakers, who dragged decayed body parts closer. Quentin and Billy kept two at bay. A zombie, bones splintering through melted skin, ran at Jenna, reaching out hands lacking digits. Machete raised, she stood poised to decapitate the creature.

With an ear-splitting shotgun explosion, the Streaker's skull sprayed across the carpet before it jerked violently and crumbled.

George admired his handy work. "See, little girls like you need protection. You should stay out of the fight and in the kitchen like women should."

Ignoring the older man, Jenna refocused her attention on Caleb's limp body. "Someone help me. Tell everyone what happened."

Billy ran back to Theater One, banging on the door for entrance.

Peter came over. Caleb remained limp and unmoving.

"What now?" Her voice hitched.

As Peter examined Caleb, the rest of the group went to work securing the lobby and reinforcing the windows. Anything moveable added to the barricade. A remote theater became the holding cell for undead body parts that would never rise again.

"He's burned pretty bad. Much worse than Victor was. I'll have to find him some sustenance, or he might die," Peter said. "Do you know anyone willing to donate some blood?"

11

TRANSLUCENT FILM DRIFTED in front of her eyes and then settled in the corner of the room and every time Jenna's gaze shifted, the haze moved.

Woozy. Must be my eyes. Why does it feel like someone is rubbing steel wool all over my skin?

Red stains permeated the bandage covering her wound. Her gaze flew to Caleb.

She had volunteered the blood to save him. Not one-hundred percent, but his burns were healing rapidly, even after a few hours.

Her gaze lingered. His skin morphed slowly from burnt charcoal to baby-bottom pink.

She didn't understand the experience. Having him suck blood from her slashed wrist wasn't pleasant in the current circumstances. It wasn't the horror movie she'd expected either. He'd needed so much.

"Jenna, are you paying attention?" Gus placed a hand on her arm. "Thoughts about the plan to get out of here?"

"Sorry. Not myself."

"You should rest."

"Why do we even need to ask her?" George rubbed a gnarled fist against his stubble.

"I'm fine." The words were as sharp as a needle. "I like the plan. I mean it's not great someone has to play decoy, but New Racers are fast and have a better chance of eluding the Streakers. It'll give us time to use the fire escape from the roof and get into the cars and out of here."

"We'll rendezvous with them in four blocks. Let's all hope the New Racers move quick, and we'll gun it out of here without a long line of Streakers in tow," Aiko said.

"What about the pile of cars?" George's voice carried from where he leaned against a wall. He hadn't washed from the Streaker attack, none of them had, and blood and Streaker remains stuck to his arms and shirt.

While Streaker bites and guts didn't infect the last humans, who appeared to have some natural immunity, bites could lead to nasty infections. Most people survived those if treated quickly enough with antibiotics. Undead also never stopped attacking, so most people perished. Dinner for the already dead.

Stay here and sleep. Humans were the last of a dying breed anyway. Why get up and keep searching for something more? Nothing better than death? Sure, the virus that killed off most of the population doesn't affect the last survivors. Thank the gods for immunity. One by one the undead took everyone important. Jenna shook the stupor away. *Snap out of this. Pray the doom and gloom wasn't a side effect of the blood donation.*

"Let's hope we'll have enough time to move any cars or junk blocking the roadway before the Streakers catch up. We have to head out of town a different way than we came in and there's no telling what the roads are like. We don't have many other options." Gus sounded like a sergeant trying to motivate his troops to head into a battle they couldn't win.

Gus was worried about their escape. It was going to be a difficult night with no guarantee of survival.

"Let's get cracking," Aiko said.

Emma vacated her comfortable theater seat and came over. "You okay to help? We have a lot of organizing to do, but I'm happy to give you a medical pardon."

"I'll be okay. I pull my weight around here." Nausea bubbled in her stomach and her arm ached, but she helped organized the supplies people had brought into the theater, making sure they were easy to haul and ready to go.

When done, fresh air beckoned. Jenna climbed the stairwell toward the roof and rested her head against the iron rail, once probably erected to keep people from trying to jump. She peered over the spokes.

Not how to go. Too horrible. The last way anyone would want to die would be to jump into the waiting pool of Streaker hell.

Below, undead aimlessly roamed but no longer crowded against the theater's glass entrance; they'd fallen out of attack mode. The hastily erected concession stand fortress was surviving well enough to create a buffer. Above, the sun sank lower. Clouds swept in like galloping horses. The wind shifted and rain was imminent.

Perfect. Everyone's job became a little more complicated with bad weather.

People became ill-tempered when rain made the most basic tasks harder to accomplish. Tonight, the rain could slow the New Racers on foot and the human drivers.

Just dandy! Jenna sighed. *Break's over.*

A few hours later, in the gloomy drizzle of sunset, Jenna's bones ached with the chill. The entire party moved to the roof with the group's belongings. Cat meowed incessantly from the duffle bag Jenna had shoved him inside. In the hours since the group had barricaded the entrance and windows of the theater, at least a dozen new Streakers had lined the street looking for entry. Now, they began to demand it. Decayed hands bulleted through the broken glass causing shards to fall alongside pieces of flesh.

They'd get inside soon enough. The group's makeshift barrier would not hold forever. Downstairs would soon become a death trap.

From the roof, the group had a bird's eye view. They planned the route the New Racers would use to lure the Streakers away and everyone agreed on a meeting spot a few blocks south. The vehicles lined the road in front of the theater. It would be easy to escape if the group could make it to them once a diversion occupied the Streakers.

So many "ifs."

"Caleb and Victor, you're staying with the humans," Peter ordered. "You're not at full strength, and we can't worry about you."

"I'm fine." Caleb said. Aiko gave him a sideways glance and he fell quiet, nodding in agreement.

New Racers, who would be decoys, started their descent. Some chose to use the fire escape ladders, cascading down like concluding a rock-climbing expedition, graceful and fluid mountaineers. The New Racers, including Aiko and John, jumped from the roof without effort. No matter what method they descended, they reached the ground with impossible speed and elegance.

The Streakers noticed. Their attack on the movie theater doors and windows came to a halt. Instead, they shambled toward New Racers who attracted their attention with taunts and threats. Aiko flung pebbles with deadly accuracy into the eyes of the undead. The exchange lasted only a few seconds before they ran, leading the undead away.

The rest of the group hurried into action, throwing supplies before descending the fire escapes.

Jenna was driving this time. *Making it into a vehicle* was a relief, but this was only the beginning. The lack of Streakers was a huge reprieve for the group. They'd all slept little and fought too many zombies in the last few weeks. And Eric was gone.

The undead would be back soon enough. Get going.

She switched the SUV into drive. Emma rode shotgun and Caleb reclined on the back seat with the duffle bag containing Cat on his lap. Jenna was surprised at the relief at having Caleb in the car with her, rather than him being one of the New Racers attempting to outrun the undead.

"You okay?" she asked in the general direction of the back seat before angling the SUV in line with the caravan of vehicles.

Emma turned and placed her hand on Caleb's forehead.

He swatted it away. "I'm fine. Just tired. I'll be ready to destroy a whole new band of Streakers after a few hours of R and R."

Jenna's body relaxed but only for a moment. Knowing they still had to get out of the town caused her knuckles to turn white against the steering wheel. Four blocks along they stopped at the intersection where everyone had planned to meet. Jenna watched through the rear-view mirror. Caleb sat and scanned the streets. Seconds later shadows turned solid. Doors opened and banged shut.

"They're all here." The line of vehicle hitched forward.

Movement outside caught Jenna's attention. *Just a shadow. Just a tree. Just . . . Damn. Not a tree. Not a shadow.* "They're here."

"You're right, and they've brought reinforcements." Caleb twisted to peer out the back window.

Streakers slunk and staggered around the corners of the buildings, beginning to fill the road in front of the line of vehicles.

"Move! Move!" Jenna screamed the words at the line of cars, even though no one could hear her in the other vehicles.

The SUV lurched forward.

Drivers hit the gas pedals, speeding away.

A Streaker crashed into her door. Fingers clawed at the

window, leaving behind a streak of human flesh. A finger bone cracked against the pane of glass. Gas pedal hitting the floor, she jammed the steering wheel a hard right and then left, throwing her passengers sideways. The crunch of a body infiltrated the interior.

"Sorry." She bit hard on her bottom lip to keep from screaming and maneuvered the steering wheel violently, slamming into the Streaker again. The feline meowed from the back seat. Caleb grunted. The Streaker staggered and fell. Jenna reversed and aimed the vehicle in its direction. Bones crunched under the wheels.

"That's how you do it." Jenna peeked over her shoulder. "How's Cat."

"You're a cold-hearted woman." Caleb said. "Except when it comes to the cat you said you didn't want."

The caravan moved throughout the rest of the town without problem. At the edge of Pittsfield, getting through the debris piled was tiring but uneventful. The group found a partially cleared area. After scattering a few tires and discarded car parts, the vehicles continued their trek. High Point Inn now only hours away.

On the highway once again, Caleb turned around in his seat, surveying the scene to make sure it was free of undead. The caravan advanced along the dark roads unencumbered for many miles. Jenna relaxed, able to laugh when she heard Caleb's snoring from the backseat.

"I'm glad you still see the humor in this situation," Emma said.

"What do you mean?"

"You are always so serious. I thought the fact we were almost eaten by Streakers might put you in a bad mood."

"Bad mood?"

"Euphemism. I was being nice."

"I'm not so horrible."

"You're able to laugh at poor Caleb snoring when he's sound asleep."

"That's different. I'm relieving the tension from almost being killed tonight."

"It was stressful for everyone. We fought hard to survive."

"We? I don't remember seeing you out on the main lobby fighting the undead."

"I was there in spirit."

"Big help."

"If I didn't know better, I would believe, Ms. Jenna, are giving me attitude."

"Maybe you should just rest too. Quiet like Caleb."

"Definitely attitude. Perhaps I will remove my stimulating conversation since you cherish it so much. Will you be all right behind the wheel? You haven't had a lot of sleep."

"I'm fine, Mom."

Emma gave Jenna a quick kiss on the cheek before closing her eyes. The hum of the car's engine and the textures of the night washed over her. For a moment it was peaceful but then Eric's face surfaced.

She let him fight, which made her responsible for his death. She should have said something and forced him back into the small theater and away from the fight.

The back seat had gone silent. She glanced in the rearview mirror to ensure the patient was still alive.

"Thank you." His gaze trapped hers for a second. "For everything. I owe you so much for today."

"I didn't do anything. You had plenty of volunteers offering to nurse you back to health. You're popular that way."

"Thank you anyway." He closed his eyes.

She'd bet her life on the fact he wasn't going back to sleep.

12

JENNA WOKE. Early morning sun drifted through the curtains. She sat, alert and then yawned and stretched. She'd slept on a real bed with sheets, pillows, and blankets.

True, the blankets had moth holes and the pillows had mouse droppings on them when they arrived a few weeks ago but making it to High Point Inn had changed everything. She wasn't afraid to face the day and hadn't had a nightmare in weeks. But it hadn't all turned out good.

A five-minute hot shower waited, one of the new luxuries she was both excited and thankful for. Hot water came via the generator at the inn but plans for a better system were under discussion. With ingenuity, heat and electricity would never be lacking.

Jenna could only describe John as a post-pandemic hipster. But no matter his fashion sense, he'd turned out to be exceedingly knowledgeable about so many useful things.

An engineer in his former life, he fashioned a gasifier, a gas generator, which turned wood into energy. The group ran appliances like the stove with it, heated the water for the showers, and powered the cars without gasoline. Making additional units took time, which meant everyone cut and hauled lumber daily to get them through the winter with heat and power.

She twirled, enjoying the luxury resort room she'd claimed. The top floor, corner room held a gorgeous view of the lake and a sense of security. A faded oriental rug rested under a huge bed. The walls were a rich, warm, taupe brown, accented by heavy drapes.

The goal today—clean the grimy window coverings.

They needed a good thrashing. She dragged them off the rods, choking on the plumes of dust smog filling the air.

She'd beat the drapes using a broom—to within an inch of their lives if she must. She'd have to borrow a broom from the supply closet.

This simple task reminded her so much of former times. When the drapes were dust-free they'd hang again and should keep the room shaded in the early morning and insulated when winter arrived. A mundane task, something deplorable in her previous life, brought joy and a little nostalgia.

Her room. A space to find solitude.

There were two large chairs. While Jenna had never been a person happy to remain idle for long periods, she hoped to start her journal again and record what went on at the inn. The chairs and the small center table between them, would be the perfect place for her to write.

She meandered into the hallway in a pair of ratty pajamas the group scavenged from some of the nearest homes though they were few and far between. The pajamas were bright purple plaid, not what the fashionista inside her would have chosen, but the soft flannel was comfortable and reassuring. Jenna came to an unexpected halt. "Caleb."

He stood at the door to his room, avoiding the milky lights filtering through the windows. "Hi." His greeting fell flat.

"How are you?"

"Fine."

"Need anything."

"No." He turned away.

Since arriving at the inn, Caleb had been silent and moody, if not downright rude. And she had no idea why. Could Eric's death have devastated him? Caleb avoided her. When chance brought them together, conversations were brief and strained. Exactly like this one.

"Sorry for interrupting the important business of heading into your room." The words lashed the air. "Go get some sleep and forget I ever said anything. Just forget I exist."

"Fine." He turned the knob to open his door.

"You are so frustrating." Tears threatened. "Is it strange I care about how you are doing?"

Jenna stalked outside, banging the front door shut and sprinted from the porch of the inn through the meadow, running from the rage within. Since settling into the High Point Inn, she had the luxury of getting mad at the living rather than the dead. With over 350 acres of forests and the natural boundaries, the inn was perfect for defending against Streakers. Dense woods on one side and the reservoir on the other, provided protection from roaming undead. The inn only had one, twisty main road and the closest town was nearly twenty miles away. The group, since their arrival, had also fortified most of the inn's boundaries with fences.

Winded, Jenna huffed, slowing to a walk, ambling around the grounds. The morning sun warmed her shoulders, but the air remained crisp.

She'd put the incident behind her. Put Caleb behind her for good and start fresh in the garden. Inside chores be damned. While everyone cooked, did laundry and kept public areas clean in collaboration, some chores were like Streakers guts. Disgusting.

Human or New Race, the common area men's bathrooms were disgusting, and that was the duty awaiting today. Sure, there were private bathrooms in each room, but people often used the common bathrooms to conserve water.

A good soldier, she never complained outright, but wished for more time to spend on personal projects.

While there was so much to like at the inn, George's words about sticking to the kitchen had enjoyed some truth. She no longer had to kill Streakers and thanks to the landscape and solid fences erected, patrols were irregular. As much as she hated it, men banded together for labor intensive jobs like cutting and hauling wood and special projects like the gasifier. She cooked and cleaned, completing mundane chores.

She'd save chores until later out of consideration to New Racers who tended to live nocturnally and sleep through the afternoon.

A lame excuse, but justification for her actions.

After spending so many months living in close proximity to everyone, wasting an amazing day was an impossible idea. It didn't even matter she ran outside in pajamas.

One thing about living through the apocalypse, no one cared if you were eccentric, as long as a beating heart confirmed you were of the living.

Jenna put a hand to shade her eyes so she could see the tilled plot of land that would become a garden. A frown formed.

What was there?

Bursting into another sprint, this time her shouting was for an entirely different reason. Rabbits and deer in her garden, sure, but this.

"Get away," Jenna yelled at the big white horses whose heads hung over the chicken wire fence she had erected. "Move, move!"

The horses failed to comply.

"Really?"

The horses looked at her with skepticism.

Out of breath once again, she approached the large, rather filthy, animals.

"How did you make it so long, out here alone?"

The horses looked at her perplexed and wary but did not shy away. They'd stopped munching the tops of the carrots which had only begun to sprout. At least they had left the beets, kale, and turnips untouched.

Jenna had started her garden the first weeks after the group arrived, finding the work soothing, but a lack of knowledge frustrating. It wasn't like she could jump on a computer and Google what crops to plant in late summer and early fall.

She was nothing if not persistent and planted, watered, and watched carrots, turnips, radishes, cucumbers, beets, and Swiss chard emerge from seed.

Proud. *Heck yes but not alone in the venture.*

There were mornings she'd come out to the garden and find the entire area watered and weeded. No one admitted to being her garden elf. She wished she could thank the person or people helping, and soon, the garden would be too big of a job for a single soul. Many hands would need to pitch in when the plants made the trip to the greenhouse.

What to do with the plants in the winter would be another challenge. Weeds triumphed daily and the greenhouse required serious rehabilitation. Broken windows needed replacement and the tables for potting the plants, repaired. She put time in at the greenhouse every day, but it was slow going.

What about the problem in front of her?

The horse's mane reminded her of her former best friend's long hair. Holding tight, she led the beast away. Large hooves clomped next to her boots. It followed willingly, bobbing its head against the flies. The second one fell in line.

I guess even summer horsemanship camp becomes useful during the ends of time.

The drafts plodded along side to a nearby field where they grazed. Hoping the horses wouldn't bolt, Jenna trekked across the field to a barn for rope. Quentin was inside, welding a broken pipe from one of the bathroom sinks. His bare, rugged arms filled out a T-shirt stained from sweat and hard work. Recently cropped sandy brown hair stood straight and spiked.

"Hey stranger." A gap-tooth smile beamed.

While Caleb had become a ghost, she'd seen a lot of Quentin.

They managed to turn up in the same place or work on the same project. The more close and comfortable they became, the farther Caleb slipped away. She hated the stilted conversation when they should be mourning Eric's death together. Every attempt to approach him and offer comfort met resistance and, at times, hostility.

"How are you today?" Quentin asked.

"Two horses have invaded my garden. Do you have something to tie them with in here?"

"Horses? Can I see?" His eyes lit with excitement.

Her heart fluttered. Maybe. A little.

"Sure. The more the merrier when wrangling horses."

"They used to have an equine program here. Everything you need should be around somewhere." Moving toward the other side of the barn, he pointed to the wall. "There's lead ropes and halters. A ton of stuff. I'm not sure what half of it is for, and I used to ride."

"Me too. I took lessons when I was younger, and I went to camp. I wonder if the two outside are ridable?"

"We could go out on a trail ride together if they are. Do they look okay?"

"A little skinny and very dirty, but we can add some weight to them in the next few weeks if they come in the barn and learn to trust us."

"You plan on keeping them here?"

"Why not. I love a new challenge. First a cat and now this." She grabbed two halters and lead lines.

"Don't forget the chickens Ford brought back last week. You're becoming the official animal whisperer."

"How'd I forget the chickens? I hope we get some eggs soon."

"We'll need to start considering what to feed all the barn yard critters, especially when winter comes."

"You are such the planner. Let's go."

"Happy to help."

She handed him a lead line. "Thanks. You handle the bigger one."

"Not a problem." Quentin quirked a brow. "For you, anything."

The blush spreading across her cheeks kept her lips sealed.

The horses were docile, obviously someone's mount at one time or another. Neither draft complained when halters went over their noses and the couple tied them on a long line to graze.

"I'll be done soon. Do you want an extra hand with those two ragged beasts?" he asked.

"I'd love help."

"I have to finish with the pipe in Emma's room. I promised myself I'd clean out the loft in the barn. You could help with cleaning, and then we could groom the horses. There might be tack and supplies there."

"Sounds like a plan."

"You'll probably want to check their feet too. I don't know how rough the weather and ground has been on them."

"Don't we need a hoof pick? Not sure I remember how to do it the right way. I don't want to get kicked."

"Give me some time to finish this project," Quentin said. "Come back to the barn in a little bit and we'll figure it out."

She sent him a wave and returned to the garden. As she plucked weeds, Cat emerged from the woods to pay a visit. He rather liked his new home but preferred to be outside most of the time. There was the occasional gift of a dead mouse on her bed, but otherwise, he failed to show her much love or attention.

He's still miffed at the fact she'd shoved him in a duffel bag when escaping the Streakers in Pittsfield.

He sniffed at her plants and twined between her ankles before heading off to the barn. Cat loved Quentin and would happily perch in the barn, watching him work.

Watching Quentin work might not be so bad.

Her gaze returned to the horses. Jenna loved the relaxation of the garden, but time dragged today. She weeded a row and then another.

Twenty minutes, maybe. What she wouldn't give for a cell phone to tell time right now. One more row and then back to the barn.

A few minutes later Quentin left with the piece of pipe and return not long after. In the barn, they climbed the creaky steps to the loft. One door lay on the ground, off its hinges. Quentin swung the other back. The weathered, antique floorboards protested loudly under his 180 pounds. The dust had settled heavily amid a jumble of objects. While there was a large, cleared space in the center of the loft, antique farm equipment and non-essential items from the inn invaded most of the area.

"How do you want to do this?" Jenna asked.

"I don't know, but it's really stuffy." Quentin drew his T-shirt over his head, exposing tight abdominal muscles and ropey arm muscles. "You don't mind, do you?"

"Not so much." She focused on the daunting task before her. "Why don't we carry anything useful downstairs and clean it up? We'll deal with the rest of it some other day."

"It's a plan." He moved to one of the many piles scattered around the room.

After hauling, pushing, and carrying, Jenna's back was sore, and her arms hurt. Her throat was parched thanks to all the dust, but she had it easy. Quentin had dragged heavy items from the loft for her to organize. Piles of usable clothes, tools, and supplies filled the space.

His footsteps battered the stairs.

"Not another pile. Let's call it quits. We've been at this forever." She sank next to her collections of books, clothes, tools, junk, and horse tack.

"You got a lot done. We'll call it a day."

"Thank you."

"I'll haul the books and clothes to the inn. You find a space for the tools and tack and then bring the horses in. I'll bring back some water."

"You read my mind."

"The room upstairs would be a great place to store all the horse tack once we get it organized, but for now it might be better here. Thoughts?"

"I like whatever you suggest if it means you'll bring me a drink. Dying of thirst."

He saluted and left.

She finished organizing the last of the boxes before Quentin returned.

"Feast your eyes." She gulped the water he brought.

The horse tack lay organized and clean. While there had been a variety of bridles, saddles, saddle pads, and tools, Jenna had picked out two western saddles, two fluffy saddle pads, and bridles she hoped would fit the drafts. An open tack box displayed brushes and other paraphernalia.

He surveyed her work and whistled in appreciation. "Impressive."

Grabbing a tack box, they ventured outside. The horses

stood munching contently in the field unconcerned at the couple's arrival.

"Let's peek at these big guys." His hand ran over the draft's flank. "What breed are they?"

The dark brown horses were large and stocky with hooves the size of dinner plates.

"Not sure, but they're pretty sturdy. Maybe Clydesdale like in the famous commercials. Remember those? Whatever they are they're solid fellas, aren't they? They don't appear worse for wear after being on their own."

"Adds to the adventure. Who wants to ride a small pony? I'll grab some brushes out of the tack box."

"Anything else we need?"

"Did you see anything like an ice pick? It's to clean their hooves."

"I'll go with you and we'll see."

"Stay and pet them. They like you. I'll search the box."

On his return, he handed off a brush and they groomed and inspected the horses. Mud and debris caked their backs and manes. One had a nasty scar, now healed, on its left shoulder. She picked leaves and twigs out of their manes and tails. The two worked in companionable silence, brushing the horses who relished the attention, leaning into the strokes, heads bobbing. One let out a giant yawn.

"Let me show you how to pick their feet."

"I remember." She reached for the draft's hoof.

"Don't ruin my fun." He moved behind, pressing close, his hand warm on hers. "Start at the bottom of his leg above the hoof and slide your hand." He angled her hand over the lower part of the horse's leg.

With a squeeze, the horse lifted its hoof. She checked for stones lodged in the frog, the soft portion of the bottom. "Their feet aren't horrible for being alone all this time."

"Could use a trim."

"I'll leave trimming to you." Her body heated with the close contact. "We better find a way to fatten them up soon."

"Isn't there a fenced in pasture behind the barn full of grass gone wild. I bet these two will mow it down in no time."

"Grab a pony. We'll bring them there. I'll figure out how to bale hay for the winter, but I'll need your help. Lots of help." He stepped back. "Let's get moving. I need to fix something for Jackie. Don't want her mad at me."

"I didn't mean to get you in trouble," Jenna said. "She doesn't like to be ignored."

The horses clomped up the hill.

"No worries, but what's the plan for tomorrow."

"Tomorrow? Are they sound enough to ride?"

"Absolutely." He held her hand when they returned to the inn. "How about in the morning?"

"Sounds like a plan."

His parting smile made the rest of her day warm and fuzzy even if she spent the last part of it cleaning toilets.

13

Jenna woke later than usual. The room was specter quiet except for the drum of footsteps below her and the muted call of birds outside her window.

Grabbing clothes off the ground, the first items touched, a flannel shirt, black T-shirt, and jeans, created her ensemble.

What is this? Happiness? Excitement?

She couldn't wait to see how the horses fared their first night in the barn after being free for such a long time. If they did well with a rider on their back, training them for work shouldn't be a problem.

Skipping breakfast, the sun was warm butter on her skin.

"Hey!" Her voice failed to carry across the meadow where Quentin was on his return from the barn.

"I woke early and let the horses out." He pointed in the direction of the field. "I had some other projects to finish so I stayed out here. I was heading in to see what was keeping you."

"Sorry. I wasn't sure when we should meet." A rash of red colored her neck.

"This is as good a time as any. Ready to ride?"

"Can't wait."

The large drafts grazed, content with their current conditions. They hiked to the old barn, gathered the tack, and then brought the horses inside. Getting bridles into the horses' mouth, turned out to be more challenging than expected.

"I thought I'd remember, but how does this work?" She struggled with the random assortment of leather straps and clasps. "Why is this so complicated."

"Like this." He grabbed the horse's mane, drawing the draft's head lower. "We have to get their head low, and then have them accept the bit in their mouth."

She tugged on the halter so the horse would behave. The Clydesdale bonked Jenna in the face when it shook its mane from side to side. She rubbed her chin. "Horse's heads hurt more than I believed they would."

He wrestled with the other horse.

"Just you wait," she warned. The large brown gelding lowered its head. The metal bit clanked against the horse's teeth, and the animal stretched its neck away. Its mane whipped at her. She tried again. And again.

"He's smarter than you." He guided the other draft forward by the reins. The oiled leather saddle glowed.

"Can you do it? Go ahead." The two switched places, Jenna holding the reins of one horse while he wrestled with the other to accept the bit. Minutes ticked by but the gelding turned stubborn. It pranced and stamped.

"Hold on," Jenna interrupted his latest attempt to coax the horse into submission. "I remember something useful. If you put your finger behind their teeth, it causes the horse to open its mouth. Give me the bridle."

Jenna soothed the horse before using an index finger behind its front teeth. The bit slipped into his mouth and she drew the bridle over the draft's head, angling the brow band and tugging the rest of the bridle behind tufted ears. "Success."

The horse pranced in anticipation. They walked into the sunlight and stood by the fenced in pasture.

"Can you get on from the ground?" Quentin asked.

"I don't know. It's been a while."

"I couldn't find a mounting block."

"They look bigger today."

"Leg up?" Quentin cupped his hands.

The first try landed her on her belly in the saddle. But getting a leg over, turned out to be impossible. She jumped to the ground. "This time you have to push harder."

"That's what she said."

"What came out of your mouth?"

"I'm not taking it back." He heaved, sending her over the side of the gelding, landing in the grass. The horse stood unfazed.

"You okay?" An unapologetic eyebrow rose once he realized no injuries were involved.

"Thanks for the help." The words snapped against the air. She stood and tried again. When in the saddle, the horse pranced and turned in circles.

Leading the draft to a rock wall, Quentin jumped to the top of the stone surface and mounted without incident.

"Not fair." The reins seesawed like waves when the giant pranced.

They walked by the lake where the sun began its rise over the water before steering the horses into the woods. Quentin was a natural equestrian, fitting comfortably in the saddle, well-worn jeans punctuating lean, muscled legs. His broad shoulders were erect when he guided the horse on a trail, a Mets baseball cap hid his normally unruly hair.

"What should we name the horses?" he asked. "We are not having a repeat of *Cat,* are we? *Horse One* and *Two*, doesn't really do it for me."

"I never realized I'd turned into a running joke. I'll never live it down."

"The horses deserve special names for surviving on their own for so long."

"This guy could be called Devil, and it would fit."

"You're so negative. I doubt he'd appreciate you naming him that."

"What about Star and Moon?"

"I could get behind those names." He maneuvered next to her.

"I get Moon. Your guy is Star." She kicked her energetic horse into a lope.

The two entered into the deep woods. It was peaceful and quiet, and they rode in a companionable silence.

She trusted him. Maybe he could help with her problem. It wasn't serious, more of a nagging concern. Nothing bad had happened.

"Can I ask your opinion on something?"

"Yes, I am the sexiest man in camp."

"This is serious."

"Go ahead."

"It's about George? He gives me the creeps, and he's been watching me."

"What's the question?"

"You have to deal with him often. Is he stable? Safe?"

"He's a little off, but he had a hard life even before the end of civilization. Once you get to know him, he's not all bad. One of the good old boys if you get my drift. I'd avoid him if he creeps you out but he's not dangerous. Sexist, misogynistic, sure. Dangerous. I doubt."

"Is he still with Jackie?"

"Not sure but neither of them makes their relationship status known. Some people like to keep their private life private around here. Caleb's been spending a lot of time with Aiko lately." He squinted hard at Jenna.

"Alrighty then." The conversation dropped.

They roamed, enjoying the thrill of ditching chores and work.

It had been too long since she relaxed and had some fun.

Moon shivered and snorted. He sucked in a breath and started dancing again. The horse pranced and pawed the ground before turning in the opposite direction, ready to bolt.

"Easy, Star. Easy." Quentin patted the horse on the neck and tugged the reins. Star's nose quivered, smelling the air, eyes growing large with fear. The horse huffed.

Branches snapped and twigs cracked. A grey squirrel ran in front of the horses causing them to spook. Jenna turned Moon in tight circles before he could bolt.

"A squirrel? Really?" Jenna shook her head before patting the horse's neck.

Relief flooded through her

Quentin made no comment, his attention focused on the prancing Clydesdale.

Star still refused to settle.

They heard the breaking of branches too late and watched in horror from their saddle when a Streaker clad in the remains of khaki pants and a green shirt, the High Point Inn's uniform, limped closer. The undead must have tracked the sounds of the frightened horses. When the creature focused on them with lifeless black eyes, Jenna shivered along with the horse.

It snorted, smelling the worth of their souls.

The dead creature staggered closer.

Moon pranced in a tight circle before rearing and bucking, throwing Jenna off.

Red dots filled her eyes and pain flooded her back when she hit hard.

Quentin, still astride, vied desperately for control. His horse skittered backwards, away from the ghastly image, hooves barely missing Jenna's head.

She rolled away and grabbed a large branch, scrambling into a sitting position. Her head throbbed, sight fuzzy. The undead hooked her boot with ghastly green, molding fingers. Her back tore against the rocks as the undead dragged her closer.

The Streaker drooled and chomped. Kicking out, she connected with the monster's mouth, shattering its few remaining teeth. The undead's mouth continued to crunch and chomp, attempting to reach flesh.

"Quentin!" Her scream bounced off the trees. Another strike caused the undead to stagger back and tumble to the ground. A loud snap made Jenna hopeful her boot had broken something in the Streaker's already decaying body.

She'd pray to the gods for small miracles.

Using the reprieve, she grabbed the impromptu wood weapon, jumped up, and bashed the figure writhing and squirming on the ground like a large putrid slug.

Quentin, finally in control of his horse, jumped off only to have Star bolt when he let go of the reins. He grabbed another large tree limb as a weapon. Hoisting the massive branch, he impaled the creature in the head. The sickening crack of rotting bone and flesh accompanied the ooze of murky green fluid.

They stared at the twitching Streaker.

"Are you okay?" he asked.

Jenna nodded.

"We were really stupid to come out here without weapons." He moved close. "We have to get back and tell everyone Streakers have gotten through the fences."

"Maybe it was only one."

"Could be but when one arrives others soon follow. We need to find out how it got in. A fence must have broken."

"We have to find the horses," she said. "They ran off."

"We will but I bet they return to the barn. They know when they have a good thing. Don't worry."

"I hurt my head when I fell from the horse," She rolled her neck causing a shooting pain in her temple."

"Be careful. You might have a concussion."

"Just what I need." She leaned against Quentin. "Not fun."

He put an arm around her. "Emma needs to look you over."

"Let's get going. It's going to be a long walk."

14

JENNA LEANED on Quentin and focused on putting one foot in front of another. Sirens exploded in her head and double vision blurred her outlook. More than two hours passed before making it back to the inn and by then Jackie and Emma were organizing a search party.

"There you are." Emma's hug made Jenna nauseous.

She stood silent when Quentin explained what happened.

"I want to see you right after this," Emma admonished.

"Both of you should have better sense." Gus's lips stretched into a tight frown. "You want to go back out and show me where this all happened?"

"Absolutely," Quentin said. "We need to make sure there are no more around."

"Let's grab some weapons and George and Ford for back up." Gus walked toward the inn.

Jenna hung her head as Emma probed and inspected. After the exam, she climbed the steps towards bed.

Waking at dusk, she meandered to the lobby to discuss how Streakers managed to get close to the inn. Her head still ached, a mild concussion. With the curtains drawn back, the night sky was on full display. The over-stuffed couch in the lobby beckoned.

She'd live to fight another day, which might be soon. So much for relaxation and peace of mind.

Emma had handed her a few aspirin from their dwindling supply, but she'd returned them. Medication of any kind was running low. Jenna was also frustrated at her stupidity, heading out unarmed like the world had reverted to pre-plague.

No medication for the undeserving. Should have been smarter. They both should have thought the horseback riding through a little more before heading into the woods.

She searched for Quentin. If the horses returned, he promised to care for them, and she wanted an update.

Not here yet.

Fluff escaped from a hole in the couch. She picked at it. Even after cleaning the inn, the furniture remained in various states of disarray. Mice burrowed into the fabric of the couches, leaving holes where white tufts of material emerged like cotton balls. Chairs, while still comfortable, lacked matching cushions or had the frames repaired with odd pieces of scavenged wood.

The group was now clean and well fed. Routine and regular meals made a big difference.

Would it relax attitudes also? Would the group be mad at them for riding the horses?

Quentin arrived and sunk onto the couch next to her. "You okay? How's the head?"

"I'll heal. Horses?"

"Back in the barn."

"Thank the gods."

"They were both fine,"

"I'm worried about this meeting. I hope we didn't piss too many people off."

"We didn't do anything wrong. Don't stress."

"Aren't you just the optimist?"

"Always. Especially about beautiful women falling for my charm and good looks."

She was glad Peter called the group to order but not so happy when he pointed at her. As was his norm, a sullen frown sat in waiting. "Why don't you explain what happened today."

She began to speak, almost blurting out "Yes, Godfather" at the older New Racer whose slicked-back, oiled hair and intense brown eyes reminded her of Al Pacino.

Jenna's gaze focused on the least judgmental of the group, Josh and Kyle. The two youngest boys were eight and ten years old and arrived in tow with Ford and Beth. Looking at the foursome who sat wedged together on a couch with the boys at their feet, she was envious. In post-apocalyptic turmoil, Ford and Beth still had each other, family, and love.

"We were overly comfortable." She cleared her throat. "It was stupid we didn't bring a gun out on the trails. But it's been so quiet. There hasn't been a Streaker close since the fences went up. The horses appeared yesterday in good shape, obviously ridden, and cared for prior, and we wanted to try them out. It was the easiest way to find out what they'd been trained to do and how we might be able to use them at the inn."

Quentin placed a hand on Jenna's knee. "The attack was unexpected. Lucky it was only one Streaker. The horses spooked and bolted, leaving us on the ground and defenseless. The horses came back so they must consider this home. Maybe someone else from around here owned them or someone stayed here before we arrived."

Jenna comforted herself by covering Quentin's hand with hers. "There's no way to tell how the Streaker got in, where it came from, or if there are more."

All eyes on her, she scanned the room, noting how intently Caleb watched.

"We went out after the attack and searched the area," Gus said. "If there are more undead, they didn't show themselves. We still need to review the perimeter of the entire property to make sure no fences are down, which is the most likely scenario. A tree fell or a deer dismantled a portion of the fence. We'll go out again first thing in the morning."

Everyone needs to be extremely cautious tomorrow when patrolling the perimeter. We can't afford more injured," Peter said.

"I'm not injured. A bump of the head." Jenna glanced to the side. "There's not much more to tell. We destroyed the Streaker and walked back. A regular day in the zombie uprising."

"I should have been smarter," Quentin said. "I'm sorry I got you into the mess."

She blushed.

Caleb shot daggers at the two of them.

What was his problem? He ignored her for weeks, and now he was acting like he wanted her dead.

"It could have been worse," Emma added. "Be happy you both made it back safe and relatively intact."

George stood, sleeveless T-shirt creased with oil and dirt, shadow of a beard on his weak chin, in contrast to his stern posture. Long, slicked back brown hair hung limp against his neck. A film a sweat covered his brow.

Like a preacher at the pulpit, he spat sermon. "If there is one, there's got to be more. The Streakers probably followed the horses in. We don't want no more people acting stupid and heading outside without guns or weapons. We need to get back into military mode. As I've been telling the group since we got here, our lazy ways are going to get us killed. It's a new world and if we don't want to be extinct, we had better be ready to fight and kill, and kill, and kill some more." He stared at Jenna with a greasy-faced glare. "Fuck your girly-girly ways."

She returned the stare.

"Be careful what you say, George." Beth reprimanded.

"We've all got comfortable." Billy had grown an inch, blond hair sculpted in spikes like Quentin, who he emulated. "It's been so peaceful. I go swimming in the lake every day and never bring a gun with me. It's the only place I find solace."

It rang true. She braided the ends of her hair to keep her hands busy. *Billy had not only grown comfortable but had grown up. Not recovered but mending. At least heading in the right direction.*

"We shouldn't have done it." She'd admit her mistake. "It was bad planning to venture into the woods without weapons. I'm sure Quentin would agree. We're both sorry."

Aiko's cat-like eyes blazed. The pout on her full red lips contrasted with her sumptuous, long black hair, straight and shiny, looking styled without the aid of hair products and a straightener. "It's obvious we need to be more careful. From now on, no one goes outside without some type of protection. It would be best if humans waited for us."

Jenna tilted her head. "We can protect ourselves."

"At least travel in pairs or groups, especially to the lake for water." Aiko's nostrils flared. "It uses a lot of water to feed and bathe all the people here. From now on when we take the trucks, it has to be in groups. We can't afford any more silly little injuries. We need everyone to pull their weight."

"Regular patrols need to start again," George cut the two women off.

Aiko's stare could freeze hell. "New Racers will patrol at night, though we do it anyway when hunting. Humans patrol in the day. Jenna, you're excused until healed. However long it takes." She flicked her head back like sniffing something foul.

"It's the start of a solid plan." Gus's voice was full of cheer. "It's getting late, so we'll figure out all the details in the morning. For tomorrow, let's go back to the last rotation we used. Emma, Billy, and I are on the first shift. Quentin, Jackie, and George, you patrol second, and Ford, you and Beth, patrol next. We'll get the rest done tomorrow. Peter, I'll let you work on the night schedule."

"Why don't we plan now." Peter nodded at the New Race who attended. "Let's meet in my room." People stretched and formed small enclaves, the meeting officially adjourned.

She stood and watched Caleb disappear around the corner. A throbbing temple forced her to sit once again. After a moment, she pushed herself out of the chair and swiveled toward the kitchen.

There might be snacks.

Quentin, carrying a Scrabble game, intervened.

"Jackie and Beth both told me to keep you out of the kitchen. Your skills with a knife are bad enough when you see straight."

"I'm not a bad cook."

"All the pieces are still inside." The tiles inside the box banged together. "The mice didn't want to learn any new words. Want to play? I bet I'll beat you."

While happy for the distraction, she really wanted a snack. "It's not really a fair game with my head the way it is and my stomach growling. If you win that's the reason."

"Already making excuses for your defeat."

"I'm a great Scrabble player. I used to wreak havoc on anyone who challenge me to a game of Words with Friends."

The game was competitive with both of them trying to prove their superior intellectual abilities. Jenna threw *foray* and *waxen* to move ahead in score early on, but Quentin had a plan of his own. Halfway through the game, he placed *taurine* on the board, earning a fifty-point bonus for using all seven tiles.

"Not a word."

"It is so a word. Don't you remember all those energy

drinks had taurine in them? It was incredibly popular before the end of the world. I used to love energy drinks. I really miss my smart phone too."

"Liar. Not about the phone, but about taurine in the energy drinks." A throbbing head made it hard to concentrate. Her fingers fiddled with the edge of the board. Like an irate three-year-old, she wanted to flip the board over and make an ungracious exit.

"Are you mad at me?" He gulped back a laugh.

"I'm not mad." Head down, fist clenched, she mumbled. "I hate cheaters."

"Jenna?" Fingers under her chin drew their gaze together.

"Have your stupid word. My turn, right?"

"I'll pull my word off the board under one condition."

"What condition?"

Freckles darkened by days in the sun highlighted his sunburned nose. His blue eyes lit devilishly. "Kiss me. For one tiny little kiss, I'll forget all about taurine."

"Really," she reached out to grab his hand. "Let me lay one down on you."

"No." He drew back. "On the lips."

This was unexpected and not the way her first kiss after the end of the world was supposed to go. She believed it would be with Caleb, at least all her daydreams had led her there.

Her last kiss had happened at summer camp with Bobby Jackson, a sixteen-year-old, braces wearing, video game playing, counselor in training.

Why not? He was sweet and kind, rode horses, and looked gorgeous in the grey T-shirt and jeans. Don't consider it.

She leaned in, closed her eyes and their lips met.

He hesitated at first, as though he thought she'd back out of the bet, but she didn't.

There was no way she wanted this to end.

Their kiss intensified and his hands traveled to the back

of her neck, playing with the wisps of hair piled into an unruly ponytail.

All too soon it was over.

No!

Quentin rested his forehead against hers. "Guess what?"

"What?"

"I most definitely won this round, and it has nothing to do with the game."

Neither of them saw Caleb watching from the corner of the room, the look in his eyes murderous. As quickly as he appeared, he vanished outside to begin a night of patrolling the grounds and hunting.

15

THE SUN SHONE STRAIGHT DOWN. The trees rustled with the light wind, leaves beginning to show the first signs of change. The forest floor was trying to hold onto summer with abundant ferns and lady slippers.

Quentin didn't mind the patrol. It gave him time to think. It had been two weeks since the incident with the Streaker on the horses, and since then the woods had been quiet. At first, the groups had stuck together and patrolled in units, but the last few days, people went on their own to cover more territory.

Life was good and nothing could come in the way of getting into settling and rebuilding. Or Jenna. She was an enigma. He liked her, but she put up walls and remained distant. After the kiss, the two continued to hang out, but it was like they were close friends. He wanted more.

A laugh bubbled from his throat and filled the woods. Wind rustled the leaves again. The trees must be laughing back at him because the idea of having a girlfriend in a world this crazy sounded ridiculous. But that's what he wanted.

If only he could find out what was going on in her head.

Ask. It was simple, but he worried about scaring her. Figure out how to get past all the reservations and find out more about her raging emotions.

While Jenna would disagree, friends at the inn had noticed their time together and considered them a couple. There were subtle signs. Two seats were always available together at dinner and meetings. Someone else coordinated their schedules. It was fun to be together, but cleaning bathrooms was anything but picturesque or passionate.

Not an everyday romantic, Quentin vowed to cook a gourmet dinner. They'd dine without prying eyes and he'd find out exactly what was going on. Hopefully, he'd like the answers.

Introspection running amuck, he hoped the group would be prepared for the upcoming winter because he had daydreamt the two of them cozied up by a fire. He knew everyone, with John at the forefront, was working on a system to keep heat and hot water flowing throughout the year, and they'd need it. Virginia winters, while by no means extreme, could include cold weather and snow. While this might be a great deterrent to Streakers, it was also harder on humans. The New Racers showed little interest in temperature changes.

He wandered. The variety of tasks he needed to complete in the next few days and into the weeks collided with daydreams of his future with Jenna. A fence stood in front of him, one portion plied open. Examining the wreckage, the damage appeared purposeful.

Time to head back and tell someone. He didn't have the tools to fix the damage.

Silence ruled the forest around him. No bird songs, no squirrels rattling through the trees. *Odd.*

His heart pumped in his ears, drowning out the scattering leaves and twigs. Rot and decay flooded his nostrils moments before the Streaker fought its way through the thicket to the right, moving slow, dragging a broken, gangrene leg.

Quentin retrieved the rifle slung over his shoulder and aimed.

The recoil threw him back, but no bullet fired.

Jammed. No time to fix it now.

Flinging the rifle to the ground, he grabbed the large knife out of its sheath, ready to battle. Moving close, circling, he watched for the best angle to attack.

"Arugula," the Streaker wailed.

Hysteria bubbled in Quentin's throat. *Did the monster ask for lettuce?*

The Streaker clearly wasn't a vegetarian. As he moved in, the undead took on gigantic proportions, towering, arms raised. A black tongue flickered out between gaping holes in putrefying lips. Broken teeth chomped. A cacophony of grunts, whistles, and groans emerged from a mouth forever shaped into a perpetual joker's grin.

Moving behind, he attacked from the rear, gripping the zombie's hair. The blade resonated against skull bone, but not deep enough. Pulling it out, he plunged again but the blood caused the knife to slip and slice the monster's neck. Black rancid goo ran down the Streaker's body and onto the blade and his hand and arm. The Streaker twisted. The knife tumbled out of his grasp.

He dove to the left at the same time the corpse reached a long, skeletal hand to his face. Rolling away, Quentin thought he'd found freedom, but the creature latched on to his leg. Pant leg inches from the creepy smile and jagged, masticating teeth, he used all his strength to kick the Streaker in the mouth. The second time, his boot clapped against the creature's jaw. With a giant shudder, it fell to the ground, sludge spilling over his pants. Crab walking away, he put needed inches between his flesh and the Streaker who regained its footing.

Quentin stood on shaky legs, searching for his knife. It perched behind a stump on the ground a few feet away.

Dodging left, the massive Streaker followed Quentin's lead. Evil reached out to him once more. Death stung the air. He dropped, found the blade, and twisted. His fingers glistened with slime as the knife blade dug deep into the undead's eye socket. The Streaker leaned into the knife, teeth angling for human flesh. With both hands and the last of his remaining strength, the blade found the corpse's decaying brain.

Pain surged from his cheek and neck. Fresh blood from Quentin's wound mixed with the black ooze of the Streaker. The lifeless corpse pirouetted before crushing him.

Using the last remnants of his strength, Quentin tilted the lifeless, mushroom body to the side. A release of gas and fluids had him heaving the contents of his meal.

At last, he stood and staggered into the forest.

Jenna bit hard on her bottom lip.

Pain to avoid the real pain. Quentin should have been back by now. Everyone from his watch shift had already returned and it was getting close to evening. Not like him.

She cornered Gus on the porch where she sat vigil. Watching the rich blue sky fading to indigo behind the line of ancient conifers, the end of the world a distant memory. But it was attacking again. The apocalypse came with a lot more than the undead. "What are we going to do?"

The hug offered comfort and reassurance.

"I know you are worried, but Quentin is a big boy. He might have wandered a little too far and it's taking him longer to get back than expected. That boy loves him some nature and tends to roam. Maybe he forgot to check in and he's at the barn."

"I checked the barn, Empty. This is not like him. He's a

good soldier and obeys orders. If he wanted to walk in the woods, he'd do it on his own time."

"The watch went out a little while ago. If he's around, they'll find him."

"I want to go out again." The words were rapid fire. "It doesn't matter I was out on patrol this morning. He means something to me. You all mean something to me. But you get it, we're close. He's a close friend."

"It's okay, Jenna. I won't stop you from searching, but I'm sure he's fine."

"I need to do this."

"It's getting late, but if you must, I won't be the one to hold you back. You'll be unbearable." He smiled at her reaction. "Let Emma know in the kitchen, so she doesn't send the search party out for you too."

She stalked to the kitchen.

Quentin gazed at the landscape hoping to recognize anything familiar.

Must keep going.

The intense neck and face pain turned the journey grueling. All the trees and landmarks blurred and the compass he carried destroyed in the scuffle. It wasn't like there were any marked paths this deep in the forest.

Would it ever end? Could he make it back or should he just wait? Wait for what? Rescue? Death?

He leaned on a tree, inhaling painfully, and staggered forward, hand dropping from the wound on his neck, arm numb and tired.

Let it bleed. One more step. The inn must be close.

His head throbbed. Unwilling legs shuffled onward. Every ragged breath and little movement caused a cloud of pain. After a dozen or so steps, one knee hit the ground before he dropped fully.

Can't move anymore. Head hurts. Done.

But after a few minutes, the pain receded. With the aid of a low tree branch, Quentin heaved himself upright.

A few more steps. Almost there.

He tottered forward. Afternoon shadows created impressions of demons on the ground. A raven screamed in the trees above. If pain had not already convinced him of his lack of luck, he might have believed the bird a bad omen.

He dropped to the ground for the second time.

Not going to make it back to the inn. This is as good a place as any to die.

Blood seeped unrelenting from his wounds, trickling along his neck, and dampening his shirt. The self-loathing of letting the damn Streaker overtake him back in the woods clashed with the pain. He crawled against a tree and closed his eyes.

If this was the end, then so be it.

His vision faded to black.

Jenna was leaving Emma in the kitchen when commotion erupted. "Let's see what's up."

The two women headed for the front door.

George and Ford carried an unmoving, bloody Quentin between them. Wounds on his face and neck trickled red covering his shirt the same color.

Momentarily paralyzed, Jenna's fear engulfed her.

She could not lose someone else she cared about. This could not happen.

Emma ran to the dying man's side.

"He must have been ambushed by a Streaker," George said.

"Where'd you find him?" Emma searched for a pulse.

"About a mile from the inn. He's been bleeding for a while. I don't know how bad it is, or how long he was out there like this."

"Get some towels." Emma met Jenna's deer in a headlights gaze. "I need something to stop the blood and lots of clean, warm water. Now!"

"Where should we put him?" George asked.

"Follow me," Emma replied.

Jenna was weary to the bone. She slouched on the couch in the main room. Three days since the attack on Quentin, and he was not getting better. In fact, he appeared much worse. She'd nursed him day and night, but nothing brought the fever down or woke him from a perpetual state of semi-consciousness.

The tranquil setting of the main room, now often called the great hall, contradicted the heated discussion. The group had worked hard to make the common area homey since their arrival. Beth, Jackie, and some of the New Race, had created a sewing circle and made new pillows for the couches and chairs. They were now working on couch covers.

How stupid. Nothing really mattered. Let them make their dumb-ass covers. When we are extinct the Streakers can enjoy them.

She stared with distaste at an old DVD player and DVDs Caleb had found and brought back to life. As a treat, the group could watch a movie since they had a gasifier and generator as power sources.

Let's enjoy a romantic comedy while someone dies. What a treat.

The group planned to scout for solar panels to increase their efficiency and offer an alternative source of energy.

None of it mattered anymore. We probably won't make it through the winter anyway. If we do, there's always more Streakers ready and waiting.

All the members of their small group, except for the two youngest boys, Josh and Kyle, were in mid-meeting. The group came together in what was now known as the Counsel. Votes decided important questions and problems, and everyone received an equal say in the final decision.

"Assholes," Jenna muttered under her breath, daring someone to contradict. The audacity of what people suggested was stunning, but her only recourse was to destroy the couch, picking out the stuffing from the mouse holes to occupy her hands. So, she did, to avoid strangling every naysayer in the room.

No one addressed her directly, but no one stopped the destruction. With all the controversy, she'd end up picking every strand of white fluff from every single usable piece of furniture.

"Should we make a final decision about what to do?" Peter's words were kind if the vote was not.

"We should leave him. Close the door, walk away, and then bury him or shoot him when it's over. I guess it depends if he turns or not," said Aiko.

Most heartless bitch on the face of the earth.

"Aiko." Beth's face drained of all color. "He's someone's son. He's our family. You don't need to be rude. This is a serious and sensitive matter."

"I'm honest about the situation, which is more than most of you are willing to be," she replied, scanning the room rebelliously.

Jenna exploded off the couch. "We can't just let Quentin die. It's inhumane and wrong. We must do everything possible to save him. Quentin's one of us. He got us here in the first place! We have to do the right thing."

"He's only human. If he was of the New Race, he would have survived this without a problem," Aiko's words lacked any emotion.

Jenna stepped toward Aiko, fingers fisting. Emma reached out, grabbing an arm to hold her back.

"Quentin needs more medicine than I have. The few antibiotics left aren't working on him. They weren't strong to begin with." Emma faced off with Aiko. "We know he won't turn undead if we keep him alive. He hasn't showed any of the signs yet, but we don't have the right medicine at the inn. We used most of our supply on the trip here and haven't been able to find more. I'm low on aspirin too. I don't know how much longer I'll be able to keep his fever down."

"We have to help him," Jenna pleaded.

"We don't know anything about his condition," Gus said. "Even with all the medicine in the world, he might not make it. We should leave it in God's hands rather than risk more people. Steakers are close. We don't know how many, but they are obviously around."

Jenna wouldn't relent. "We have to try. There are pharmacies in every town. The medicine we need can't be far away. What about going back to Pittsfield? There must be medicine at both the grocery store and the drug store on the main street."

"It's a long trip demanding supplies and manpower," Peter reasoned.

"Or womanpower." Jenna scowled. "You're worried about supplies? It will be worth it."

"For the humans," Aiko interjected.

Jenna ignored the comment. "You heard Emma say we were low. A scouting group would be going out soon enough. This turns it into a priority. I'm sure the medicine we need is out there. Every store in the city cannot have been ransacked."

"You know what's there?" George answered his own question with a cruel smile. "A shitload of Streakers waiting for any dumbass to set foot in that reeking hell again."

"We're worried about you coming back too, not just supplies." Peter placated.

"Antibiotics? Really?" Aiko's words cut through the air like a sword. "Are we trying to rescue the same person? Never mind all the Streakers running around in the stupid town almost got us all killed, but antibiotics and aspirin aren't a guarantee he'll get better. Even with medicine, he's probably going to die, especially if you run into trouble or delay even a couple of days. If you even make it back."

Small conversation erupted throughout the group, but Jenna didn't like the dribs and drabs of words she heard. Most of the New Race and humans agreed with Aiko, even if they did not condone her harsh presentation of the facts.

"We can't risk sacrificing a bunch of people to save one," George said.

Jenna had an overwhelming desire to gut punch him to shut him up.

The pock-faced man continued. "We don't know what will happen to Quentin when he gets the medicine. We could lose everyone we send back into Pittsfield. Going into the city once was more than enough."

"Not to be rude George, but I'm with Jenna," Billy said softly from the other couch. He jutted out his chin, attempting to look more mature, but instead, looking every ounce the young and rebellious teen. "Quentin is family. You do everything you can to save family."

"You're too young to vote on this." George sneered. "You must realize if it was anyone else, Jenna would be voting with the majority. It's the fact Quentin's her boyfriend."

"That has nothing to do with this. I would save anyone in this room," Jenna charged. "Except maybe you."

George shot out of his chair and lunged. "You little bitch. I should knock you a good one and show you what happens when . . ."

Caleb and John each grabbed one of George's arms, hauled him back to his chair, and dropped him into it. They didn't move away. Instead, both men hovered, standing guard.

Emma pulled Jenna back to the couch.

"This is getting us nowhere." Peter swiped a stray strand of hair away from his forehead. He should have been eating at an Italian restaurant directing stooges who to put the hurt on. Instead, he organized the vote. "At this point, let's find out what people want. We'll do it by ballot, so no one's uncomfortable about how they are voting. Billy, you get a vote too."

Gus nodded in agreement, and Peter and Aiko went to find paper and pens. Jenna, full of restless energy, paced alone in the corner of the room. She was thankful when nobody tried to change her mind or console her. If they had, the tears would have arrived.

Each person received a piece of paper and a pen and furious scribbling began.

She wrote *Save Quentin*.

The collected and sorted ballots formed two piles with one larger than the second. Peter gathered all the paper fragments, read them, and addressed the group.

"We did this the fair and democratic way. After I tell everyone the decision, there's no more discussion on the matter. By a two-third majority, the group will not go to Pittsfield to find antibiotics. I'm sorry, Jenna."

She sank to the floor and covered her face with her hands.

She'd end in tears if she saw their looks of pity or worse, they betray of the people she trusted the most.

"He might come through. Stranger things have happened," Emma sat next to her and rubbed her back.

"He might also die a slow and painful death." Jenna opened her eyes, letting the tears come.

This is angry crying. Quentin will not die as long as I live.

"You can't believe what you just said. You don't know God's plan."

"God? God's plan? Emma don't start. There's no plan. There's only Streakers and one chomped on Quentin. Now he's dying. His death will be on your hands and everyone here because they are cowards."

"I'm not a coward," Caleb said, joining them in the corner. "I voted to find the medicine. If it means so much to you, we can still do it."

"What?" Emma narrowed her eyes. "There's no way you two are going to Pittsfield alone. We won't let you."

Caleb smiled. "As far as I'm aware, I am a legal adult who will do anything I want, whether that be leaving or never coming back. If I want to go to Pittsfield and get antibiotics, I'll damn well do it, or anything else, I please. Do you have a problem?"

Jenna wiped away the tears.

He'd never appeared so handsome. And he'd been damn hot before.

Emma shrunk back. "No problem but stop being pigheaded. I love you two. You're family. I don't want to see you get hurt or worse."

"I'll care for this one. I always do," Caleb said.

"You'd really follow me to Pittsfield for the drugs?"

"If you're up for it."

"Can't freaking wait." She stood and pulled him into a hearty hug without an ounce of embarrassment.

"We leave tonight," Caleb said. "Get packed."

16

DARKNESS RESTED COMFORTABLY by the time Caleb and Jenna settled in the vehicle.

Emma peered at her through the open driver's side window.

"Thank everyone for offering the use of the car." Jenna's fingers combed through her ponytail, which reached her waist. "We are off to save Quentin. It's a mission like none other and one we promise to return from."

"I have misgivings." Emma placed a hand on the car window frame. "Obviously, the whole group does, or the vote would have been different. But we can't stop you. Can we?"

A brief smile reached her lips. "My mind is made up. Sorry. I have my sidekick for safety."

Caleb tugged on the sleeve of her camouflage jacket. "You're the sidekick."

"You want to fight about it?"

"We might have to."

Emma stepped back. "I see you two have this under control. Come back safe." She blew them both a kiss before heading back into the inn.

The car purred to life. He navigated the winding driveway in the dark with ease, the only noise coming from the engine and the crunch of the tires on the gravel.

Jenna hugged herself.

This coat better still be a good luck charm. Haven't needed to wear it much of late, she thought, *but it kept me alive when I traveled alone. Let's hope jacket magic still exists.*

Should she start a conversation with Caleb? Where to begin? Caleb ghosted her. *How did one communicate with a ghost?*

But he was here now. She couldn't thank him enough. If only it wasn't so awkward. She wasn't a great conversation-alist to begin with. The more she considered it, the more strained the silence became.

My high school friends always used to joke with boys or talk sports. There were no sports to debate unless zombie killing counted. That left being funny. Not her forte, but witty banter it would be. She had to try something. The void was driving her crazy.

"Hey?" She frowned at her ineptitude.

"Hey, yourself."

"How are you?" She bumbled along. "We haven't really had a chance to talk in a while." *This was going brilliantly.*

"Losing Eric was harder than I thought it would be. Let me rephrase. Death is never easy, but Eric was like a brother to me. Losing him after the death of all the other people in my life, hit hard."

"I understand, but everyone was there for you. I would have helped any way possible. We were all grieving the loss."

"I had to mourn in my own way. It was easier to confide to Victor. He understands the depth of New Race emotions, which might sound odd, but once you change, it's intense."

"What do you mean?"

"Think of it this way. The world is all primary colors. Vivid and intense. Love has depth I didn't understand when human, but it makes the emotions dangerous. You become connected to a person's life in ways you couldn't when they are human. I'm not sure if it's the heightened senses or something else, but pain of loss hurts a hundred times more than it did before the change."

"Called maturity."

"Could be, but with the world the way it is now, it would be a lot easier to turn my emotions off. I wanted to die alongside Eric."

"Maybe what you say about your emotions is true, but I was in pain too. We all were."

"I'm sorry."

"We used to be friends. Or something akin to it."

She couldn't believe she was about to hold a confessional. What happened to light, witty banter. That went out the door quick. This conversation was anything but.

"Only friends?"

She ignored the question. "I missed you. I could have helped too. I wanted to be there for you."

"I had to deal with it my own way."

"I should have made more of an effort to break down the walls and let you know I was around."

"It wouldn't have made a difference. It wasn't a great time for me, but I don't plan to repeat my bad behavior. I'm here for you now. I'll protect you."

She wasn't sure if she was happy Caleb wanted to protect her or angry, he believed she needed protection. "Really?"

His smile transcended the dark. "You're as tough as nails, but you can't decapitate every Streaker in Pittsfield. Even you need backup once in a while."

"I guess I'm glad it's you. There's no one else I'd want behind me."

"I could read your comment so many ways. Are you sure you don't want to rephrase it?"

The tension dissolved between them. A gap-took smile emerged. "There is no one else I'd want to support me. Is that better."

"I'd definitely need to support you if I was behind you."

"Stop being such an oversexed jerk."

"What are you reading into my comments? We're talking about support against Streaker attacks, right?"

The vehicle chopped through the darkness.

"Whatever." It was time to change the subject. "Do you ever miss the ease we lived in the past?" she asked. "Sometimes, I wish I could go back to high school and flirt with the guy sitting next to me or I wish I had a college class tomorrow, and I could learn about physics or economics. I'd even take one of those math classes I hated in high school."

"I miss television. I wish I could be with my sisters, bugging them to get off the couch. Mom would bring us hot chocolate and they'd tune into their girly shows every week, and we'd fight over the remote control. When I remember, I miss them so much. I try to avoid reminiscing about the past."

"I didn't know you had sisters. Sorry. I was an only child. I hate what happened to my family too, but I'm thankful you are all my new family now. I would be dead if the group hadn't found me. I'm sure of it. I'm trying to enjoy the little things like Cat and the horses. Keeps me going when stuff like this happens."

"That's why Eric's death was so hard. It was like losing my family all over again. I'm not letting another person die." He shook his head, exorcising demons. "Tell me more about the horses. I see you working with them."

"I've been trying to figure out how to harness them to the wagon. I found all the stuff needed in a shed but have no idea how to make it work. I wish there was internet or at least a book somewhere on the subject, but no."

"You'll have to go riding with me soon."

"I'd love too. The horses are so well behaved. Someone obviously owned them at one time. What have you been doing to keep busy?"

"I've been working with Peter and John on alternative fuel sources for the inn. A gasifier is great but needs constant attention and burns so much wood. We must replenish our supplies daily. Peter's also wants to create a wind turbine at the inn and we're scouting for solar panels in nearby areas. It takes time. Most are too damaged to use, but if his ideas work, you'll never run out of hot water or heat."

"Sounds wonderful and amazing. I love my hot showers."

"There you go again, putting images into my brain."

"Stop it."

Was he flirting with her?

"Can't help myself."

The long but uneventful ride returned them to the dreaded car pile-up, but after exiting Pittsfield already, it was easy to navigate through.

Jenna's palms began to sweat when the two entered the city. She didn't want to lose Quentin, but she was also risking a lot coming for the antibiotics. Time gardening at the inn had given her a false sense of security. This was reality. She had to remain hard and ready to kill.

Driving along Main Street, finding a drug store wasn't difficult. The ransacked building sat on the corner, dark and seemingly empty. Caleb cut the engine and Jenna grabbed a shotgun from the back seat before slinging it over her shoulder. A 22-inch machete and a 12-inch bowie knife cradled her belt.

Caleb grabbed for a shotgun. Instead of knives, his weapon of choice was a large, wooden, baseball bat. They listened and Caleb scanned the area through the open windows. When he gave her a thumbs up, they exited the car, leaving the doors slightly ajar for a quick escape.

The drugstore, with broken windows and a battered front door, was a mess. The dim beam of their flashlights created eerie shadows on the walls and floor. Jenna prayed the light would not attract the attention of unwanted visitors.

Easy to steal items were long gone. Jenna had hoped for left-over sweets, but little merchandise remained on the long-toppled racks What survivors hadn't looted the vermin finished off. Jenna focused on finding the lifesaving medicines. Living day to day for years had taught her and the group to never pass a chance at any new supplies.

Nothing was insignificant.

The duo combed through the shelves along the route to the pharmacy in the back. They kicked aside debris and turned over discarded boxes, searching for anything of use.

"It appears safe enough. Let's split up to search the last rows and meet at the pharmacy in five," Jenna said.

"You sure you want to go it alone?"

"We'll get out quicker."

The store remained secretive, cloaked in darkness. Heading in the opposite direction, Jenna's flashlight licked the floor.

Out of the darkness a sudden shriek pinned her to the floor. Within a heartbeat, Caleb drew to her side, faster than humanly possible. With a hard shove, she stumbled through a swinging door that separated the pharmacy. She righted herself and glared.

"Find what you need. I'll worry about whatever is out here," he said, hauling the bat into position.

She found the mostly empty bins and began rummaging through bottles, looking at different drug names. Not one of the labels sounded familiar. How was she supposed to find antibiotics in this mess?

Take everything.

She threw vials, bottles, and cardboard boxes into the drawstring bag.

Two Streakers rambled toward Caleb. He dropped the bat, aiming the gun. A rally of shots puckered the undead's faces before splatter hit the walls and floor.

She returned to her search, reading the generic drug names, not one of them sounding like the needed prescription. Out of an abundance of caution, she packed every medicine.

Who knew when you might need something?

She fumbled with a large container, the exterior print reading *amoxicillin*, something prescribed to her for strep throat.

"Got it." She swept whatever else was in the vicinity into the bag. "Let's go!"

They didn't get far. It emerged from the recesses. Shielded by the inky blackness dominating the store, Jenna couldn't fathom the Streaker's size or shape.

She stared at the stunted, hunched figure. Shadow and hair covering its features. That didn't stop the demonic moan calling for additional undead to join the party.

Not what they needed.

Caleb approached, bat in hand. Jenna pulled the drawstring bag on like a backpack before covering him with her firearm.

All the while, piteous, high-pitched moans crowded the tight space. The Streaker edged along the dark aisle, closing the distance.

Too close for comfort.

"Do you want me to shoot it?" she asked.

"Hold tight for as long as you can. I don't want the gunfire to become an invitation. I'd like to make it to the exit without the arrival of more Streakers. Let me try to quiet this moaning banshee first before you use your gun."

Jenna tracked the figure with her flashlight.

Wrong move.

Noticing the light, the undead's pace quickened. Its head shot up and for the first time, Jenna could see its face in the flashlight beams. She reeled back.

A child. A small girl younger than her at the time when the pandemic craziness started.

Long-dried blood smeared the rose-embroidered dress. Vacant eyes held no expression. Its mouth hung open in an eternal pout. But its upper lip was now mush and puss.

The Streaker child stopped moaning and shifted its head pensive. It could not figure whether to attack Jenna who stood immobile in front of it or Caleb who had woven his way through the aisles to emerge from behind.

Predator and prey faced off in the stale, still air. The creature charged at Jenna. Caleb grabbed an arm before the creature had darted two steps. Bits of flesh tore from the bone, slipping between his fingers.

The undead turned, teeth snapping close to his flesh. Caleb shoved it back. It stumbled and fell. The baseball bat slammed into the Streaker's skull and reverberated. A second blow lodged in its brain matter and the little girl collapsed to the floor.

It could have been her lying on the floor, a monster lacking intellect and emotions.

He yanked the bat out of the Streaker's head. The slick, wet sound caused Jenna to squirm.

"Good to go?" Caleb appraised her.

"Can't leave quick enough." She moved along the aisle to the front door. Once at the exit, he held her back with his hand, peering into the night before signaling all clear. The two raced to the car.

Huddled in the safety of the front seat and snuggled in the warmth of the camouflage jacket, she expelled a sigh of relief.

From the blackness moans and grunts reached inside the

147

car clashing with garbage cans crashing to the ground close by. A bloody hand smacked against the window. A body slammed into the taillight, then a Streaker lunged onto the hood of the car. Teeth gnashed against the window.

Jenna suppressed a scream. "Go. Go!"

The car squealed off the curve. The Streaker's body flew off the hood. Seconds later the two were back on the road, heading out of Pittsfield, medication snuggled on her lap. Pride surfaced, surprising her. With Caleb by her side, they'd faced a challenge no one else had been willing to complete and it turned out successful.

He glanced her way as if he could read the thoughts, which ran amuck. "Good work back there."

"Thanks, but it was all you. I just stood around and looked pretty."

"And deadly, holding a gun ready to shoot anything in the way of you bringing back the medicine."

"Don't mock my bad ass persona." Jenna wasn't sure if she should be happy or mortified. "Look who's talking. Did one of the perfect hairs on your head fall out of place when you tackled the crazy, moaning, Streaker baby in the store? Nope. Not one."

After he leveled her with another inscrutable gaze, the vehicle squealed to a stop on the side of the road.

"Not another cat." She peered out the window.

"Not this time."

The vast emptiness accentuated her confinement within the car. The highway was void of life, holding nothing more than the shells of burnt out and overturned cars. Inside, things were different.

He cupped Jenna's face in his hands. Unable to turn away, she stared into his eyes, and what she saw their made her shiver.

"I can't stand having you around." He broke the silence.

Not the opening line she expected.

"Excuse me?" She tried to pull away.

"I can't get you out of my mind. Everything you do and say is attractive to me. I often wish I never met you."

"You aren't making sense."

"I'm different. Other. New Race. I've been changed by this stupid virus and you're human."

"I admit it. I was not supposed to like you. I was even scared of you at first but not now. Maybe I'm still a little scared, but only a tiny drop in the ocean kind of way. I didn't fathom we'd ever make it here."

"I can't stop my feelings for you. When I told you about Eric earlier, I explained. For me, love is consuming."

"Is that supposed to reassure me?"

"Let me finish. You're much better off with Quentin, but I don't care anymore. I had to tell you."

"Clarify for me."

He released Jenna and ran a hand through his hair. "I want you more than anything. I care about you and need you."

"I'll tell you about Quentin." Her hand rested on his thigh. "I love him."

Caleb's eyes dropped from her face. "I see."

"Like a brother. Big problem. I wanted there to be more so everything could be normal. I'd have a life and find love. But I can't. Not with him. He's one of my best friends. I would do anything for him, but there's nothing romantic between us."

"What about us?"

"You abandoned me when Eric died. I don't know how to process that. It could happen again."

"Never. Don't say anything else." He moved to kiss her.

Jenna slid back.

"Let's see if I'm right and there's something worth fighting for between us."

He tasted her lips.

149

Jenna didn't want him to stop. Her mouth demanded more.

In the darkness, they yielded to temptation.

THE FIRST HINT of sunlight hit the horizon when Caleb and Jenna trudged the steps to the inn.

"They're back." Tears laced Emma's eyes when she opened the door.

People swarmed to greet them, and Jenna was suffocated at the center of a tight, group hug.

"Don't break me. I just arrived home." She held out the bag full of medicine, Quentin foremost in her mind.

"I'm on it," Emma said.

"Let's hope for the miracle."

Winning over death would be significant. It would mean things had changed, and the group had a chance for a real future.

Jenna followed the physician assistant into Quentin's stuffy room where he lay buried under a heavy quilt, a glass of water and an empty bottle of aspirin by his bedside.

She'd visited before leaving for Pittsfield but seeing him was a shock.

"He doesn't look good." Her voice trembled.

"The meds you brought will perk him right up."

Quentin's brow was greasy with fever, skin dank and sallow.

They had to have made it on time. The antibiotics had to work.

Jenna wasn't even sure he was conscious. "We did it. We got the antibiotics. You'll be as good as new in a couple days."

"Thanks." Quentin's eyes were puffy, swollen. The whispered word evaporated into the air before a cough ensued, and then his breathing turned shallow and disjointed.

"What do we do?" Jenna asked, tears threatening.

"It's going to be okay. We're doing everything we can." The older woman went into medical mode, tallying the products in the bag and selecting a large bottle of antibiotics. She read the information and retrieved two capsules.

Jenna watched Emma prop Quentin's head and prompt him to swallow the large pills. Then she brushed the lank hair off his forehead and fluffed his pillows, all the while chatting about how he'd be better soon.

Grabbing Jenna's arm, she guided the younger woman out of the room.

"Off to bed with you." Emma's voice was motherly. "You must be exhausted and there is nothing more to do. We won't know anything for at least twenty-four hours."

"Let me sit with him."

"You'll just bother him."

"I want to be with him. He shouldn't be alone."

"Quentin has not been alone. Someone is always with him." Emma looked offended anyone might consider her care substandard. "Aiko volunteered first and is one of the most common visitors. Other than you and me, she's been with him more than anyone else."

"Seriously?" Anger leaked into the words. "She probably wants to be the first around to shoot him if he changes. Get some target practice in."

"You most definitely need some sleep and to wake up with a different attitude."

"I want to sit with him for a couple hours."

"Fine, but don't bother him. Let him sleep."

"Thank you." She gave the other woman a quick squeeze before returning to the room, settling comfortably on a chair next to the bed.

While he slept, she whispered all the details of what happened in Pittsfield. He did not stir and after a while she drifted into a doze.

Jackie woke her and Jenna hurried to her room. She washed, changed, and attempted to sleep but light filtered in from behind closed curtains and rest eluded her. After restless minutes, she was back in Quentin's room, forcing Billy out and once again settled comfortably in the deeply cushioned chair.

"Jenna!"

The murky room made her wonder where the day had gone.

Had she dozed off for a long time? Why had no one come to relieve her? Where were they all?

Darkness snaked across the floor, slithering up the chair Jenna nestled in and capturing her in it. It overtook the bed too, inking its way across Quentin's toes, his foot, and up his torso.

She reached out to save him, but couldn't move, mired deep in the dark malevolence.

Quentin opened his eyes in fright and sat. "Please save me!" The blackness slid down his throat causing him to retch. He was dying and there was no way to help. The gags turned muffled and then stopped. The body on the bed lay rigid and unmoving.

Evil will find you, a voice screamed. *Something wicked, this way comes.*

Jenna shot out of the chair, panting and fully awake. The nightmares were back. She gazed at her hands to see if the evil had left a mark and then approached Quentin, fearing she had predicted his demise.

It couldn't be true.

His shirt was soaked through with sweat, but he was breathing. She swiped at the stray hair hanging across his eyes.

"Hey, beautiful," Quentin whispered. "You make a lot of noise when you sleep."

"How are you?"

"Awful." He managed a pained smile. "I'll make it." A raw, hacking cough claimed him.

"I must have fallen asleep for a while." Jenna moved to the bed to give him some water. His cheeks were hot and damp. "You still have a fever."

"You were sleeping when Emma came in and gave me a few aspirin and more horse pills. She says I'm doing better."

"How long have I been in here?"

"A long time. I don't mind. They tried to make me eat lunch and dinner so it must be evening."

"I slept so long. I must go check on the horses. Will you be okay without me?"

"I'll manage." He cracked another small smile and yawned through dry, chapped lips. "I'm going to nap like you've been doing all afternoon."

"I'll check on you later."

Quentin had already dozed off. She planted a kiss on his check and found Emma on her way out of the inn.

"How's the patient?"

"I'm hopeful." Emma said.

"Me too. He's going to make it. I feel it in my bones."

"Keep sending those positive mantras his way and he will."

"If only positive thoughts worked all the time."

Maybe she had enough positive thoughts to keep her nightmares at bay. It was just a bad dream, her subconscious crying out, nothing more.

She wandered out to the barn brooding about Caleb, which started her heart pounding and palms sweating.

What was she going to do with that situation? Not consider it. Find a distraction. Visit the horses. They'd help.

They'd thrived on the overgrown grass in the big paddock where they spent their days, but Jenna was already worrying about winter. There had to be a way to cut and store hay, and maybe she'd convince Caleb to go forage for some grain after their successful raid in Pittsfield. Exercising the drafts would be a bonus before tucking them into the safety of the barn for the night. She'd free lunge the horses outside. It would rid all of them of excess energy. When done, the treat of a shower waited.

Boy, did she need it! Not worth wasting water before going to play with ponies.

She might extend the five-minute limit to seven, the scalding water cleaning off both the anxieties of the raid and the pungent smell of equines. While she found the smell of horses an improvement over Streaker, other people didn't share her fondness and she would soon reek with the powerful combination of the draft's sweat and manure.

Working with the equines also meant missing the communal dinner, but for now she preferred to be alone. Even though the rumbling in her gut had started hours ago, anger over the group's decision not to help Quentin left her not wanting to socialize. People would demand details of the raid in Pittsfield. Jenna was not in a mood to share.

Leftovers in my room it will be.

In the barn, Jenna made her way to the loft, where she stored the tack after hours organizing the bridles and bits, scraping horse pads free of mice droppings, and cleaning the gear. The oiled leather on the saddle shone. She grabbed the lunge whip and brushes.

Pivoting in the gloom of the loft, the slam of the door had her scooting backward and dropping one of the brushes she had been juggling.

"You scared me. What can I do you for?"

George removed a long blade of grass from between his teeth with mud caked hands. His greasy shirt hugged his paunchy stomach. Liquor was rare to come by, but George never lost the beer belly he had developed well before the Streakers. Stories about when George had first joined the group continued to circulate. He arrived with guns, cigarettes, and cases of beer. While the beer and cigarettes had run out, George was still fond of the guns. He did not mind the inn too much either, since the group had found the wine cellar and broke out a good bottle of red or white on special occasions, which was every day the Streakers stayed away.

He stared, making his assessment obvious, eyes lingering too long on her breasts.

"You're making me uncomfortable. How'd you find me, anyway?"

"I followed you here after you left the inn."

"Why?"

"I've been meaning to meet you 'bout a couple things going on here." He dragged his eyes to her face. "You got a moment?"

This is not normal. No, I freakin' don't want to talk to you alone in a hay loft.

"Why don't we discuss this at dinner tonight. I'm heading back there soon. I'm sure it's stuffed the whole group wants to hear about."

"No, not really. This just involves you and me."

"Oh," she said. "Have I done something wrong?"

"Now that you ask, I believe you have."

The hair on her arms prickled, defenses heightened similar to when a Streaker arrived. "Really? What?" The lunge whip thumped the ground.

His eyes meandered before answering. "You've been whoring yourself out to all the men in camp. First you lead Quentin on, but then he gets sick and so you turn to Caleb, a no good, dirty New Racer no less."

Her mouth dropped open.

Where to even start?

He continued his rant. "The way I see it, you're pretty willing to be with anyone, human or otherwise. If it had just been Quentin, I might not be here. He's a decent kid and deserves a good woman, but here you are, deserting him the moment he falls ill and spreading your legs for the undead."

"What's wrong with you?"

"Being of the New Race is only one step from being a Streaker. Go ahead and let them turn you too if you're so interested in fucking them."

"Not that I need to explain myself to you," she retorted, "because my personal life is none of your business. I do not spread my legs for anyone. The New Racers s you appear to hate so much are the same people who kept you alive all these months."

"I kept myself alive!" George roared.

"Caleb was the only person willing to help me!" The high pitched screamed bounced off the walls.

"The New Race might be good for some things and have a place in this world, but they can't be mixing with humans. You should know better. You have to save the race by having human babies. Lots of human babies."

"As I just said," Jenna emphasized every word. "What I do, and who I do it with are none of your damn business."

"Well, I beg to differ." He closed the distance between them. "What you do concerns me a whole lot. It hurts me to see you make stupid choices, but if you're going to be stupid, I'll take advantage of it. Since you're making it free and easy for any man to get a turn at you, I want my chance."

"Don't even think about it." Backing away, she searched the room for something she could use for a weapon.

Too far away from the baseball bat that lay propped at the door. The hoof pick perched in a bucket to her right. She'd run for it.

Jenna sprinted. Rough fingers yanked her back before she

could reach the hoof pick. He pinned her flailing arm and twisted her around, before throwing her to the floor. Her head hit the rough wooden planks and sparks of pain erupted before her eyes. His weight was upon her, suffocating.

She kicked and pummeled but did little damage. "Stop."

His hard slap filled her mouth with blood. Hands pinnacled hers.

"Fight and this will get ugly. You'll make this worse, little lady."

Her knee jammed into his thigh.

A fist rammed her nose. Blood trickled from it.

"Let me go. Please. I won't tell anyone." Each inhale was torture, words hard to enunciate when blood ran down the back of her throat. She flashed back to the person who gave her the scar on her stomach, all the former horror rushing back. The last man who attacked her had almost succeeded. Before she'd been able to run, he sliced her and left her for the undead to feed on.

George anchored both her thin wrists in one of his own chunky hands, and then secured them with rope, leaving her helpless. Rough meat paw traveled under her shirt to her bra and shoved under. Tasting of onions and alcohol, his mouth clamped over hers. Jenna's scream died as Georg rammed his tongue against her teeth.

Trying to twist away, she writhed beneath him, but the movement aroused his desire more.

Play possum.

Even her breath hushed as Jenna forced herself to go limp. When Jenna met George's eyes, he dropped his gaze to her exposed belly.

"Whatever you're plotting, don't try it." He moved a hand from her chest. It slithered to the button on her jeans.

"Stop, please."

"Shut up. You're going to enjoy it."

Jenna waited. His hands forced the buttons of her jeans. Her knee came up hard. It was a weak attempt, her legs partially trapped, but his grunt left her with a small wave of satisfaction.

He yanked her ponytail forcing her cheek to scrape against the wooden board. Once again, stars littered her sight. Nausea threatened. His hand roamed across her breasts, and she closed her eyes in hopelessness.

The worst would come.

Fresh air graced her face, and she inhaled a full breath. George's weight eased off. She opened her eyes to find him gone. Lifting herself to a sitting position, she peered around.

Caleb dangled George by his feet, out the window in the loft.

His eyes held murder.

"You don't understand, Caleb," the hanging man cried.

"I understand perfectly. Do you want me to drop him or not, Jenna?"

George begged for his life.

Relief flooded her. She sat and pondered the situation, enjoying the fact the would-be rapist was about to plunge to his death.

"I'm waiting," Caleb shook George by the legs.

"I'm thinking." She wriggled her hands out of the rope, fixed her shirt, and rebuttoned her jeans.

Caleb watched her do so, his lips a tight line.

He deserves to die. But he's one of us. Is he? He's a rapist piece of shit. Can you have his life on your soul?

"I'm dropping him," Caleb announced.

She swallowed the blood in her mouth and swiped at the same covering her face. "As much as I'd love to see you do it, there are so few of us. Each and every death is a horrible thing, even if that death would be George."

"He tried to rape you," Caleb pleaded with her. "Let me drop him."

"You'll make sure he won't try it again, right?" She stared into his beautiful eyes and couldn't believe she once found them menacing. They were red with anger but something more. An emotion she'd never believed could exist after a zombie apocalypse.

Caleb hauled George into the loft—the man's pock-marked face as bright as an apple. He dropped George onto the wooden floor, then bent down, his face inches away.

"If you ever come near Jenna again, I won't consider what she wants. Listen close and believe this. You don't go in the same room, don't speak to her, don't get close to her, or you will wish I dropped you from this window. Do you understand?"

George nodded.

"Say you understand." He growled the words. A wolf protecting his pack.

Dank fear radiated off George. He whimpered his answer. "I understand."

"Get out, now, before I change my mind," Caleb said. He picked the man up and threw him into the door.

George slid down the steps and was gone.

Caleb rushed to her side. "Are you okay? Really okay?" He brushed hair and blood from her face.

"I don't feel so good," Jenna said. The light in the room strobed, then the world vanished into darkness.

When she opened her eyes, he was an angel hovering above.

"Am I dead?" she asked.

"You passed out for a minute, but you're fine."

"Am I going to die?"

"No, but you look like you might."

Blood splattered the floor. She lifted her shirt to examine it. More blood. "That's what every girl wants to hear. How bad is it?"

She'd be okay. He was here, which was nice. But she was strong.

160

There'd been much worse in recent times to deal with. This was a walk in the park.

"You have a cut on your lip, and it looks like your nose was bleeding and maybe still is. There's a nice bruise on your cheek, a bump on your forehead, and some small cuts. Are you sure you don't want me to kill him? I want to kill him more than you'll ever know."

"No. No killing." She sat tall. "The Counsel can deal with this. I'm fine."

"You're not fine and it's his fault. Are you able to stand?"

She wobbled to her feet. "I owe you. Between going into Pittsfield for the medicine and now this. I don't know how I'll ever repay you?"

He hugged her carefully, wary of aches and pains. "I'm sure I'll devise something," The whispered words departed before he stepped away with a smile.

THE COUNSEL CAME CLOSE to banishing George, but in the end, didn't. He stayed far away, and Jenna never even had to pass him in a hallway. After Emma confirmed all Jenna's injuries were superficial, she spent her extra time with Quentin, who continued to improve, each day gaining stamina.

Caleb thought of numerous things for her to do to repay him. They were all to her liking. He made a plan for them to spend free time together. They played boardgames in front of the large picture window in a grand room off the main lobby, which provided a spectacular panorama of the tree line and reservoir below.

The next day, they sat reading the limited supply of popular paperbacks pre-pandemic. She'd picked up a teen vampire romance, more so to have fun with Caleb than having a true interest in reading the novel.

"You guys are supposed to sparkle in the sun," Jenna said, reading lines out of the book.

"We don't sparkle because we're not vampires." His mouth turned into a thin line. "It's fiction."

"Fact is stranger than fiction these days."

"What else does it say?"

"All vampires are gorgeous and sexy. Not."

"Gee, thanks. Glad to know you find me attractive."

"You said you weren't a vampire." Her eyebrows rose in question. "Are you recanting your position?"

"Not a vampire."

"I must disagree, but I still find you only slightly attractive. I guess that will have to do thanks to the exorbitant number of Streakers, all of whom are rather homely." Jenna dropped the book to the ground. She sashayed close, moving like a predator cornering its prey. With a wide-eyed stare, he appeared so lost and befuddled, Jenna had to force back a smile. "Here, let me show you."

Her hands stroked his chest, searching for the belt threaded through his jeans and grasped the belt buckle.

Confusion radiated off him.

"Gotcha." Jenna sprung away.

He yanked her into his lap. "Not nice. I'll so get you back."

"Caleb, we need you in the office," Billy called from the next room, as if not wanting to disturb whatever was going on between them.

With that, he dumped her on the floor and left.

The next day Jenna plotted revenge, offering to play Caleb in monopoly, one of the many abandoned games at the inn. The two turned out to be competitive, and the contest raged on until early morning when Jenna was finally out of all her fake cash and had mortgaged all her property.

"I'll loan you some money," he offered.

"I'll cut my losses and head to bed."

"You're no fun. Are you?"

I'm tired is what I am. It's way past my bedtime. I have

horses, a garden, and chores in the morning. Not to mention, I'm still in recovery."

"Don't remind me, or I'll start plotting ways to murder someone in their sleep again."

"I haven't laid eyes on him since the incident."

"Incident? Understatement of the year."

The duo returned pieces to the box, closed the lid, and put the game back on the shelf. She waved before heading for the door, but he grabbed her hand.

"Let me walk you to your room."

"Why not."

"We need to discuss one more thing about the George incident."

"I don't want to rehash it anymore. I'm fine."

"You and I both know there is something seriously wrong with a person who could do that. He could be dangerous for everyone here."

"The Counsel decided. It's over. Don't ruin an otherwise great night."

Caleb didn't press about the situation when they climbed the steps. At her door, his lips met hers. He smelled of exotic spices and tasted like honey. She wanted more. His strong hand framed her face, and his lips stole her breath.

When he stepped back, she understood loss.

Gentle fingers traced a heart on her hand. Their lips met again. He reached under her shirt, hand tickling her side and moved to her stomach, accidently touching the scars.

Jenna went rigid.

"Did I do something wrong?" he asked.

"This is moving fast. I need some time and to set things right with Quentin. He can't walk out of his room before I explain what's going on."

"We'll go easy." His hand under her chin. Her eyes met his. "Don't ever forget how beautiful you are. You're Venus, and

I'll wait as long as you want just for a chance to bask in your splendor and taste your lips one more time."

Why did he say things like that?

He was gone before her hand turned the doorknob.

Their attraction ran deep.

No denying that.

. Whether she admitted it or not, it had been obvious since fighting the Streakers together at the school. For a moment, just one moment, she'd been wrapped in a flame, like a dynamite keg ready for ignition. After tonight, she assumed Caleb had felt the same way and now wanted for her to take the next big step, the serious move forward in her own time.

When she hunkered down to bed, her dreams ran rather randy.

Life turned routine, something long forgotten and wonderfully mundane. The garden, the horses, visits to her sick friend, and time with Caleb all claimed Jenna's energy. She saw Quentin every day but avoided talking about anything emotional, wanting him to heal. But with every new visit, her discomfort rose. Many times, Aiko sat Quentin's bed, whispering to Quentin on her arrival and sending her the evil eye until one of them departed. Aiko's exit strategy usually included a kiss that appeared to be more for Jenna's benefit than his.

Had Aiko been telling Quentin how much time Jenna and Caleb were spending together? Was she filling him in on other details?

Jenna hadn't asked Quentin about Aiko only because she wasn't ready to explain her relationship with Caleb, but it had to be soon. Guilt about not being completely honest made tossing and turning in bed a nightly ritual.

So angry. That woman was the one who had suggested the group let Quentin die, but now she nursed him back to health.

If that wasn't enough, Aiko fed Quentin information about Caleb out of spite rather than true concern for Quentin's emotional state. She was sure of it.

Two weeks had passed since the trip to Pittsfield, and it was time to come clean with Quentin. When she arrived, he was out of bed, showered, and sitting in a chair, clean T-shirt over his flannel pajama bottoms.

"I'm so happy to see you up. This is great." She made her way over to the chair and gave him a hug.

He refused to meet her eyes. "Thanks."

"Are you okay?"

His hands remained limp at his side. "You don't have to keep coming to see me. I won't be offended."

"I want to be here and love hanging out with you. I'm happy you're better." Her hand covered his.

Quentin drew back. "Let's face the truth."

"The truth? What truth?"

He gathered his words. "I appreciate all you've done for me. I would be dead without you, but even recovering, I worried I might change, be susceptible to the virus from the bite. If that happened, I didn't want you witness it after all you went through to get the medicine. I might still change."

"You won't. People have survived the bite before. We've both seen people in the group heal fine when bitten or scratched."

"We don't know anything these days. Maybe I am changing now. It could happen years from now. I didn't want to be close to someone only to lose them, but after Aiko told me about you and Caleb . . ."

"Why couldn't she keep her mouth shut."

"It was better I found out. At first, I believed it for the best. It would be easiest to let you go, but now I don't know what I want."

"What do you mean?"

"What happened to us? We had something real."

"We have a real friendship. That's rare."

"I want to be clear. I can't be your friend. I've been in this stupid bed with nothing to do but think, and I've finally got my head straight about this whole situation."

"I don't understand. You say we had something real, but the only thing I've seen this last week is you're happy to be around everyone else but me. Aiko's always in here. If you like her, I'm happy for you."

"It's different with her. She's immune. The virus has already changed her."

"Changed her into a cold-hearted bitch. She's the one who wanted to do nothing."

"She explained, and I understand her point of view."

"You understand her but not me?" Frustration and sadness played tug-of-war. "I'm your friend. I was there for you when she wasn't."

A deep rattling cough from Quentin sent Jenna into panic mode. She brought him water.

"I'm fine," he said after a few sips.

"I don't mean to sound angry. I'm confused. You're so distant. I want us to be friends like we've always been."

"Always friends. Wasn't there more?" Quentin stood.

Jenna followed his lead, inching closer. He reached for her, laced his fingers behind her neck, drawing her in. Their lips met.

With all her heart, she tried to create the excitement of their first kiss, but all she managed to do was to muster camaraderie. She had mistaken comfort and caring for something more. While she cared for Quentin, their relationship lacked passion.

He crushed their bodies together, bruising her lips. Jenna could do nothing to stop him. At last, he drew back.

"Well?" His gaze met hers. "Tell me you didn't feel anything?"

She dragged in a long breath. "My emotions for you are real, but I'm not in love with you."

"No?"

Was this all about his jealousy? "What do you want me to say?"

"Aiko and George both told me." A muscle twitched in his jaw.

"What exactly did they say?"

"Details. Lots of gory details." His eyes registered pain.

"It's not what you're imagining." Her hands shook, so she balled them into fists.

Her gut clenched knowing she was an awful person for not hashing this out sooner.

Fear of losing him made her delay. Now he's angry and jealous about Caleb. Maybe he had the right to be, but these stupid emotions are impossible to control.

"Caleb and I never planned any of this. I can't explain how it is when I'm around him."

"I understand." He held her gaze. "No. I don't understand."

"Let me explain what happened."

"That's the last thing I want to hear. Don't come to see me anymore."

"You're my best friend and more. I'm coming back here every day until you kick me out."

"One day, I'll do it." He bit at a thumb nail. "I need time. Can you just leave me alone for a while?"

When the door closed, the separation became permanent.

How could she have destroyed her relationship with him?

Throughout her chores and work with the horses, their conversation haunted her. Later in the evening, Caleb became the needed distraction. Once again, skipping the communal dinner, the two dined alone on the back patio. While a beautiful night, a fall chill danced around them.

"How's Quentin?" Caleb asked.

"Better. The bites need more time to heal, but he's doing well. No fever, no problems. He's walking short distances, but Emma has him on bed rest until next week because of a lingering cough. It really effected his respiratory system and ability to breathe."

Should she tell him the rest. The urge not to was overwhelming.

"Good news." His gaze probed hers. "What about George? Has he come near you?"

"I haven't seen George since that night, and every time he sees me at the end of a hallway he turns and runs the other way."

A savage smile crept across his mouth. "Just the way I like it."

There needs to be honesty if this relationship is to have a chance.

"Quentin's heard about us from Aiko and George." She refused to make eye contact. "We need to step back. I don't want to hurt Quentin anymore than I have."

"Tell me what really happened today when you saw him. You're sad."

She pushed her plate away, relived the conversation with Quentin, and by the end, tears threatened.

Caleb moved around the table, sitting close, and drawing her in for a hug. "I'm not confused." The words tickled her cheek. "This is right, and I can't stop how I feel about you. I'm not going away. You're stuck with me, and you better learn how to deal with that."

His words caused a shiver to run through her.

What they were building together was different from anything she'd ever known. So intense when compared to her emotions for Quentin, but he represented the normal world, comfort, and friendship. Chemistry with Caleb promised something much different. She'd drown in the physical ache running through her and go willingly.

She had to be with him. It was like she had no alternative. But damn it, if she'd expose her weakness to him.

"Promise me one thing, Jenna."

"What?"

"You'll give me one more date."

She studied him. "One date."

He grinned like he'd won an Olympic Gold. "I'd better plan then." Gathering up the dishes, he headed back inside.

Jenna sat watching the clouds shift in the dark sky, enjoying the night and the bracing wind.

"It's happening today." Caleb stopped her in the morning before she left the inn.

"We only made the agreement last night."

"I don't want you to back out."

"I wouldn't."

"You can't. Meet me by the lake at eight."

Her flashlight lit the steps down to the man-made slim strip of sand surrounding a large reservoir. The beach wound between the water and the dense woods that cloistered the lake on three sides. In the darkness, the woods developed a supernatural quality. A still functioning kayak lay next to boats and canoes s half buried or torn apart by the harsh weather.

An abandoned house perched forlornly on the lake's edge.

"Are you sure we're safe here?" Jenna asked, enjoying the magnificent lake view. After her battle in the woods and the recent Streaker attack on Quentin, she remained uneasy.

"It's been two weeks since we came across any indication of undead. Even if they have some way of smelling us out, the woods are too dense for them to make it here, and the lake protects us. Plus, I've got a gun."

"Romance and a gun. What more could a woman ask for."

"Strange times call for strange dates. No telling what an apocalypse will do to traditional dating rituals. Relax and enjoy."

"Relaxation isn't really my strong point. I'm usually doing laps around the inn if not engaged in chores or outside." She fingered the holes in her sweatshirt.

Should she wear something nicer? Not a lot of options in her closet. At least the jeans are clean.

"We'll work on relaxing together." He sat her on the blanket. He pointed to a fresh salad.

That's thanks to your garden. The casserole is from me."

She eyed the pan. "Interesting. What's in it?"

"Don't look so skeptical. Made it myself." He chuckled. "Not sure what it will taste like, but Emma swore by the recipe and we trust her. Right?"

"We trust her with medicine, but not sure about her cooking. Still, she's all for this union so I'm sure she wouldn't steer you wrong."

"Let's dig in." He doled out meals and handed her a plate.

Jenna relished the dinner and relaxed, enjoying the scenery and company.

"This is our official first date." He broke into a boyish grin and added, "How's it going so far?"

"What makes today different to previous times?" She put her fork down.

"Because I'm going to go hunt. If you don't go running back to the inn, it will be because you don't find me utterly repulsive."

"Putting it to the test. Go for it. After killing Streakers, I can deal with sitting here while you go find some more food. Before you go, explain why you want to do this now."

"I don't need to hunt at this moment, but it's important you understand what you are getting into."

"And that is?"

"New Racers are driven by a need for blood, be it animal

blood or human, but human blood is more fulfilling. No matter what kind, the virus brought about an evolutionary change linking us to Streakers. We all need blood. If I don't hunt regularly. I really would go insane. Lucky for us, there's plenty of deer and bears around."

"Deer and bear?"

"And squirrels and rabbits but they aren't filling."

"Obviously." She frowned. "Off you go for a late-night snack. Find something tasty."

"I'll try." Caleb kissed her on the cheek before he sprinted into the woods.

What to think about this?

Her boyfriend drains the blood from poor woodland creatures. It should disgust her, but she was a fan of fresh venison steaks and never turned down a hamburger when they were available pre-pandemic. Damn, she was making herself miss dollar-menu fast food right now. Was it really so crazy in this bizzarro world she called home?

The rustle of small animals scurrying away turned loud amid the silence. And then two pinpricks burned scarlet in front of her. As they drew closer, they grew into demonic red eyes like seen in old photos. Those eyes stared into her soul. Caleb was but a blurry image when he approached, back by her side before she could blink. She hadn't known what to expect but his clothes remained clean. She'd wondered if he'd returned covered in blood and guts. He appeared healthy, happy, and sane.

"That's it?" she asked.

"What did you expect?" He shrugged his shoulders before sitting on the blanket. "I had an extra meal. I'm a growing boy."

"I'm not sure how to react to all of this." The darkness hid her heated cheeks.

"It's a strange new reality. All of us needed a while to come to terms with what we are now. Accepting this new life is liberating. Discarded my old self for an improved one. At least that's the line I'm selling to myself."

"Who were you before all of this?"

"I was in college, liked music, played guitar, and had started a band. My goal was to be a rich and famous rock star or a music teacher."

"Seriously?" Jenna stared at him in disbelief.

"Average, normal person just like you. Hated math just like you. I was on campus when the virus invaded. They didn't even have time to evacuate us and send everyone home. By the time I was able to get in the car and leave, half the campus was in the infirmary infected or dead. Coming home wasn't much better. My parents and sisters were already gone."

"I'm sorry."

"Everyone still kicking has a story like mine or yours or worse." He shifted, gaze intent. "I didn't bring you here to make you sad or talk about the past. What can I do to make you happy in the present?"

"Would you play something for me. There has to be a guitar somewhere in the area."

"That's what you want?" He pointed at himself. "Out of everything you might have had."

"It's what I want."

"I have a guitar in my room but haven't played since the outbreak. I might not remember how. I'm not sure I want to play anymore."

She moved close. "It's romantic and if you want a second date, you're going to have to woo me."

Caleb chuckled. "Woo you? What pandemic have you survived? We're not back in the flu pandemic of the early 1900s." His hand moved to her knee. "I'll woo you if that's what you really want. Your wish is my command."

"Really?"

"You. This. Whatever we have going here is keeping me sane, so if I need to woo, I'll woo."

"Please stop saying the word *woo*. I'm so sorry I started this."

He leaned in and Jenna moved expecting a kiss.

She shrieked when Caleb's fingers found her side and tickled her stomach. Jenna kicked out, but he refused relent.

"Mercy. Mercy," she begged and sat wheezing, leaning on his strong shoulder.

"How's that for being wooed?"

"Not what I expected, but I guess it will do."

More.

Jenna packed the remains of dinner, placing plates and cups in a picnic basket. She walked next to Caleb, heading back to the inn. Once there, she held his hands, breathing in the electricity between them. Their fingers danced.

"It was a great date." His eyes caught hers.

Heat simmered in her core. "I'm in one-hundred percent agreement."

"Would you consider another? Let's do some exploring and check out the empty house at the beach."

"I'd like that very much." Her husky whispered words embarrassed her.

Caleb grabbed the basket from her, climbed the steps to the inn, and opened the front door. "Coming?"

What's he doing?

She didn't want to consider the end of the night but loved the emotional high he gave her.

She watched him step inside, moving far away.

Damn, not the way I expected to end the night.

"I need you to come back for a moment." Her voice sounded loud in the quiet evening.

He retraced his steps and held out a hand to help her. She resisted, drawing him to her and planted a kiss on his lips.

She'd take what she wanted.

He drew back, but then his lips melted with her, and his hand brought her close.

The kiss was exotic and intoxicating. A cliff dive off the edge of her reality. She wanted to keep the intensity and security forever.

A noise from inside the inn startled her. She eyed the windows to determine if someone was spying. Forcing herself away, she scurried around him, hopped the steps, and disappeared inside.

She blew him a kiss from the lobby and headed to her room.

Her fingers brushed her lips, and she wondered if Caleb wanted more. She did. In bed, she tossed, replaying the date, and contemplated why she'd been the one to kiss him.

Did he have all the feelings he claimed to? If he did, what comes next?

19

In his room, Caleb studied the guitar. He stared at it, poked it like roadkill with his foot before picking it up. It had survived the outbreak, his travels, his only constant companion, and keepsake from the past. His father had given it to him and taught him how to play.

At the arrival of the pandemic, Caleb understood it was adapt to the new world or die. When he'd woken up, disorientated from the fever, and of the New Race, he'd refused to look back. He'd slammed the door on the past, but then Jenna showed up and made him want to share.

Caleb wanted more, but she was skittish. They could share whatever this new life would offer, but only if she made the choice to do so. Jenna had to pick him. To want him. A hard lesson to learn by herself, but Caleb would help her down the road a little bit.

The guitar rested against his knees. Thrumming the strings and tuning the instrument, he began to play. The notes and chords sang cherished memories. Transitioning into the song he wanted to share with Jenna, Caleb considered writing a song for her. It would have to wait. It would take time to compose it, but the inn just might give him the needed respite.

Gorgeous in a quirky, kick the living shit out of a Streaker kind of way, Jenna differed from his initial impressions. From the day the group came across her in the cemetery, she'd been moody, independent, and wild, but the tough exterior hid a fragile nature and tragedies. Tragedies were the things they all shared the most of these days.

She rebelled against this existence, and he could tell, she still mourned her old life. While it was tough to crack her hard exterior while on the road struggling for survival, now she'd revealed a gentler, nostalgic side. As the last notes echoed from his guitar, Caleb could not help but wonder when he had fallen in love.

He lowered the instrument and crossed to his bedroom window overlooking the lake. The first hint of the sun, ready to rise, diminished the darkness. Exhaustion clung, and he sprawled across the big bed. Before allowing sleep to dominate, he planned their next date.

A week had passed, and for Jenna, the days dragged slowly. She tended the garden, removing the weeds that no amount of plucking had been able to eliminate, to abate her insecurity about Caleb. She was happy, still riding the high from her time with him. Her garden, that was producing something good as well. The maturing plants supplied a variety of vegetables.

On autopilot, Jenna plucked weeds and considered about how much of a farmer she'd turned into. Alongside Jackie, Beth, and Emma, she learned different canning techniques. Even Aiko joined in and their little party experimented with preserving food for the winter. Now the group had fresh milk thanks to a recent discovery of a nanny goat in the woods, and they planned to find recipes utilizing milk and cheese.

While tempted to join with the scavenging party leaving to explore new, not-so-nearby residences, the garden, the horses, and new goat, eradicated any free time. Cat, who nudged a hand every time she put it down, was also very demanding.

She spied Emma crossing the field in her direction.

No surprise there.

Tonight, she had a big date with Caleb, but she hadn't caught a glimpse of him. The man had to be plotting with the older woman.

"Can I help you?" Emma asked.

"Of course."

She sat cross legged on the ground and began to pull at weeds. "What's new?"

"Since yesterday, nothing."

"What's new with you and Caleb?" Her voice trilled.

"I'm looking forward to tonight. Isn't that what you really came out here to talk about?"

"You know me so well. Tell me everything. What are you doing? Where are you going?"

"It's not like we can watch a movie or go to a Broadway play." Jenna shook her head in disbelief. "Weren't you in on it anyway. I thought you were part of the planning committee."

"He's kept it secret from me too. You must have some inkling."

"He won't tell me anything."

Emma's eyebrow shot up. "Not one clue?"

"I swear."

"So romantic."

"It's frustrating. And this is all so weird because right outside our little utopia Streakers rule and people, if there are any left, continue to die."

"More reasons to enjoy what you have and the fact you can have it."

"I'm worried about one thing. Remember how I was alone and injured when I met the group?"

"You had scars on your stomach. I was scared it would get infected. I'm always looking out for you, girlfriend."

"I'm afraid to tell Caleb the entire story."

"Why?"

"It's ugly."

"Tell me and let me be the judge."

"When the pandemic was in full swing, we stowed away at a school that was supposed to be a safe house. As time went on, there were less and less of us. Some died and then when supplies got low, many left."

"I'm sure many people went through the same situation."

"By the end, there were a bunch of kids and maybe five or six adults who stayed with us. When we finally left the school, no one had a solid plan. It was awful, and within two weeks we lost half the group. We were unprepared and ill-equipped. It was akin asking kids, and teens, and financial analysts to become zombie killers. It's not like the television shows made it appear."

"Preach, girlfriend."

"At the end it was me and this guy named Danny. He was older, and one night, we were in a house. He was scared and mad and tried to, you know. He tried to . . ." The words died on her lips.

"Take advantage of you?"

"Yes." A tear slid down Jenna's cheek. "When I fought back, he took out a knife and sliced me. He wanted me dead if I wasn't going to give in. That's the reason I have the scars. I ran and by some miracle escaped. Then you came to my rescue in the graveyard."

"What a horrible story, but why can't you tell Caleb about it?"

"What if he looks at me differently? What if he sees the scars and decides I'm hideous inside and out?"

"Silly girl." She gave Jenna a motherly hug. "You're so beautiful, and Caleb knows how lucky he is."

"Sure." She bit her lip.

"It's getting late. Don't you have to get ready?"

"Let's head back." She stood and dusted her hands on her jeans.

Once inside, the women parted ways. Aiko sauntered by in the hall carrying clean dinner dishes.

Go away guilt! Doesn't matter Quentin's out of danger.

It didn't matter how good a friend or how often she visited. No matter how much they talked about the horses or the petty squabbles at the inn, it wasn't the same.

One best friend gone. Pathetic.

Quentin had become more and more distant. Worse, every time she went to visit, Aiko refused to leave if present. While the woman remained polite, Jenna wanted to bring her down if only because Quentin preferred Aiko to stay. In fact, he pretty much hinted Jenna could stop coming and he would be fine.

Getting ready for tonight would cheer her. She wanted to look good but didn't have much in the way of options. Most of her clothes tended to fall on the practical side: rugged flannel shirts, sweatshirts, and jeans along with serviceable steel-toed boots.

Jenna had saved a single dress rolled in her ratty shoe box. Her mom's favorite, she'd been unable to get rid of it. The little black dress had followed Jenna no matter where she moved. There'd never been an occasion to wear it, but tonight was the time for a change.

She dug under her messy pile of shirts and carefully unpacked the dress from in between tissue paper. Along with the garment, a shiny silver tube fell to the ground. Jenna had forgotten it. Mom's favorite red lipstick. The wrinkled black dress was in good condition. The memories it brought to mind were also well preserved, yet somewhat painful to relive.

Mom. Dad. Miss you so much.

She headed to the bathroom, a tear sliding down her cheek, wondering if the sleek garment would fit. Jenna had found Caleb, and she was ready to deal with her past in hopes of creating a future. She stripped and showered. The black silk was a little big but slid like rose petals along her skin. The neckline plunged lower than she remembered, but there was little she could do to remedy that or the wrinkles. Black boots and a beat-up leather jacket finished the outfit.

Call it a fashion statement.

Braiding her hair in the mirror, she almost didn't recognize the person who stared back. The woman was thin, had circles under her eyes, scars on her cheek from where the glass cut her, but her gaze remained strong.

Cherry red lipstick adorned her lips. It gave her hope her old world and new world might somehow find balance. If she could reconcile the past with the present, happiness might also exist. She bore witness to both steel and softness in the reflection.

Outside, Gus and Emma enjoyed the evening weather.

"Wow," said Emma. "You clean up nice, girlfriend."

"Thanks. Have either of you seen Caleb?"

"He's the good kind. You two getting pretty close?" Gus asked.

"Sure," Jenna said. She had a sinking suspicion Emma had given Gus a little too much information.

Caleb stepped outside wearing a dark blue button-down shirt. Left untucked, he looked more like a model out of an Abercrombie catalogue than a mutant from the apocalypse.

"There she is." He wore a huge smile. "Ready for tonight?"

"You two don't belong in this world. So gorgeous." Emma clapped when Caleb clasp Jenna's hand.

Heat rose in her cheeks.

Too many people staring and grinning.

She managed a smile. "Let's go before Mom and Dad here give us a curfew."

This would be normal if he wasn't carrying a nail-studded baseball bat. Oh well, got to take what you can get.

Jenna trailed Caleb along the pebbled pathway, through the ancient line of trees and toward the lake. She wondered if they were going on another picnic, but before getting close to the beach, Caleb turned onto a path in the woods. It dipped precipitously, causing Caleb to clasp Jenna's hands on occasion and direct her. With each nudge, memories of their first kiss made her long for more.

They arrived at the lone house that perched by the water like a cormorant ready to catch its prey. It was the one they noticed the night they picnicked at the beach.

"What are we doing here?" Jenna asked.

"I was curious. I came here after the hunt a while back and explored. This way we'll have some privacy. There is a great view of the lake from the back. I set it up so we can hang here tonight."

"Could be fun."

"Fun will be the understatement of the evening."

The two climbed the front stairs and headed inside. Most homes showed abandonment and neglect, furniture, and remnants of past lives in disarray and covered in dust, mold, and cobwebs. Broken and overturned lives and furnishing the norm. The entrance of this house, on the other hand, looked like someone could move in. The room was spotless.

"You cleaned for me."

"One time only. You're the woman. You should be doing this," Caleb teased.

"You did not say that." The smack of her hand against his well-muscled arm filled the air. "You'll get nothing if you act like a cave man."

"Look at this." He opened a door to a patio suspended above the water. A bouquet of wildflowers sat on a table with two chairs perched near the railing.

She stepped out into the night air and peered over. "The world is at peace here. I wish I never had to go back to reality."

"It would be nice if it was like this all the time."

"This is too perfect. Nothing this good is permanent. Something's bound to come along and destroy it," she said. "And not only our date. We found an amazing place to live at the inn. I found you. I can't believe it will last. Not in the world we live in now."

He held a bottle of red wine and two glasses in his hand. "You're always a pessimist, aren't you? Maybe this is exactly where we're supposed to be, and this is how it's supposed to work out. We found each other. That's fate, destiny, serendipity. Let's enjoy every minute of it." He poured wine into chipped, mismatched glasses.

"How did you get the bottle? Doesn't Jackie guard the wine cellar like every bottle was akin to gold and jewels?" She tasted the jewel-red drink, enjoying the little luxury. "Tasty."

"You better enjoy the treat." A grin worked his lips before he sipped. "I'm responsible for pretty much everyone's cleaning duties around the inn this month, but it was worth it. You're worth it."

She took a large drink.

"You did it all for me." The warmth of the wine hit quickly. "Are my cleaning duties included in the deal you made?"

"You're enjoying the benefits of the bottle." He raised an eyebrow. "You want to be excused from cleaning too? Gold digger."

"A woman's got to do what a woman's got to do." She sipped the wine, enjoying the view of the lake.

Caleb moved close, breath on the nape of her neck, proximity both comforting and disconcerted her. Bolstered by the drink, she leaned back against his broad chest and rested. His hands massaged her shoulders, teasing her senses.

His voice broke through the reverie. "Hungry?"

"Always."

"Let's eat."

They moved to the table and Caleb offered her chair with a flourish. For having survived the apocalypse, the chair was in surprisingly good working order. She slipped off her jacket and slung it behind her.

Caleb stared, his look appreciative. He drew matches from his pocket and lit the two candles he'd wrangled from the unknown. Candlelight danced, creating magical images, and added to the fairytale atmosphere.

As they ate, Caleb related tales of growing up in rural New York. His family had been close knit and the stories wove the tapestry of his life.

"We lived on a farm, but my dad wasn't really a farmer. He made a lot of money working in the stock market and decided it would be better to raise his family in the country. He retired early, bought some land, a few cows, sheep, and horses, and called himself a farmer. He was the biggest disaster, but my sisters and I loved him more than anything. Mom, too. She put up with all his crazy ideas. He was really smart, but a bit insane. I say that in the kindest of ways because he was my dad."

"Like father, like son," Jenna joked.

"Exactly. He taught me to play guitar and piano and encouraged my love of music even when I wanted to do it for a career. What did you want to do when you grew up?" Caleb poured her more wine.

Her eyebrow shot up. "Are you trying to get me drunk?"

"Maybe. Answer the question."

"I wanted to be a journalist." A chuckle escaped. "I wanted

to save the world by writing stories exposing the corruption in the government and big business. I was into causes. Save the polar bears. Save the whales. Stop rainforest destruction. Before everything happened, I was on my high school newspaper. I thought I could change the world for the better. Now, I'm happy to get through the day without running into a Streaker. My new cause is to save the humans."

"The world isn't so changed, Jenna. You make a difference every day by helping people."

"I'm not the person I was before, and I can't fathom a pre-pandemic life anymore. Too much has changed. I don't know if I can help anyone. Some days I can't help myself. For so long it was survival mode. It's hard to get out of the mindset with Streakers right outside the fences. Our safety here is an illusion. One that I'm happy to buy into at the present but still an illusion."

"You have gorgeous eyes." He changed the subject abruptly. "They reveal whatever you're passionate about."

"You don't want to discuss Streaker invasions? The inn's safety? Set up a plan for the perimeters?"

"Don't even joke. We are not going there tonight. Instead, I'm going to tell you how beautiful you are, and how much I want you. Those lips are killing me. They look so luscious, like a ripe raspberry I want to nibble on."

"Who are you?"

"I'm the person you enchanted with those red lips."

"It's my apocalipstick. I found it with the dress. The lipstick was my mom's." Jenna thought about how far she'd come to be willing to go on a date tonight with Caleb, the man who intimidated her not so long ago. "It represents the new me."

"You're stunning." His hand covered hers.

Her pulse raced and only intensified when he ran a finger across her cheek. It lingered on her neck for a brief moment before it trailed off. His gaze heated her.

What had started as contentment when their hands met, now turned into a primal emotion. It thrilled and scared her. In need of a distraction, she sipped her wine, all the while hoping Caleb would kiss her.

Instead, he rose, grabbed the plates, and went inside. On his return, he brought forth chocolate cookies.

"Are you serious? Where did you get this? How? I love you." She blushed at the last statement.

"I've told the scavenging parties to keep an eye out for anything chocolate, and they brought back cocoa powder. I knew you had a liking for the stuff, so Emma and I figured out a way to make you a special treat—for all you do with the garden and the farm animals." Caleb handed her a cookie, then he sat once more. His chiseled legs clad in rough blue jeans extended under the table, his knee making contact with her bare leg.

Jenna's mouth watered. "This is so delicious. You are my favorite person."

"I guess the way to a woman's heart is through her stomach too. There are more back at the inn. We made several batches, figuring most people would enjoy them."

"You're amazing." She leaned over the small table and planted a kiss on his cheek before finishing her cookie with gusto. "So good."

Caleb picked at his dessert. "Glad you like it." He stared at his folded hands, suddenly intent.

"A penny for your thoughts?"

"Currency is worthless now adays." His eyes danced red in the night.

Bewitched by them, Jenna stared. "Tell me anyway."

She wanted to know this man. He was charming and funny, loving and kind, but whatever else Caleb was— Jenna couldn't wait to embrace it.

Caleb stretched. "How crazy is it the two of us survived and found each other after everything that happened?"

She pushed out of her seat, sitting on his lap, and cuddling against his chest. "I wouldn't have it any different."

"It's like we were meant to be together. It's our destiny." His arms wrapped around her, caressing her through her sheer dress.

"I don't know if I believe in destiny anymore."

"I do."

His lips pressed against her hair, his honey breath making her lightheaded. His hands set Jenna's skin on fire. They roamed down her back and across her side, dress shifting beneath his fingers.

"I really like your dress, but I would like you out of it more. What do you want?"

"Nothing."

"Really?" A smile played on his lips. "That's a disappointment."

"I only desire what you freely want to give. This isn't about taking anything."

"I freely give you my love." His fingers cupped her chin, so their eyes met. "I want your love freely given. I can't imagine this world without you next to me."

Jenna's mind raced.

Did he really love her after the little time they spent together?

Could he mean it?

His hand moved to caress her shoulder while his lips tickled her neck. "Don't go quiet on me."

"I want this to happen."

When their lips met, her world spun out of control, and she lost herself in the sensation.

Was this desire? Love? It was her first real taste, never having the luxury of experiencing such emotions before.

"You're beautiful." Caleb drew her close, tracing the pattern of Jenna's dress as it danced on her thighs. "Stay with me."

"Yes." Jenna trembled at the idea.

"Are you scared?" Their bodies collided. Sparks might have well flown between them and burned off her dress, she was so hot.

She'd never felt anything like this before. Sure, she lacked experience, but this was something, all right. And she wanted to pursue it, at least her lady parts did.

"I'm nervous." She whispered words against his neck. "But more scared about losing this opportunity to be with you."

"Are you sure?"

"Absolutely."

"I love a decisive woman." He carried her into the bedroom, letting her slip onto the mattress. Joining her, his hands and lips roamed her body, distancing the outside world from this protective cocoon.

He drew close, and she leaned into the kiss. His lips tasted like chocolate and fervor. Irresistible. Caleb worked her dress up and over her thighs, hands roaming her stomach, fingers tracing the line of Jenna's scar. They separated, and he liberated her from her clothing. She pulled at the buttons on his shirt until there was nothing between them.

He kissed her shoulder, and then slowly trailed down her body, tracing her form with fingers and lips.

She flinched when his lips touched her scars, but then he kissed her navel and murmured, "Exquisite. So perfect."

He loved all of her, the good and the bad, the beautiful, and the ugly. Caleb could be her future, and she could not deny the need.

His kisses drove any last rational thoughts from her mind, and she moaned. His eyes begged for permission.

"Don't stop. God don't stop what you're doing." Her voice had a deep, husky quality she'd never heard. To make sure he understood, she shifted on top of him, enjoying his gasp of delight. From her vantage point, she made demands with her hands, her nails raking across his abs. Body relishing his touch, she pressed against him.

"You'll be the end of me, woman." He flipped her to the side and was instantly above her.

When their lips met again, her heart thundered.

"Jenna?" Caleb's need was evident, his body straining. "Are you sure?"

She unbuttoned his jeans. "I want to. I need you. Why are you still dressed?"

Something primal lit in Caleb's eyes, and they spiraled from red to purple to black. He buried his face in Jenna's neck. His teeth nipped against her fragile skin. She bucked with wanting under him.

"I'm yours." Her hands roamed his beautiful body.

"Are you sure?" Caleb stared into her eyes.

"Don't ask me again. I want this more than anything. I love you."

The words undid them both. Tangled together, long moments of pleasure blanketed them together.

Afterward, the pair lay, legs twisted like vines. Jenna's body burned so hot while Caleb's coolness stood in contrast. The two didn't return to the inn for many hours.

20

THEY RETURNED to the inn before morning arrived, exhausted but without the desire to part company. While it would be easiest for Jenna to complete her normal routine, little desire to do so remained. As they ambled through the hallway, Quentin exited Aiko's room with her in tow.

Jenna was unprepared for a moment like this. She almost raised her hand in greeting but forced it down to her side and balled it in a fist.

His gaze hammered her. "Walk of shame." He spit the words. Anger turned into a disappointed frown. "I see you made your decision." Resentment crept into his eyes.

"Leave them," Aiko said.

"Let me explain," Jenna's words were little more than a whisper.

Caleb forced her fingers open when their hands merged. "Quentin. You're a good friend, and Jenna would do anything for you. She did. She saved your life. You have no right to talk that way when you are involved with . . ."

"My life," Quentin interrupted, "is none of your concern. If it wasn't for you, things would be different between Jenna and I."

Her eyes grew owlish. *What were they yammering about? Neither of these men owned her thoughts or emotions.*

"Let's go." Quentin turned to Aiko. "I'm done with this conversation." They disappeared around the corner.

"Come on. Let's get to your room, and I'll explain." Caleb propelled her forward.

Jenna nestled in an armchair by the window, jiggling her foot while waiting.

"Remember last night?" A huge grin ensured he did.

"Of course," Jenna blushed thinking about some of the things they had done.

"Some New Racers want to do more than what we did. They want to share human blood."

Her mouth dropped open. "What?"

"Humans and New Racers find it enjoyable. I swear. There is something different about human blood. It's compelling and leaves the New Racer with a complex high, I guess you would call it. There isn't really a good way to describe what both people experience. It's unique to the individual. It's also addicting. New Racers s have to be careful."

Jenna's nostrils flared. "Seriously?"

"There is something about the way we've changed that makes the experience pleasurable rather than painful. The antithesis of Streakers."

"Why are you telling me all this now?"

"I'm telling you all this because Quentin and Aiko are in a relationship. It's based on mutual need. Aiko wants to feed off human blood, and Quentin enjoys the experience. I'm not sure how long it's been going on, but Peter brought it to my attention last week."

"You didn't tell me about this sooner?" Jenna's voice was squeaky.

"It's not really my business to tell. They are both adults, capable of making mature decisions."

"How do we know Quentin is making his own choice?

How do we know Aiko isn't using some New Race power to persuade him?"

"We aren't vampires, werewolves, witches, or devils. It's not a Shakespearean tragedy. We don't cast spells on people or compel them to do whatever we want. We don't enslave humans. If she's using anything, it's her feminine mystique."

"You sure about that?"

"Quentin is a big boy. He makes his own decisions."

"I don't like it. Should I speak to him?"

"It would only make him feel worse. He's mad right now that we're together. His ego is bruised, but Aiko is a good person."

"She told everyone to let him die!"

"She was rational. Maybe she didn't say what she wanted to in the most politically correct way, but her heart was in the right place. She was watching out for the group."

"Why did she get so close to Quentin once we got the medicine?"

"Guilt. She realized your way might have been the better way to deal with the situation."

"What should I do?" She stood and paced the confines of her room. "Is there a way to stop it?"

"Don't get involved. He's an adult who understands exactly what he's doing. Aiko isn't forcing him into anything. She can't make him do it. New Racers aren't vampires. We don't compel people."

"Really?"

"I'm positive you'll do whatever you want, no matter what I say. It's one of the reasons I like you so much."

"You could get me to do almost anything if you asked nicely," Jenna's voice turned husky. Her hair was in wild disarray from the previous night, and her bootlaces untied. He stopped her in the middle of the room and led her to the bed.

"You're an absolute mess." Caleb's eyes radiated heat.

Insecurities streaked across her face.

"It looks perfect on you." He tousled her hair. "I love my women wild, and I love you."

Caleb began to remove the few articles of clothing she wore, boots first.

Jenna didn't get around to starting her chores until it was past noon. This was unlike her, and she hated the rush. Luckily, after months of hard work, most of her routine was easy to complete.

She scrubbed the water bins for the horses and goat, filling them anew. Her flannel shirt quickly became covered with mud and animal hair. The Clydesdales still had plenty to graze on in the meadow, but the group had left two fields to grow. With cold weather right around the corner, they would cut and harvest hay for the winter. In addition, Jenna had planted corn and soybeans. While the group used some for food, the animals could also benefit from the excess in winter.

After tending to the animals, she began working on the garden. She was surprised to find most weeds gone and assumed someone had competed the chore in the morning. She wondered who had worked in the garden and if Caleb would have to do something in repayment.

No complaints.

.

Between the equines and the harvesting in the garden, hours flew by. She was surprised Emma or Gus hadn't arrived to interrogate her, but, for once, they granted her some time. She was sure that would change at dinner. Wiping dirt from the garden on her jeans, she headed back to the inn.

The view from the front porch was riveting with the lush meadow leading into dense woods. She sat, stalling before going inside and facing everyone with their good intentions.

Was this a hallucination? One. Two. Four. Six.

They moved through the meadow.

Panic flooded her system. She stood and ran, pushing open the front door.

"Streakers." Jenna grabbed a gun kept in a nearby closet. Ford was first at her side, also reaching for a weapon. The two headed out to the porch.

"Where?" Ford asked.

Jenna pointed to the figures moving toward the inn. They moved quickly and efficiently in a straight line.

"They don't appear to be Streakers, do they?" Ford asked.

"No," Jenna squinted

More people joined them on the porch, weapons in hand. As the figures reached the middle of the field, people could recognize strangers not Streakers. A blond, angular woman shadowed a tall Hispanic male, both charismatic and carrying weapons. Four people followed.

Word spread and everyone crowded on the front porch. Some held weapons at the ready while some stared in awe.

Peter stepped forward to greet the new arrivals and no one stopped him.

"Good evening," the strange, blond woman addressed Peter, her voice lilted with a strong accent.

"My name is Peter," he said. "It is not often or ever we receive visitors to the inn. We're happy you're here and safe. Everyone is healthy?"

"Of course," replied the woman. "My name is Tundra."

"Come inside and share some dinner. Welcome to our home."

Jenna shifted from foot to foot. *Was Peter sizing them up? Determining if they were friend or foe? Shouldn't there be a test before allowing strangers to enter?*

The pressure of Caleb's hand on her back gave her instant comfort. She could not resist leaning against him.

"Thank you," replied the blonde, clearly of the New Race. "These are my companions, David and Gunnar." The blonde pointed at the two men next to her, also of the New Race. David was Hispanic, well-muscled, with tattoos running in sleeves along his arms. Gunnar, his polar opposite. Bright green skinny jeans and an oversized jacket that hung listlessly about him amplified his skinny frame. Long, shaggy brown hair covered one of his eyes and reaching to his shoulders.

"Of course," Tundra continued, finally recognizing the humans in her group. "These are our humans . . . human companions. This is Lilly, Jim, and Mack."

The three humans issued quiet hellos. It was obvious the travel and stress of the Streakers had worn on them. Jenna was excited to learn more and hear their stories. A babble of voices erupted from the porch when the new arrivals entered, everyone curious to find where they had been and what it was like on the outside.

Peter led the group into the dining hall where Jenna helped ladle out bowls of hot soup with fresh vegetables, broiled venison, and some recently found, canned pineapple. Jackie had attempted a new bread recipe and rolls perched on each table.

Tundra spoke while the humans in her group ate quietly but with vigor. They were skinny to the point of emaciation, obviously suffering from worse conditions than at the inn. The two New Racers next to Tundra stared at her with adoration, and there was no doubt who kept the group together.

"David, Gunnar, and I hail from New York City," Tundra began to tell their story. "New York is now a wasteland, but I'm originally from Belgium. We are some of the very few who made it out, but not before losing many of our companions. We have been searching for quite a long time for a quiet place to call home." Tundra addressed the members of the New Race, avoiding eye contact with the humans.

Feels great to be ignored. The bitch keeps staring at Caleb. What is going on here?

"My companions and I found Jim and Mack on the road together about a year ago. They joined us, and then Lilly was a surprising find about five months ago. We see less and less humans as time goes by. We don't often run into anyone these days, except, of course, the Streakers."

English is her second language. Maybe that's why it sounds like Tundra refers to Lilly as a pet rather than a person, Jenna thought.

"How long did it take you to get to Virginia?" asked Aiko. "How did you find us?"

"I assume we had a similar idea to you," Tundra said. "The colder states would have less people and less Streakers but would also be harder to survive in. We decided to venture south, hoping to find more survivors, and run into less Streakers by staying away from big cities and off major highways."

"How'd you end up here?" Peter asked.

"We're actually on our way further south. We hope to find an island off the coast of Florida. David and I noticed this place from a distance and considered staying the night. When we moved closer, we smelled wood burning and were curious."

"It is a nice place you have here," Gunnar added.

"It speaks," Billy joked, and Josh and Kyle snickered.

"You don't address us that way." David jumped out of his seat and turned a malevolent stare on them, pale eyes spiraling to red.

The boys quieted, fear apparent on Kyle's face.

George, gun in hand, rocketed out of his seat. "You don't talk to anyone here like that ever. This is our home, not yours." The gun barrel was mere feet away from David's head.

Peter and Tundra stood in unison.

Tundra aimed her gaze at David, voice cold and venomous. "We are guests here. You need to control yourself." She placed a pale hand on his shoulder, fingernails digging into his flesh.

"I'm sorry," David met Tundra's eyes before the group. "I am sorry for the comment. It was not my place."

To restore normalcy, Peter steered the conversation to his own experiences and spoke to Tundra about the group forming and traveling together. George sat and the conflict dissolved.

As the evening wore on, Lilly, Jim, and Mack became more communicative. Lilly, tiny and thin, was roughly the same age. The two rehashed life before the pandemic while Quentin, George, and Gus showed Jim and Mack the improvements to the inn. The New Race went to bond on the hunt.

Jenna loved having another person her age to reminisce with. It brought back reminders of sleepovers and gossip sessions. Lilly was sweet and shy but warmed when the discussion focused on the years before the virus.

Emma came over with a bottle of Chianti and poured it into three mismatched mugs.

"You broke out the wine for a special occasion," Jenna said.

"Nothing more special than finding people." The older woman pulled them both into a hug.

"We were reliving the past. I hated middle school when I was in it," Jenna said. "I was thirteen and such a geek. Who would have thought I would give anything to go back if I could."

"I'm sure all the little boys were dying to give you your first kiss," Emma teased.

"Not at all. I was tall for my age in middle school. All the boys were shorter than me for a year or two. Just imagine me bending down for my first kiss?"

"You're lucky," Lilly said. "I was always a midget. Everyone towered over me or jostled me out of the way. I tried so hard to be cool, always into make-up and trends, but hated the fashions. It was all leggings and short skirts when I wanted to be different. Now, I just wish we were all the same. Human. No Streakers."

"Amen, girlfriend," Emma slugged back her Chianti.

"Hey."

Jenna and Lilly jumped, and Jenna wondered once again how Caleb moved so soundlessly, she failed to hear when he came near her.

"You scared me," Jenna studied him. "You finished with the hunt?"

"I didn't want to stay away too long. Dinner was a little tense, and I wanted to make sure everything was okay here."

Jenna introduced Lilly. Caleb stuck out his hand so she could shake it. Her face turned white, and she stared at his fingers like she didn't understand the social protocol.

"Are you okay?" Jenna asked.

"Sorry," Lilly replied. "Stupid of me. Nice to meet you, Caleb." She shook his hand.

Caleb joined them and after a few more glasses of Chianti the conversation erupted. Lilly came out of her shell and told funny stories about her past life as a band geek. It was obvious Lilly was intelligent and sweet, but she acted nervous and scared around Caleb. After Lilly retired to bed, Caleb and Jenna returned to her room.

She jumped on her bed and motioned Caleb next to her. Her hand drifted to the leg of his jeans and she let her hand drift along the fabric when they conversed.

"What do you think of the newcomers? Especially Tundra? She's different."

"I like Lilly. She's charming. I didn't really get a chance to meet Jim and Mack tonight. The hunt with the visitors was intense. Tundra and her crew are pretty extreme, but I guess you need to be that way to live in the world these days. We've gotten soft at the inn."

"I don't like her." Conviction permeated the words. "There is something off about her and her group. She must have been a good leader because they all survived, but I find her really condescending."

"How so?" He entwined their hands.

"Like Lilly was less important than the New Racers in her group. She made it apparent she doesn't like me or maybe all humans. Tundra addressed Peter and the New Racers, while ignoring the rest of us."

"You're reading too much into it. Peter stepped in to introduce us. Its natural Tundra would consider him in charge. Plus, it must be easier for New Races to relate to their kind and humans to humans."

"Really?" Jenna asked, freeing her hand from his. "I guess we are done." She stroked his washboard flat stomach. "Unless you'd like to articulate what a New Racer is doing with this human?"

"Good question," Caleb teased. "Maybe I should dump you now that some new blood is in town."

"Don't joke." She swatted him.

"Sorry." He lowered his eyes. "Seriously, Jenna, there is no one else I could ever imagine being with, and no one I want more than you." Caleb's gaze intensified and his eyes darkened to the color of thick blood.

He leaned in and kissed her. She was suddenly aware of how small she was against him. His scent, musky from the hunt, made Jenna tremble. At first, Caleb was gentle, nuzzling her neck and arms, causing them to tingle. Then he let his desire be known.

Jenna met his kisses with equal fervor, something she

never would have imagined. She ripped at his clothing, wanting to touch skin, feel his nakedness next to her.

Caleb, on the other hand, took his time, easing Jenna's shirt over her head. His hand leisurely trailed from neck to navel to tackle the single button on her jeans. He liberated Jenna from those.

He nuzzled her neck.

Jenna's pulse raced. Her body longed for his and whatever existed between them was real. As the night advanced, Caleb found a way to bring her joy she could never have imagined.

Afterwards, Jenna snuggled in the tangled sheets against his broad frame, his arms wrapped around her. She fell asleep to the sound of his whispered words.

Harsh banging on the door roused her and Caleb before dawn the next morning.

"Group meeting in fifteen minutes. Move yourselves sleepy heads." Victor's baritone boomed.

Caleb and Jenna arrived late, entering a crowded main hall where closed curtains sealed out the light. Tundra stood in the corner politicking to Aiko, Victor and John, who laughed, captivated.

The hairs on Jenna's arms rose, and she grabbed Caleb's hand for support. He smiled reassuringly and found two seats.

Peter brought the group to order. "Tundra and her group are happy to find us. They never thought they'd find people settled and doing well and want to join. Let's start the discussion with concerns. Every situation has both pros and cons needing to be addressed."

Jenna had plenty of concerns, but she didn't want to be the first to speak and come across as negative. She liked Lilly, Jim, and Mack, but was already ill at ease around Tundra and her creepy sidekicks. There were more base concerns too. More mouths to feed, more people to house and keep healthy. Until the inn was fully functional, they'd drain resources. Saying that to everyone would sound childish and petty, especially after her campaign to save Quentin.

"It will be fine." Caleb squeezed her hand.

Luckily for Jenna, George decided to play the role of jerk for the day.

"You know we have limited supplies. Six more mouths to feed could drain our surplus quick." George's gaze focused on the new arrivals.

"Consider what you said. We all know you're more concerned about the wine than the food. Three of the group are New Racers. They can help defend us and bring in deer meat with the hunt," Jackie said. "They won't be using much of the medical supplies because they are always healthy."

George scowled.

"As for Lilly, Jim, and Mack, I am sure they will be useful around the inn." Jackie sent a smile in their direction. "We have so much we need to get done before the winter sets in. We need the manpower. Sorry, Lilly—and the womanpower —to survive."

"I'm just one voice," George said. "I still have concerns."

"We all do with important issues." Peter stepped into the conversation. "And we should. Debate is healthy. Thinking about all sides of an issue is important. Does anyone else want to speak."

Aiko made the case for the new arrivals to join.

"We are good on medications," Emma added. "If anyone does get sick, we'll handle it. I do wish one of you all had been a doctor though. It's stressful caring for this lot on my own."

"Let's vote," Peter said. "What would you want to happen if you were in the same situation?"

Jenna helped pass out slips of paper and writing utensils once again. Tundra, Gunnar, and David sat whispering together in the corner. Lilly, Mack, and Jim gazed around with saucer eyes.

What would life be like out there? And the struggle e to survive day-to-day? Fighting Streakers and scavenging for food and supplies must have been horrible for everyone.

As concerned as she was about Tundra in her home, she couldn't live with herself if she forced them out.

The votes were collected and tallied, revealing the vast majority of people wanted the new arrivals to stay. There were only two votes against them. Jenna assumed George had been one of those, but she was curious about who had cast the additional negative ballot.

When Peter announced the decision, Lilly gave Jenna a hug, and a celebration started. People milled around conversing or went to the kitchen to help prepare a meal. Gus and Jackie began to plan new work rotations that would help everyone settle. Lilly would shadow Jenna for a few days until she was comfortable around the inn on her own. Gus would show Mack and Jim around, and Peter, Aiko, and Victor could help the others.

The celebration lasted into the morning with wine flowing and conversations about the future. For a moment suspended in time, everyone appeared happy and slightly drunk on the wine from storage.

Caleb and Jenna left the party early, but it was not to sleep.

When Jenna and Lilly headed out into the morning, Jenna's head thumped heavily, and she wondered if she had a little too much wine. The air was crisp, and winter appeared much closer than it had only a few days ago. Without a calendar, it was hard to keep track of time, which now passed in small spurts or rushing waves, never in a consistent flow.

"This is Moon and Star." Jenna introduced the woman to the Clydesdales.

"They're beautiful. I can't wait to help you with the

animals. This is the most wonderful thing after being on the road forever."

"Was it tough?"

Lilly's face shuttered over. "Yes."

"I'm sorry. I know it's hard."

"But I'm here now."

"Do you think you'll be okay helping here. It's dirty work, and some people don't like it."

"One hundred percent yes."

The two women dug into mucking the stalls. As the days trudged forward, Jenna and Lilly became a strong team caring for the animals and the garden. With the additional help, Jenna had time to focus on the greenhouse project too.

Jenna and Lilly quickly established a close relationship and happy work routine. Each day would begin with the two started with barn chores and then migrated out to the garden.

"Tell me more about how you survived on your own," Jenna asked one morning while she pulled out small weeds invading her pumpkin patch.

"One of the main reasons I was able to survive was my background being a naturalist and my wilderness training from camp." Lilly filled Jenna in on her back story. "I was trained at a survivalist summer camp. My parents were extremely religious and believed God's rapture was soon to arrive. In a way, I guess they were right. They were worried for my soul and sent me to learn to survive if I was left on earth."

"Maybe they were smarter than the rest of us."

"When the pandemic got bad and I lost them, I set off alone in the woods with my camping gear. It was tough going, but I know all the edible wild plants and how to trap small animals for food. Being alone all the time is awful, especially not knowing what was happening in the world. It was worth the trade off, meeting Tundra and her group."

"What trade off?" Jenna queried.

"You know," Lilly waved her hand around in a vague gesture.

"I really don't," Jenna looked up from the pumpkin she held.

"We share."

"Share what?" *This conversation was getting weird.*

Confusion turned Lilly's eyes owlish. "You really don't know what I'm trying to tell you?"

"I have no idea."

"You have to promise not to say anything if I tell you about it. Tundra would be so mad at me, and you do not want to make Tundra mad. She has an awful temper."

"I promise."

Lilly tore back the collar of her shirt. Scars clearly stood out against the pale pallor of her skin.

"What happened? Did someone attack you? Did Tundra do this?"

"I saw marks on Quentin. Aren't you and Caleb in some sort of relationship, too? I thought the same thing was going on here, but you all appear happy. Not scared like I am. Am I wrong?"

"I'm in a relationship with Caleb. We're in love, but he'd never force me to do anything I did not want to do. I haven't done that." She put a hand to her neck.

"I'm sorry I brought this up." Lilly's face colored. "You're with Caleb. What about Quentin. He has marks on his neck. I assumed his situation was the same."

"Quentin had a recent near-death experience. He needs something or someone to help him recover. What they do in the privacy of their own room is none of my business."

"The dark haired one, um . . . Maybe her name is Arlene."

"You mean, Aiko."

"Aiko told Tundra about him. She said Quentin was a regular. I believe she called him a donor."

"A donor? Shit. Harsh."

"You won't say anything, will you?" Lilly knotted her hands together.

"Of course not," Jenna replied. "I'm just confused. I've been so concerned with my own little world I've lost touch with everything going on around here. Listen though, the New Racers here are our friends and family. They would never make us do anything we don't want to."

"Good to know." Lilly smiled, but the light didn't reach her eyes.

The women worked in the garden until lunch time, conversation shifting to how the inn ran and the low-down on the people who lived there, relieving some of the tension between them. Jenna told funny stories about the group's adventures before reaching the inn. Lilly's tales were much darker, and she didn't like to expand on the months she'd spent roaming with Tundra.

Throughout the conversation, unease chomped at Jenna. At lunch, Lilly joined Mack and Jim, and Jenna went to seek out Quentin. He was in the kitchen helping to fill Jackie's version of tortillas with meat and vegetables. Jenna drew him aside.

When she had to speak, she wished she'd planned a little more. "Can I ask you something?" Her eyes flew to the marks on his neck. *How could she have missed those?*

"Sure," Quentin said. "I think it's time we all forgive and forget."

"Then you might not like what I have to say. I've heard some rather weird stuff lately and wanted to know if it was true."

"What gossip is going around the inn now? People need to keep their mouths shut and their eyes on their own business."

"You and Aiko."

"You know all you need to. The details of my relationship

are really none of your business. You're perfectly content with Caleb. I bet the only reason you come to see me is because I'm happy and with someone who cares about me the way I do about them."

"Unfair. Think about it. Does Aiko care about you, or is she using you? Lilly said Aiko called you a donor when she was speaking with Tundra. What does that mean?"

"You should ask the same thing about you and Caleb. Maybe he's the one using you. Maybe you're so caught up being with him, you let him use you any way he likes."

"It's not like that with Caleb."

"You know what, Jenna? I don't care. Be with whoever you want, whenever you want. You believe the new girl but ignore what I have to say. Just leave me alone. You make this so hard."

"Because we're friends. I don't want to see you hurt or used." She reached out a hand to him.

"We were friends at one time, and I actually thought we might be again, but you obviously can't let me be happy. I don't want to be friends. If you won't leave, I will." Quentin stomped out of the kitchen.

Jenna stood hurt and angry, a cascade of emotions running through her. Finding an empty table in the dining room, she sat alone. Flinging away her plate drew curious stares. She pulled it back and forced a couple bites.

What's the right thing to do?

After lunch, she and Lilly joined up again for afternoon chores where they endured the joy of laundry duty. Lilly worked hard to make Jenna laugh with funny stories of the times before the pandemic. Afternoon merged into evening. When the women had finished their work, she sought Caleb out even more sure Lilly didn't deserve this.

Caleb made her wait. First, he had a project to plan with John, and then he forced her participation in a long and feverish game of Parcheesi with John and Victor. Jenna conceded defeat early because John and Victor spent the entire game claiming good naturedly the other cheated, and she had more fun watching them bicker than attempting to win.

She finally coerced Caleb back to her room. He arrived with a change of clothes and guitar. Could it be he had plans to move into the small space with her? His dirty socks, toothbrush, and tattered books had already found a place to call home amongst her possessions.

This was a very different discussion they needed to have, but it would have to wait.

"Planning on playing your guitar for me?"

"Not tonight."

"Then why bring it here?"

"I'm going to practice later."

"You could practice now or in a few minutes. We need to talk."

"I'll work on it later. It's not ready."

"What's not ready?"

"The song I wrote for you. Soon. I promise. What do we need to talk about?"

Caleb yanked her on his lap and kissed her neck, but she shifted back. "Can't I distract you?"

Snuggling against him on the chair, Jenna said, "Talk first. I need your help processing a conversation I had with Lilly earlier."

"Someone's serious?" Caleb teased her hip with his fingers.

"This is serious. There is something weird going on with Tundra, but I promised Lilly I wouldn't say anything. If I tell you, you have to keep it between us."

"Anything," Caleb said. "You know that."

"Something wrong with the New Racers in Lilly's group."

"What's wrong?"

"Lilly spotted the scars on Quentin and thought Aiko

used him to donate blood. She thought you controlled me the same way and used my blood for your own pleasure."

"Can't be right." His brow knotted into a V-shape. "You must have misinterpreted what she said."

"She said Tundra and the rest of the New Race in her group make her, Mack, and Jim do things they might not volunteer to do otherwise."

"What things? Are we talking in addition to blood?"

Jenna's head snapped up. "Blood donations definitely. I didn't want to push about what else. I explained to Lilly we're a couple, but we do things differently here. She got all embarrassed and didn't want to say more. Something bad might be going on with them. I don't know what to do about it."

"It does sound strange." Caleb rubbed his forehead. "Could Lilly be fabricating the story because she didn't want you to know she was having a relationship with someone? Maybe she was embarrassed about it and thought if she made up a story, you'd think better about her?"

Jenna tilted her head. "Lilly knew something was going on with Quentin. Why would she fabricate a story if she was in a relationship? Quentin's in one, and we're in one. It's pretty normal around here."

"There might be alternative explanations."

"The reason she said anything in the first place was because she observed scars on Quentin and assumed the same thing was going on here. It doesn't make sense she would lie to create such a crazy story and get the New Racers in her group in trouble unless it was real."

"If this is true, we need to do something. Let's ask Peter about it. I promise no one else will hear any of this. Maybe he knows more about situations like these. He was alone longer than anyone else in our group, and he traveled with New Racers before joining us. He's never openly discussed what went on with them."

"I promised not to tell. What if it gets out that I'm a snitch? Let me think about it tonight. I'll try and get information out of Lilly tomorrow."

"I'll talk to Tundra over the next few days and find out what is going on from her. Aiko likes her. I'll get her opinion without letting on about what you said."

"Aiko likes Tundra. Shocker. Make sure they don't suspect anything."

"I have perimeter duty in a couple minutes."

"Why didn't you tell me earlier?"

"Absence makes the heart grow fonder and all. How about we meet before sunrise. Do you mind waking early tomorrow?"

"For you, anything."

"Thanks." He flashed a smile.

Her gaze lifted, and she found him waiting. There was an unspoken question lighting his eyes.

"Don't you need to leave?"

"If I'm a few minutes late no one will care."

She pushed closer to him, and the movement was all he needed. He kissed her, and she kissed him back until his taste became part of her soul. His fingers caressed her cheek, heating her spirit and her skin. She drank him in, knowing she'd never get enough. His kiss, urgent and demanding, challenged her to give him more.

He nipped at her neck.

She groaned.

"I want to taste you. I want you to share your life with me in every way."

She was confused. "I want it too, but I'm scared."

"I'd never hurt you." He nipped at her again.

Every part of her body warmed, ready. The emotions overwhelming. Jenna pulled back, dizzy, and out of breath. "We should stop."

"We should," he agreed, "but I don't want to."

"Do you always get what you want?"

"Usually, but for tonight, you're right."

Another groan escaped. This time, she wasn't sure if it was from disappointment or desire, yet she said the most rational words she could muster. "You need to go on watch."

The erotic tension building between them melted away like snow on a warm morning. He headed for the door.

One part of Jenna wanted to drag him back and let him do everything he wanted to, but thoughts of Lilly invaded her mind and made her realize they needed to figure out what was going on.

"I'm really worried. I hope Lilly's not in any danger. Be careful when you question Aiko and Tundra, but I need answers."

21

CALEB LEFT A FEW MINUTES LATER, but sleep wasn't in Jenna's future. Grabbing a sweatshirt, she went to find one of the new arrivals, if any were still awake.

She checked the work schedule. Tundra, Aiko, and Caleb would be on first watch tonight together. Jealousy scratched from under the skin. Of anyone available, Caleb had to get Aiko and Tundra, Jenna's least favorite people. Still, that might give her a chance to approach the humans in Tundra's group without interference. If what Lilly said was true, Jenna wondered how she could have missed the signs with Mack and Jim. Her preoccupation with Caleb did this. Losing her edge could mean her death.

She had to remember the world would never be safe. For anyone.

All three were hard to find. As much as they liked the accommodations at the inn, they tended to avoid gatherings in the evenings. She banged on each of their doors before finding the three in a secluded corner of the inn.

"How's everyone?" Jenna asked.

Lilly jumped at the words, gaze lifting from her cup of

instant coffee while liquid sloshed over the side of the cup. "Good."

Mack and Jim remained stoic and silent.

"Can I join you, or are you in the middle of something important?"

"Sure, sit," Lilly said.

She sat cross legged on the floor. "How is everyone settling in?"

"Good," said Mack, sending her a rare smile. A big, burly guy, his black beard had grown long, and he'd kept it that way. Dark hair peppered his arms and sprung from under his shirt. His muscular build, tattoos of waves and mountains, and crooked nose spoke to the possibility of a life of extreme sports. "You most definitely have better food than on the road. I hear you have a green thumb and have become a garden master. Must be a lot of hard work, but it's so worth it. Dinner was amazing."

She tried to look for marks on his neck, but if the bites existed, they stayed hidden. "Thanks. The group has really come together to make this place home," Jenna said.

"Your group is lucky." Jim sat stiff. His face was clean-shaven, and he'd buzzed his hair back to a crew cut. His intelligent eyes assessed Jenna when he spoke.

"We support each other, and I love the garden almost as much as the horses. I hope we'll get a whole menagerie of farm animals soon." Jenna smiled. "Lilly's already pitched in. Anyone who wants to weed is more than welcome. Some mornings, I get outside and my work is done. Someone around here must have a secret green thumb. I wish they'd tell me, so I could thank them."

"I loved the greenhouse too," Lilly said. "It was great to see. and the plantings are going to be amazing when up and running."

"I'm working on it. The windows are all fixed and the

flats for the plants are up. If anyone wants to move plants with me in a couple of weeks, I'd love it."

All three of her companions were eager to help with the greenhouse project, but when the conversation continued, Jenna's gaze wandered. Scars dotting Lilly's thin, pale neck and arms were the most obvious. When Jim's long-sleeve shirt rode up, she could see scars running along his arm. If Mack also had marks, he hid them well.

The evidence against the new arrivals was weak. The scars appeared healed or healing. They could have easily been part of the rough time on the road. Everyone has scars these days, both internal and external.

Jenna chatted away with the group and was beginning to think maybe the situation had been blown out of proportion. Once relaxed, they all seemed happy and thankful for their new place to call home.

The hand squeezing her shoulder had Jenna pivoting. Aiko stood behind her.

"Sorry to interrupt your little pajama party Jenna, but a word please."

"See you guys later," Jenna said.

Aiko flicked her plaited hair behind her, one hand balanced on her sculpted, curvaceous hip. She puckered candy pink lips.

"I thought you were on watch with Caleb?" Jenna asked.

Aiko ignored her question. "You have no right to get involved in Quentin's life, or ask him what he's doing, and who he is doing it with. You made your choice, and Quentin made his. Believe me, Quentin made the best decision."

"No offense to you, but he's my friend. I didn't try to upset him. I wanted to make sure he was doing the right thing for himself. Maybe the problem is a lack of communication between the two of you. He's always welcome to come talk to me. He's a big boy and can express his own opinion on the subject."

Aiko chuffed. "I know all about you. You believe you're tough, you'll get any man you want, but face it, you are only human. You're nothing when compared to us. Why would anyone want you when they could have someone better, someone from the New Race? Caleb is only with you for one reason. A food supply. Once he gets over the initial thrill, don't doubt for a minute, he'll return to one of us. Get ready for disappointment."

"Caleb and I care about each other." She spat the words through gritted teeth.

"Listen and listen well." Her icy voice froze the words she spoke. "Tundra has a whole new philosophy, and I admire her for it. There is a new way of life coming, and humans are at the bottom of the food chain. Enjoy your time with Caleb now, because when he sees the light, he'll recognize you for what you really are—a tasty treat." Aiko cackled and tore from the room.

Jenna stood alone and confused. Tundra and her group were serious trouble, but she had no idea what to do about it.

As the days went by, trouble did not visit the inn. In fact, everything ran efficiently and without problem throughout the weeks following. Temperatures dropped, but the New Race could install solar panels and gather enough wood to last the winter. The greenhouse was up and running thanks to Lilly, Mack, and Jim. Emma, Jackie, and Jenna perfected their skills at canning foods and learned to make killer tasting preserves. Gus brought back chickens to add to the menagerie, and all the animals thrived. They'd be able to feed the animals over the winter with all the hay the group gathered, and corn grown. Even Streakers had turned rare, with only one far-away sighting when a scavenging party went out.

Mack, Jim, and Lilly didn't complain, worked hard, and became more social. Yet, Jenna worried. One day when Mack took off his coat, his shirt rose high, and Jenna couldn't help but notice bite marks. It incensed her no one else shared her concerns, but she felt like a hypocrite being involved with Caleb. Similar marks appeared on Quentin too. New Racers feeding on humans had become normalized. While Caleb had discussed the issue, it might not be voluntary with Peter, he hadn't heard anything and was reluctant to go to Tundra. No one had a problem with the new arrivals, except for Jenna.

Jenna kept her angst about the new arrivals at bay but wanted to understand what was happening on a rational, scientific level. As her relationship with Caleb deepened, she decided to trust him. If he needed to share her blood to make him stronger and healthier, she'd let him.

Maybe there was something sensual to the experience, and that's why the newbies let it continue.? She was curious, but curiosity kills the cat.

If she went through with it, she'd understand what Lilly had to endure.

Don't lie. Beyond the experiment and the curiosity, there's a desire to do it. A need to share every part of herself with the man she loved.

She wanted him to know all of her and trusted him with her life.

When he knocked, she let him in and pushed against him the moment the door clicked shut, pressing her arms around his back.

Don't back out.

She raised her chin so her lips could meet his and melted into their kiss.

"I missed you too, but what's going on?"

"I'm ready," Jenna said.

"Ready for what?"

"To let you share my blood."

"I'm fine with the hunt."

215

"I want you to know all of me." She felt the wealth of muscles under his brown shirt.

When his tongue challenged hers, she melted. His hands worked her curves, teasing. They caressed her arms and then dropped down to her thighs. He kissed her neck and unbuttoned her blouse in a deft movement. When he finally released her, it took a moment for the world to steady.

He smiled wickedly. "I really missed you." His fingers returned to her shoulders, gently massaging the tired muscles, until he pushed her shirt to the floor. Taking her by the hand, he led her to the bed.

"What are you doing?" Her heartbeat exploded in her chest.

He nibbled her ear lobe. "Exactly what you want."

His fingers ran down her neck. She trembled in anticipation.

Jenna was ready. One part of her couldn't believe she'd only met Caleb after the end of the world. It seemed unfair. But a voice in her head screamed it didn't matter. "I want you to."

She didn't want his hands to ever stop caressing her. As much as he wanted to know her, she wanted all of him. His finger traced the pulse on her neck, and then his lips were there.

Whispered words kissed her skin, but she lost herself in the sensation.

A pent-up moan escaped her lips. There was a moment of pain, and then a tingle of pleasure built into a tidal wave. She wrestled for control, but rode the sensations, losing herself in them. Unable to hold back, she blissfully went over the edge.

∼

Days later, on a crisp day when autumn had nearly fled, Lilly asked Jenna if they could go riding. They met at the barn after breakfast. Cat kept them company. The air was cool, but the sun still warm enough for only a heavy sweater. Jenna showed Lilly how to groom and tack the horse, and they mounted using a block she had created with Caleb's help.

She brought a gun though Streakers had been scarce.

The two set off, enjoying the peace of the forest even with most of the trees now bare. Lilly showed no desire to turn around, and the two ventured farther from the inn than Jenna had been in a long time, but the woman remained quiet. Jenna didn't pressure her.

"We're friends, right?" Lilly asked.

"Absolutely."

"I need to tell you something, but nervous."

"I guarantee I've witnessed a lot worse in the past. It can't be that bad."

"It is."

"We'll deal with it."

"Mack, Jim and I love it here, and Tundra's been good since we arrived. She's told Gunnar and David to lay off the whole power trip thing, but she has a plan."

"Like a master plan of death and destruction?" Jenna joked.

"I'm serious. Tundra's been working hard to get close to certain people here. She started with Aiko, Victor, and Bethany."

"What do you mean?"

"She wanted to persuade the New Racers humans are beneath them and take control. Tundra wants the power to take what she wants whenever. Do you understand?"

"I think so."

"If someone of the New Race wants human blood, Tundra believes they should take it. They don't ask for it."

"We're a close-knit community, no matter what problems and disagreements arise. I can't see anyone from here agreeing with Tundra. Aiko wouldn't turn on us. She's with Quentin. They care for each other."

"Think about it. If someone called you the most powerful creatures alive, and you should be able to do what you wanted when you wanted, you'd buy into that logic. Tundra's extremely persuasive."

"Sounds far-fetched."

"Why would Mack, Jim, and I have stayed with her if it was unbearable? She used me like a snack. But she's smart. She knows how to get into your mind. She'd remind us how awful it was on our own and explain how they needed to feed to stay strong and protect us. Tundra would tell us to go because there were Streakers at every turn, and we'd be dead in hours. She is a great manipulator, and we all bought into it because it was easier than fighting. There was nothing to fight for, but now there is."

"You think Tundra wants our friends at the inn to do the same thing. Make humans food and slaves? That's what it sounds like you were when traveling with her."

"Tundra needs to be in control, and she's strong and powerful. I hate to admit it, but on the road, she was our best chance for survival." Lilly paused. "There's more. You're a threat."

"Why?"

"You're in a relationship with Caleb. It goes against everything she is saying because Caleb treats you like an equal. She hates it. It doesn't help Tundra has grown bored of David and Gunnar and now wants him for herself."

"You can't be serious." She drew back on the reins and forced her horse to stop. It pawed the ground restless and waiting. It pranced and snorted, excited to continue.

"Why would I tell you all this otherwise."

"This sounds like something out of a bad pulp fiction

novel. Tundra's plotting to turn my friends against me and use me like a food source. She also has a personal vendetta against me. She's jealous and wants my boyfriend."

"It sounds crazy when you put it that way, but every word is true. Why would I lie?"

Jenna turned her horse around, motioning for Lilly to do the same. "We should get back."

She and Lilly began the trek back.

"What should I do?" Jenna asked, realizing she believed Lilly.

"I have no idea. If I could have thought of a solution, I would have tried to handle it. That's why I'm telling you about it. I'm afraid to go to Mack or Jim."

"Why?"

"I'm not really sure where their alliances are. They've been with Tundra for longer than I have, and she's been trying to make them believe things will change now."

"Will things change?"

"I don't know. Not the way they hoped for. Tundra tells them life will be different from when she used their blood to stay strong and healthy to fight Streakers, but Tundra still visits them from time to time even with the evening hunts. I think she's forbidden the other two to do anything. At least with me."

"I noticed the marks. Maybe Jim and Mack like it. Could they be doing it without being forced into it?"

She rather enjoyed it.

"I wouldn't say they're forced. More so coerced these days. Tundra claims sharing our blood allows her to do more for us. To be the leader she needs to be. By supplying the New Race, we better our lives." Lilly's voice dropped into a whisper. "It was always awful, especially with Gunnar. He thought his liberties extended farther than they did."

Jenna paled. "What should we do?"

"I don't want to leave. They told me if I don't share blood

with them again and soon, they will find a way to get the group to kick me out of the inn."

"It would never happen." Jenna shook her head.

"You don't know how convincing Tundra can be. Be careful. Tundra has developed a close relationship with Aiko, Bethany, and Victor. I've seen her hanging out with John, too."

"I'll watch my back, but I'm sure nothing will come of this. Peter has a sway with the New Race here, and Caleb would never do anything to hurt me."

"You don't know how devious Tundra is. She'll get to Peter and Caleb, give her time."

"You make Tundra sound like pure evil."

"She wants power."

Jenna had reached the large meadows that ran parallel to the inn. The horses pawed and pranced, wanting to show their speed.

"Do you want to let them lope?" Jenna asked.

"Sounds fun." Off they went, Clydesdales galloping through the meadow, hooves beating steadily on the ground.

For the moment, she forgot the plot Tundra spawned. The wind rushed against Jenna's face and the horses' muscles danced under her. She and Lilly raced across the open field, enjoying the moment.

PERFECT MOMENTS DON'T LAST, she thought after tucking all the animals away in the barn for the night. Cat twined his way between her feet, preferring the hay loft to the indoors. The air was brisk when the sun sank behind the horizon, and she wished for a jacket.

She went to the kitchen, grabbed a battered, chipped bowl and headed back outside to collect what little remained of the vegetables. Jackie could add them to the salad planned for dinner or use them tomorrow. While easy to gather, the vegetables were fewer in number. The group would soon have to start using the canned and preserved ones, but at least now, they had a large food supply. What a change from the previous year, scavenging along the roadsides, living day by day.

Jenna glanced at her feet and realized she needed to scavenge some new socks unless they found sheep and a loom. With cold weather, they needed to stockpile many items besides food. While plans were in place to plant wheat, soybeans, and corn in the spring, this winter might be a lean one for the group in many ways, especially if more people appeared at their door. They had survived worse times, but winter was all about death and destruction.

Footsteps approached from behind. They'd been so quiet, Jenna didn't even have a chance to turn before the bowl with vegetables hit the ground and shattered. The rough sack thrown over her head scratched her cheeks. A powerful blow rendered her unconscious.

When she emerged from the blackness, waves of nausea rolled through her.

"We've got the bitch where we want her. No escape from the dump we're going to drop her at."

Jenna's head pounded, her tongue stuck like glue to the inside of her teeth, sealed by the metallic taste of blood. The words she heard made spiders crawl under her skin.

"What are we going to do with her?"

"We'll have some fun, and then make sure no one ever finds her. Without this one in the way, the New Racers at the inn will be easy to convince, even do-gooder Caleb."

She dry-heaved behind the sack, lurching side to side.

They were on the move in a car. Jenna recognized Tundra's voice in front of her.

"Do we really need to get rid of her? She was causing problems, but there has to be other ways to make our point?" Gunnar's words were deferential.

"I've explained this to you before. I'll try and make it simple. We're superior, and the little bitch will never buy into that. Always causing problems. New Racers are the future of the world. Humans serve us. Humans are not equal, and we need to demand their blood. They have a sweet setup at the inn, and I'm going to claim it. I will lead the new world. If you are of a different opinion, tell me."

"No," Gunnar said, but he sounded unsure. "You're right. I just hate to waste perfectly good food."

"We don't need to get rid of her quickly. She'll be around

for your use for a while. Take what you want when you want. Have some fun for once," Tundra said.

Jenna's skin crawled when she listened to the conversation, but the lull of the ride made her slip in and out of consciousness.

"Wake up sleepyhead," Tundra's voice rung in her ear.

Jenna couldn't imagine where she was, or how long she had been unconscious during transport. She had no memory of being hauled from the car.

Wrists tied, she couldn't move her hands, and when dumped onto a bed, she couldn't cushion her fall and landed heavily.

"Are you awake?" Tundra slapped her.

Jenna couldn't hold back the gasping cry.

"There's nowhere to go. She'll never find her way back to the inn from this shack," another male voice, this one belonging to David, said. He was much too close.

Cold fingers caressed her neck and arms like worms across a corpse.

"I can't wait to have a taste. What I could do to you." He bent and sniffed her skin and her hair. His mouth traveled to her ear. "Human fear smells so yummy."

Jenna screamed into the void only to choke back her fear.

"Get ready for your worst nightmares to come true." He moved away, laughing.

Her mind worked feverishly. She'd have to find a way out or be dead soon. She might be able to wrestle free from the ropes that bound her arms, but she couldn't defeat the three New Racers, especially without a weapon. Even with a weapon, it was doubtful.

Her only hope would be to find a time when they all went back to the inn and run. Or pray Caleb would search for her. Time moved in and out of nightmares. When she heard voices once again, Jenna could not tell if minutes or hours had passed. She balled herself into a fetal position, the cold consuming her.

"Glad you're finally awake." Tundra yanked the sack off and met Jenna's eyes. "You thought you could stop me. You and your cute boyfriend. I'll be getting me some."

Jenna remained mute.

"I can't wait to suck you dry," Tundra continued. "You'll be as withered as an old hag. I'll drink the last drop of your blood and let Gunnar and David bury you somewhere in the woods where even Streakers can't find the body, but first, Gunnar and David will have some fun with you. I'll be back for the final drink."

Jenna stared.

"Nothing to say for once." Tundra laughed. "Maybe we'll keep you for a day, maybe a month. Depends how cooperative you are, and how much you scream. Do be careful about screaming too much, you don't want to attract Streakers when you can't fight them off. Though, I think David likes to make his humans scream. You'll tell me all his dirty little secrets, won't you?"

Tundra placed a gag in her mouth, patted her head, and left. Thirst began to override her thoughts. David's laughter filtering in from the other room.

How long have I been here?

"She's mine first," David said. "I'll come get you when I've had my fill."

David entered the bedroom and removed the gag.

Jenna sucked in air, at the same time, choking back sobs. She kicked out, but her bound legs merely grazed David's thighs.

For the first time, the nondescript bedroom in the dilapidated house, registered.

When her eyes met David's, his glare was hard and cruel. Despair settled in, rooting deep within her.

"Humans," David said. "You all believe you're tough. But

wait until I start this little party. I've had to be gentle with our three companions to make them last, but Tundra doesn't care about you so much. She hasn't set any limits on what I'm allowed to do with you. Your friend Lilly was so hard to resist. I just wanted to chew on her flesh so bad. With you, I don't need to resist, do I? As long as I don't kill you, anything is fine."

Jenna swept the dark, dank room with her eyes for a weapon. Trash, an empty pack of cigarettes, a book of matches, discarded magazines, a chair, and the rickety bed. Her mind raced searching for ideas. The surrounding houses around the inn were few and far between, with thick forests sheltering each from the neighboring homes. The dejected, deserted house met her equally despondent mood. No one would rescue her.

"People will notice I'm gone," Jenna spat. "You shouldn't do this. They'll find me and kill you."

David grabbed her arm, dragging her into a sitting position close to him. Reeking of tobacco and evil, he pawed her. "Screw them all. You're mine, bitch."

"Let me go. I'm sure if you change your mind now, everyone will forgive you. We could go back to the way things were. It would all be fine."

David ignored her. Instead, he flicked a strand of Jenna's dark hair behind her ear. His hand pressed against her face, and she shuddered. Fury caused her vision to blur and then clear.

"Where to start?" David asked. He bent and dragged Jenna's legs closer to him. "Much better." He cackled and unknotted the ropes securing them.

"You could start with a nice cup of coffee, maybe three eggs scrambled." She kicked out with her free leg.

He grabbed it, painfully tightening his hand around her ankle. "You're the only food here."

"You'd be surprised what I can do with limited ingredients. Maybe you want to let me free and show me what's in the pantry."

"I'll show you something alright."

"Just be prepared for me to bite it. I'm that hungry. No. I'm that angry."

Pandemonium erupted in the next room. David planted his hands on her calves, confining her more tightly than the ropes had.

"Where is she?" Caleb's voice echoed through the house.

"Here! In the bedroom!" Her horse scream filled the room.

David grabbed a serrated knife and headed to the door but didn't make it to the entrance.

Caleb, face transformed by fear and anger, entered. His eyes had turned demonic, pupils and irises black-red void contrasting against his ghostly translucent, skin. He pounced liked a rabid wolf, ramming David in the chest with a fist and grabbing his other wrist.

Jenna heard the crunch of bones. The knife clattered to the ground.

Caleb picked up the knife and hacked at the other man's chest. Ribbons of flesh mixed with blood on the floor. Every footstep they took, puckered with the liquid gore. The man she loved raised the knife and sliced.

David wobbled, his hands flying to cover the spray of blood weeping from the wound.

The dark liquid poured from his neck, but with fierce resolve, the New Racer slammed into Caleb's shoulders, forcing him on one knee, the knife skittered across the floor.

Jenna compelled herself to stand and pitched herself into David's back, knocking him off guard, causing all three to fall. Caleb threw the man off and grabbed the knife, but he didn't need it.

David barely clung to life, but Caleb grabbed him by the hair, forcing his head up. He finished the work he had started, decapitating the man, and lobbing his head across the room.

"Did he hurt you?"

Her eyes focused on the headless corpse on the floor. "What did you just do?"

"Took care of the problem."

"You are efficient." She pulled her eyes away to meet his.

"Stop avoiding my question. Are you hurt?"

"Just my pride for being unable to escape on my own. I kind of suck at being a hostage."

"I'm sure you did just fine."

"I'd rate my performance a D+"

"You're a tough taskmaster, but I knew that. Kind of sexy."

Jenna sent him a weak smile. "Are you trying to make it all better?"

"Is it working?"

She shrugged. "A little. Be a lot better if you got around to untying my hands. I can't feel my fingers."

Caleb worked the knots. Shouts and animal sounds moved closer. Aiko and Quentin forced Tundra and Gunnar into the bedroom.

Caleb jumped to his feet to do battle. Jenna joined his side.

Aiko was bloody.

Not so beautiful now. Jenna was unable to determine whether it was her blood or someone else's.

Quentin staggered in behind her. He was wounded, barely able to stand, but wielded a knife. He pitched sideways and then sank in the doorway.

"I need a weapon." Jenna crawled toward his slumped form.

Caleb blocked her. "I got nothing but the knife."

"Give it here. You've got your super-human strength."

"Quentin needs you more."

She started towards the wounded man, but the fury of fighting left her without a path.

Caleb hoisted the serrated blade.

Madness radiated from Tundra, who screamed out with each thrust of the hatchet.

"We could have ruled the new world." Tundra slashed at the air in front of Aiko, holding the woman at bay.

Aiko parried. "I came to realize I wouldn't want you in charge." A gash running down her side, dripped dark blood.

Caleb moved in front, becoming a buffer. "Got to agree with Aiko on that one."

Tundra hissed and cleaved the hatchet she held. "You're both dead and that little human bitch is bound for an early grave unless, she returns as something fouler than her stupid mouth."

Jenna searched for a weapon. Anything to beat the woman's brains out with. "Just because you don't get my sense of humor, doesn't mean you should put it down. Take all types."

"Nope." Aiko moved to Caleb's side and swung at Tundra. "I think we can definitely do without her type."

Tundra was a strong fighter, even against two opponents. She thrusted and countered her opponents moves. Lines of red began to crisscross Caleb's and Aiko's arms and chest.

Gunnar, who until this moment stood on the sidelines, kicked Quentin's slouched body aside and grabbed Aiko's arms, pinning them behind her.

Tundra sidestepped Caleb and sliced into the woman's side, burying the weapon there just as Gunnar let Aiko go, and she slipped to the floor. The weapon clattered next to her.

Gunnar and Tundra turned to Caleb. Jenna forced herself into action, grabbing the only weapon close, a discarded plank of wood. She ran forward, swinging the timber. Tundra ducked the blow and backhanded her.

"I'm not done with you." A fist smashed against Jenna's cheek and again into her mouth. Red dots overtook her vision, then she crashed into the wall.

Caleb pounced on the woman. The two collapsed, and he pounded Tundra's head to the floor, but her hands went for his face, fingers ready to gouge out his eyes. His hands found her neck, but she broke his grasp, jumped, and stood above him.

Jenna crawled along the floor, found the hatchet Tundra had arrived with and stood on wobbling legs. She pitched herself forward, and the hatchet landed square in Tundra's back.

"I guess it's too late to bury the hatchet between us," Jenna said. "Bitch." Tundra's hand reached behind her, attempting to pull out the offending weapon. A gurgle escaped her lips, and she crashed to the floor.

Caleb faced Gunnar. Fear registered in the man's eyes. Lost without Tundra's directives, Gunnar backed out of the room, turned, and fled into the night. Caleb followed.

Jenna inhaled twice, taking in the moment of silence.

The boom of cracking wood had her straining to see what had arrived.

Glass shattered in the next room and footsteps crunched over the broken splinters.

What had once been a tall, middle-aged man in a business suit, was now a bloated corpse in rags crusted over with blood and pus.

The baked-by-the-sun Streaker wore a wrinkled face with the consistency of an old raisin. His right arm hung limply, dislodged from the socket, but both hands made continual grabbing motions. Lacking any grace, the creature staggered to the bedroom door and stopped. It sniffed, searching out its next meal.

Blood poured from Jenna's lip, where Tundra had hit her. She wiped it away, then retrieving the piece of wood. Sensing the movement, the Streaker turned its undead eyes on her. Some of its skull had been torn away, exposing the rot. It lumbered and stumbled over the chair in its path, giving Jenna desperate seconds to ready herself.

Arm raised, eyes dead and unblinking, it came, dancing with death. It reached out to grab her.

Jenna ducked, then swung low and hard.

"I must have gone brain dead. I can't think of one good zombie joke right now."

The creature staggered back, but then surged forward. Jenna rammed the edge of the board into its stomach.

"No comeback from the undead. There's a no brainer."

It writhed against the constant pressure of the wood. A trail of intestines spurted out, staining the tattered remains of clothing.

Jenna gagged at the stench. "You, my good sir, are too gross for words."

The undead groaned, plowing forward. Decaying brains leaking from its nostrils and eyes.

"That all you got for me?" She stepped back, hoisting the board, and swung. The head of the creature flew sideways, but it continued forward, emaciated fingers scratching. She drove the Streaker over to the left with a repeated, steady swing. The wood sank into a shallow layer of skin covering the undead's overripe, bloated belly.

Upon Caleb's return, he moved to Jenna's side. She stepped back and leaned against the window. Caleb, hatchet in hand, forced the Streaker into a corner. A noise at the window had her spinning around. A hand shot through the glass and into the room to claw at Jenna's face.

Outside in the darkness, lifeless eyes found her.

The undead rammed against the window, spraying glass. Jenna stepped away, and seconds later, a loud crack caused splintered wood and glass to fall to the floor along with pieces of the zombie's fingers. With a catatonic stare, the

Streaker pushed through the opening, tearing its flesh against the jagged edges of the frame.

Jenna flashed back to the cigarettes and matches she saw in the room. Fire was exactly what she needed now. She searched for the matchbook that had laid on the floor, but the room was in disarray thanks to the fight.

Something bumped behind her, and panic rose inside her. Dropping to her belly, scanning the floor, her fingers reached under the bed.

She snagged the small, cardboard matchbook and hauled it out of the darkness. Gathering the discarded magazines, fingers shaking, she twisted a match from the book and lit it.

A small flame burned, and she put the edge of the magazine to it. The dried pages flared instantly.

Caleb, still battled in the corner, but Jenna had no time to help him.

A pale sea of rotted flesh and decay advanced on her. Against her own survival instinct, she let the putrid beast come close enough to hear the gnashing of its blackened teeth.

A boney hand reached for her, and she let the burning magazine ignite the rags barely covering gangrenous limbs. It pawed at her arm. The burning magazine arched toward its mouth. With desperate strength, Jenna twisted to free herself. Sizzling flesh indicated the flame worked to devour the undead's ear.

Black lips smacked her shoulder, and Jenna wrenched free, shoving the remains of the burning magazine into the Streaker's face.

As quick as tinder, the Streaker ignited. The creature turned in circles, unable to comprehend its own burning body. The overpowering smell of charcoaled flesh filled the room.

Jenna dropped to the floor, rolled out of the way, and joined Caleb. The room erupted in flames.

"We need to move now. Grab Quentin. I'll get Aiko," Jenna shouted.

With a final surge of strength, Jenna ran to Aiko. Caleb shoved the Streaker he'd been battling into the burning corpse. Both bodies tumbled to the floor, igniting the remains of the bed.

"Move." Caleb lifted an unconscious Quentin as if he weighed nothing.

Stumbling, dragging Aiko, ash-laden fumes filling her nose, Jenna exited the bedroom, dense smoke hindered her vision.

Rancid odors from charred corpses and dense flames overwhelmed Jenna's senses. She followed Caleb, dragging Aiko into the darkness.

Once outside, Caleb lowered Quentin to the ground, and then staggered over to Aiko. Jenna searched for a pulse in Quentin's neck. The suffocating heat from the burning house billowed and caused her to hack.

With her touch, Quentin stirred.

"You scared me." She ripped off her sweatshirt, pushing fabric against the worst of his still bleeding wounds.

"I had to save my bestie, right?"

"I'm sorry for everything." Jenna forced Quentin's hand down on the fabric. "Hold this tightly. I'll be right back."

Unsure if he'd passed out again, she moved away to check on the others. The sight of them made her want to weep.

Aiko had a large gash in her stomach and side. For any human, the wounds would have meant instant death.

Caleb knelt next to the silent, injured New Racer. As Jenna bent to console him, she spotted a long, ragged gash weeping blood.

Applying pressure, her hands seeped red. "You're injured."

"I'll be fine. Let me help Aiko." Caleb shouldered Jenna aside and kept pressure on Aiko's stomach.

"What should I do?" Jenna asked. "We have to get them back to the inn for care."

"It was Aiko who told us where you were. She came clean about Tundra's plan to kill you and turn against all humans. If it wasn't for her, you'd be dead."

"Why are you telling me this? We have to get them back to Emma."

"You're the only one who can help her. She'll die if you don't offer her some blood. Quentin's lost too much. He can't." Caleb attempted to stand, staggered, and sank to a knee.

"You're hurt, too." Jenna stepped to his side.

God damn it. Can't help anyone. Useless. Must give them both what they need.

"I'll be fine," Caleb said.

"Don't lie to me. Are you asking me to make a choice— your life or Aiko's? I won't do it. I won't let you die on me."

"You don't have a choice. I won't live if it means letting Aiko die."

"You'll both have to do it. You both have to drink from me."

"It could kill you."

"I don't care. If you both don't do it, I refuse." She met Caleb's eyes. "I can't live in this world without you."

"You have to."

"Not when there's an option. You'll both die out here if you don't drink."

"Only enough to survive and make it back to the inn."

"Whatever you need. I'd rather be dead than without you."

Jenna nestled between them, holding out a small pocketknife. She offered both wrists in sacrifice. The knife stung. It dug into her flesh. She moved her hand toward Aiko, who sensed the blood. The New Racer's teeth latched on, digging in—the pain intense.

After a moment, she offered her other arm to Caleb. He kissed her wrist and then the pain of tearing flesh.

Jenna swayed and tried to focus on a part of her body not in pain. She noticed a mark.

Was it a bruise or a bite? Could the Streaker have bit her when she torched it?

That was her last thought before the world went black.

23

JENNA WOKE in her bed back at the inn, confused and disoriented. A hammer pounded in her head. Caleb sat at her side, and when she saw him, the memories rushed back.

"How'd we get here?" Jenna's throat felt parched. She signaled for water. When he handed her the glass, she guzzled the liquid.

"Welcome back. I was able to go for help. Emma and the crew drove out and rescued us."

"How long have I been out?"

"Three days." Caleb grasped Jenna's hand. "I'm so happy you're awake." He leaned in to kiss her cheek. "Worried is the understatement of the year."

"What happened?"

"Aiko saved you. She overheard Tundra debating what to do with you. None of the options were good." Caleb's sad smile relieved a little of the pressure in Jenna's pounding temple. "She went to Quentin with the information."

"Lilly told me Aiko and Tundra were planning on trying to turn New Racers at the inn against the humans."

"True. We learned about her plan from Lilly and Mack. Aiko might have liked the idea of it, but not the reality. She has real feelings for Quentin. A lot of her anger against you has been from jealousy. When she realized Tundra kidnapped you, she was ready to mount a war."

Jenna narrowed her eyes. "Not sure I believe it."

"Truth. As soon as they came to me, we set out. Quentin was also smart enough to let Lilly know what we were doing, and Lilly went straight to Peter."

"How did you find me?"

"It wasn't too hard. Tundra and her group wouldn't venture too far from the inn. There's just not enough gas and resources. They wouldn't want to go closer to town where there might be the chance of running into a lot of Streakers. We found the vehicle they stole and tracked it."

"How'd you do it?"

"It's amazing what you can do when motivated." Caleb frowned. "They were at one of the houses in the woods."

"You found me." Jenna traced a near-healed wound on Caleb's cheek. "That's what matters. You were there when I needed you."

"Thank God we found you. Do you remember the rest?"

"Most of it. The three of you fought against Tundra and her sidekicks." Jenna stiffened. "How are Aiko and Quentin? Are they okay?"

"Both doing better. Aiko was fine after you gave her some blood. You saved her, and she's grateful."

"Better be."

Caleb laughed. "She appreciates it. Really. She's been less than friendly to you because of her feelings and those Quentin still has for you. She needs a good therapist, but they are in short supply."

"Even after the apocalypse, some things don't change."

"Aiko would never tell you this. It's our secret, she was jealous of you."

The pain in her head ramped to jackhammer levels. She closed her eyes and continued to listen. "Go on."

"Quentin was injured but on the mend. I'm sure he'd love you to visit soon."

"I'll go see him, but tired now. I'll nap for a little bit." Jenna slipped into sleep even while willing herself to stay awake.

∾

The moonlit shadows painted ghosts throughout the room. The nightmare had returned.

"Jenna!"

Wraithlike forms closed in on her and something prowled. As much as Jenna searched, it hid, preferring the shadows.

"You can't help me now. Something wicked is inside you."

Trapped in the tangle of blankets, she tried to sit. The bed sheets turned into hands, clutching her, pulling her into the fabric, and skeletal fingers dug into her flesh. She pushed them away, but her hands were useless and rotting. Shooting up, shifting into consciousness, Jenna sucked in labored breaths.

The dream. What did it mean?

She slid back down on to the mattress and yanked the covers over her head to ease the throbbing pain. Upon awakening, Lilly sat next to the bed.

The acidic scent from fingernail polish laced the air. When Jenna moved, the woman squealed with joy and leaned over to give her a huge hug, wet nails, and all.

"You're awake." Lilly's cheerful words rang loud. "You've been sleeping on and off for days, and Caleb's been guarding the door like a rabid dog. He wouldn't let anyone in until you woke yesterday. I've been here since morning."

"What time is it?" Jenna asked.

"Late afternoon. Do you remember waking yesterday when Caleb was here?"

"He told me what happened to Aiko and Quentin. I'm happy they're both okay."

Lilly held the bottle of nail polish in front of Jenna's nose. "Look what Jackie found on a scavenging expedition. I thought I would paint your nails to pass the time. You need a little glamour in your life after all the adventure. You could use a shower too but that can wait until tomorrow."

"I don't think it can." Jenna threaded damp, limp hair behind her ears. "I'm disgusting right now. Maybe we could do this another day?"

"This is the best therapy for you. Give me a few minutes. I want to tell you about some of the changes since Tundra's defeat."

"I'm all yours." She held out a hand.

Jenna could imagine what her hands looked like after being in a battle with the Streaker. Lilly painted each of her nails methodically, chattering like a chipmunk.

"After your rescue, a meeting was called. Sorry you missed it, but you weren't awake at the time."

"What happened?"

"Peter and Gus called us out and made us explain everything. I mean, everything. The whole situation about how Tundra used to feed from us, and how we didn't always agree to it. I was so scared. Even though Tundra was dead, I kept waiting for her to storm in and kill me or something. But it was worse that I was at fault for what happened to you."

"Tundra takes all the blame."

"But if I'd come forward earlier. Told people sooner."

"You did what you thought was right."

"Aiko explained what Tundra was trying to do, and how she wanted to convert people to her way of thinking."

"What did people say?"

"Everyone was dismayed and angry. At the end it was a huge love fest, even for us, the newcomers. We can stay. For good." Lilly's delighted laugh clung in the air. "The group decided to create a charter stating no New Racer will ever use a human for blood without consent. It's the first official document of the new government."

"Great." Jenna stared at her hot pink fingernails.

Lilly relinquished one hand and picked up the other. "Everyone thought things would get back to normal, but no."

"What happened?"

"Gunnar returned yesterday. He begged forgiveness and asked to stay at the inn. There was a ton of debate about letting him stay, but everyone voted, and he earned the right to stay by a single vote."

"He tried to kill me. Who voted to let him stay?"

"We don't know. I am so curious who voted that way, but we'll never know because it's all secret ballot. Stupid, right? But he's under constant supervision for now. He can't go anywhere or do anything without someone else watching him. There's never been a need for a jail, but they're trying to figure out what to do."

"How'd you vote?"

"I voted not to let him stay after all he did. I guess I'm not a forgiving person. Though, I will say, between Gunnar and David, Gunnar was always the nicer one." Silent tears streamed down her cheeks, and she dropped Jenna's hand. "I'm sorry I got you involved in any of this. You could have died. Can you ever forgive me?" Lilly wept.

"None of this is your fault." Jenna reached for Lilly and gave her a teary hug. Damn the nail polish, which left traces on the back of Lilly's shirt.

"I'm sorry," Lilly said again.

"If I want to blame anyone, I'll blame Tundra, and she's no longer an issue. You're a good friend. Don't worry about any of it."

She hugged Jenna again, effectively smearing the rest of the newly painted nails in the process. "I'll leave you now. I know Caleb has been waiting patiently, and I don't want to deprive him of his *Jenna* time. I'll visit tomorrow."

"Sounds good. Can you bring me something to read? I have a feeling Emma and Caleb aren't letting me out of bed for a while."

After Lilly left, Caleb entered, carrying Cat. Both made themselves comfortable on the bed.

Cat deposited himself on her lap, kneading a spot, and then curled into a ball.

"He's happy you're alive," Caleb said. "I'm happy we all made it thanks to you."

"You saved my life."

"You're the hero." He held her hand, admiring her smeared nails with a lopsided grin. "Don't ever scare me again."

"If everyone is so grateful, why'd they'd bring Gunnar back?" Bitterness crept into her words.

"Lilly told you?"

"Everything."

"It wasn't my decision. You know how I voted."

"You could have fought it."

"I tried. Lilly tried, but the vote was in his favor. He'll never get close to you. I promise."

"I can't talk about this anymore. At least not now. Can I clean up? I'm ready for a shower."

"Good call. You still have Streaker gunk and soot from the fire all over you. Take all the time you need. No five-minute limit."

"How nice. Send my thanks to everyone for the big treat." Her head pounded and muscles ached.

Caleb removed Cat from her lap and set him on the bed. Refusing to let Jenna shamble the few steps to the bathroom, Caleb picked her up in his arms and carried her. He stripped off her pajamas and got the water steaming. A fog sprayed forth. She stepped into the hot, misty shower.

Caleb left her alone in the bathroom, and Jenna reveled in the water. Each drop fluttered like rose petals and the lathered soap tingled when rubbed on her skin. The silky, fresh scent was so intense, she could have been sitting in the middle of a flower garden. She would have stayed in the shower all day soaking in the experience, but a knock on the door shook her from her near trance.

"You okay in there?"

"Enjoying the moment." Her aches had diminished and the throb in her head had dulled.

Jenna turned the water off. Steam and the fragrance of flowers lingered. She stepped onto the chilled tile floor, dried herself, and put on the fresh pajamas Caleb had left for her, returning to bed a much happier person.

After that day, Jenna's healing took a surprising turn, and she recovered quicker than expected. Her bumps and bruises stopped aching, and she yearned to return the animals and the greenhouse. While Caleb tried to get her to take more time recuperating, she refused, happy to revert to her normal routine.

Jenna padded to the greenhouse early one morning, thick fog creating a damp gloom, surprised at how the winter's chill had invaded. Her camouflage jacket failed to shield her from the gusts that sent her hair flying in front of her eyes, wind cascading the leaves through the air.

Quentin was waiting for Jenna in the greenhouse. She'd thought about the moment when she'd have to face him, but she had avoided it. She'd ignore him, Aiko, and Gunnar whenever possible. It had worked up until now.

This dreaded, unwanted conversation was bound to be awkward, and she didn't have a speech planned. No escape route existed. No quick getaway this time.

Quentin offered her an awkward, partial wave, and then fiddled with a trowel, mutilating some of the most prized, potted plants.

"Hi, stranger," Quentin said.

"How are you?"

"Beginning to believe I'd never see you again." His smile didn't reach his eyes.

"I needed some time to figure everything out."

"Would it bother you if we weren't friends anymore?"

"It was heading in that direction anyway before all this happened. I missed you, but that didn't seem to matter to you or Aiko." She kicked at the dirt floors with the toe of her boots. "There's so much that happened, so much to consider."

He nodded. "I'm sorry about how it went down. You mean the world to me, and my emotions were the problem. You hurt me even if you didn't mean to. I want all this stupidity done. I'm here for you. All you have to do is yell, and I'll come running." He swiped at his shaggy hair in need of a cut. "What I really wanted to say is I'm glad you're okay. Ecstatic. You look really good. I mean healthy. Losing you would have been devastating, but it made me realize what an ass I've been."

"I'm glad you're okay, too. We all played a role in this fiasco."

"I want to apologize for everything. I should have been more aware what was going on with Aiko."

"I should have gone to Peter when Tundra's insanity first came to light."

"I never thought Aiko was serious about any of the stuff she'd rant about. Obviously, she didn't tell me the whole story until afterwards when she begged for forgiveness."

"We don't need to rehash this. I care about you. You were a good friend, and I hope we'll be friends again?"

"I'd like that, but I have to tell you one thing. It's the reason I forgave Aiko. She went after Tundra. When Aiko found out you were missing, she got everything organized and led the rescue. Caleb couldn't think straight, he was in such a panic. They worked together to figure out how to find you. I don't know what might have happened without her."

"Caleb told me a lot of this. He gave her a lot of credit for the rescue. Can I ask you something personal?"

Quentin nodded. "Anything."

"Are you two still together?"

"We're trying. Sounds like something from couples therapy." He shrugged. "She's a good person once you bypass the insecurities."

"If you like her, I'm sure I'll find something to appreciate in her." As much as Jenna rationally understood how it was not Quentin or Aiko's fault, a small part of her remained petty and angry, but she'd give being a better, bigger person a try. "It's just going to take some time."

Quentin gave her a hug.

Why did everyone feel the need to hug her?

"You're the best," he whispered before turning and heading back to the inn.

Jenna worked until lunch, putting thoughts of the recent experience out of her head. She focused on the plants, soil, and growing things. When she left the greenhouse to head back to the inn, a chilly rain coated her hair against her face and neck, her jacket weighing her down.

Inside, a fire roared in the main entry, the hearth aglow, alleviating the damp. Warmth and the scent of smoky, seasoned wood had her creeping near the heat. She warmed her hands and marveled at the colors she had forgotten existed. The fire blazed, not only red and yellow, but with shades of blue, silver, and gold.

"What are you up to?"

Caleb's words made Jenna jump. He stood beside Peter, Gus, and Ford.

"Nothing," Jenna sent them a quick wave of her hand. "What about you? Not sleeping?"

"One of the solar panels doesn't work. We need to figure out a way to fix it. Dinner still on for tonight?"

"Absolutely."

First step toward normalcy, she thought.

After saying goodbye, she headed to the kitchen and grabbed a cup of leftover soup. While the warmth of the broth was soothing, she did not have her appetite back. Normally, soup alone wouldn't have filled her, but today, she struggled to empty the mug of its contents.

Most of the group had eaten earlier and the kitchen was quiet, but she preferred the peace. Between being sick and all her friends' confessions, sitting alone appealed to her. But all good things must end. As Jenna rinsed her mug, Emma bounded over, curls swinging, full of vitality and pent-up energy.

"Hi, Girlfriend. I was wondering when we would get a chance to catch up." Emma felt her forehead before dragging Jenna down into a seat. "How are you?"

"Weren't you in charge of my care? Didn't you get hourly updates from people babysitting me?"

"True, but I wanted to hear it from you."

"I'm fine. Feeling better and up and around. Is my improved health the reason you're so happy and perky today?"

Here we go again. It was understandable everyone was concerned, but how many times could she explain she was okay physically and mentally.

"The attitude's a good sign. Tell me all your dirty little secrets though. I didn't interrupt my day for niceties."

"All my aches and pains are gone. Lilly and Quentin both came to see me, and everything is perfect other than the fact they let Gunnar return. Whose stupid idea was that? How'd you vote?" She shook her head. "Never mind. I don't want the truth. I also learned Aiko rescued me, so I can't be angry with her either. Everything is fine!"

"I see that from your calm and rational rendition of things. You and Caleb? All hot and heavy still?"

"You have no boundaries," Jenna huffed. "Caleb and I have a dinner date tonight. Can't wait."

Emma kept the conversation going, and when she did impersonations of Peter, Gus, and Ford at the recent meeting, Jenna relaxed, and almost fell out of her seat with laughter.

Had it always been this way? Or did Jenna need her near-death experience to understand how precious life was?

Joy overwhelmed her, and she wondered how bad the bump on her head had been. Maybe she was still in a coma or had a brain tumor?

Did she have the right to be this happy after everything? Where was the old Jenna who worried and fretted?

24

JENNA WORKED the horses into the late afternoon and had them pulling a wagon. Hauling wood and needed items would soon be much easier. Once darkness fell, she stabled them, and then headed home.

Back in her room, she changed into clean jeans without rips, tears, mud, or horse manure, and her favorite sweater, a grey cotton pullover with pink and red stripes. As a final addition, she added Mom's favorite lipstick to her ensemble.

A book sat on the table. It must have been the one she asked Lilly to bring her days ago. How could she have missed it? Jenna hitched a breath. *Macbeth* by Shakespeare.

Of all the books to bring her, why the tragedy? She was being stupid and paranoid again.

She placed it back on the table. It signified nothing.

A loud knock on her door signaled Caleb's arrival.

"Missed you." She leaned in for a kiss.

Jenna melted against his frame.

"I have a surprise. I made it."

"Cute and crafty."

"Cute?" Caleb stole another kiss. "Crafty?" He shoved his hands into the pockets of his jeans. "It was anything but cute.

You have to come to the kitchen to get it. I've been so worried about you since everything happened. You need to start eating better. You're losing weight."

"I eat." She scowled.

"You're not eating much of anything. Are you still not feeling well?"

"I'm fine. Better than fine." She shrugged. "I haven't been hungry. Maybe I'm in love and can't fathom something as trivial as food."

Caleb's eyes danced. "Promise me you'll make an attempt to eat a few bites of the surprise. It took a lot of hard work. Ask anyone who was in the vicinity."

"Don't ruin it. Let's go see."

"Promise?"

"I promise to eat everything on my plate but only if I get something in return."

"What would you like?"

"You." Jenna ran her hand up his chest.

"I walked right into that one, but I am happy to oblige your request. Come with me first."

They entered the empty dining hall. A plate sat on a wide-planked, wooden table. The dish contained heart-shaped cookies with her name etched in icing.

She turned to Caleb. "You made them? Beyond cute."

"There's the word again."

"How about adorable, wonderful, beautiful. Thank you."

"We're so glad you're fine. Everyone helped, but I stirred the batter and baked them with supervision, of course. I want you to know, getting cookies into the shape of a heart is harder than it appears. So is writing with icing."

"How did you do all this?"

"We had most of the ingredients, and I had some extra time to go looking for the rest."

Jenna's heartbeat trilled. "You went scavenging?"

"It was fine. I had a lot of help, and the inn constantly

needs new provisions. We're not anywhere near self-sufficient yet."

"I keep forgetting." She wished for safety, security, and hoped the outside world never intruded again. Those thoughts made Jenna lose her appetite, but to make a point, she devoured every crumb of one of the masterpiece cookies.

"Good?" he asked before taking a bite of the cookie he held.

"In another life, you might have had a chance at being a chef."

"In another life, I'd be the stay-at-home dad, and you'd be the tough-as-nails business executive, bread winner."

"I like that alternate reality."

"Me too. I dig hot women in tight business suits." Caleb smirked and moved closer. "What do you want to do tonight? A rousing game of Monopoly or Risk? Nothing too strenuous, you still need to rest up."

"Any chance you'd want to play a certain song for me?"

"Soon. I have the music, but it's not perfect. I need a few more days."

"I don't need perfection. I need to hear it."

"What you need is patience." He leaned over and kissed Jenna on the nose. "We can save the rest of the cookies for a midnight snack." He leaned in for a real kiss. "It's your night, what would you like to do?"

"How about a walk? It's not too cold out, and the weather looks like it cleared up from earlier."

"A walk. I was thinking something a little different."

"We'll do a lot of that later."

"I guess I couldn't stop you if I wanted to." He chuckled. "Are you sure a game of Battleship isn't an option."

"I've been spending too much time inside recuperating. Fresh air will do me good."

"Yes, Ma'am." He bowed and followed her to the front porch. "But I think it might rain soon."

"Do you want to risk it?"

"A little water can't hurt us."

Caleb got her, whether she was happy or miserable, and everything was bright and shiny around him, or at least, had the potential to be.

The moon was huge with silken threads of silver-gray clouds easing their way through the sky. The soft glow framed Caleb in shadows. The trees across the field blended into a Matisse painting, inviting Jenna to become part of the canvas.

They sat on the front steps, enjoying the stillness of the night, broken only by the occasional wind-driven, fallen foliage.

His fingers intertwined with hers, and she rested her head on his shoulder. A few minutes passed. He caressed her back and neck, and then drew her in for a kiss.

Jenna's stomach warmed, and with the meeting of lips, she understood his love.

Caleb lifted her and sat her on his lap. His kisses continued, first light and playful, but soon demanding more. And she desired more from him too, her hands roaming over his shoulders.

Sitting back, his gaze returned to the overripe clouds. "We should go inside."

"It's so beautiful out here tonight. Where is your sense of adventure? Let's take a walk."

"I'll be adventurous in bed."

Jenna stood. "Coming?"

"If I must."

The two traipsed down the stone stairs and out into the meadow. Cat met them in the field, loud purr disrupting the peace. The feline twined between their feet.

"Do you see this? He's intentionally trying to trip me," Jenna said. "He has an evil side."

"You're telling me, I got you a devil cat."

He was teasing her of course, but it brought forth shreds of her dream.

Something wicked is inside you. Just a dream. She shook off her unease.

"I never know what your evil mastermind plan is. World domination. New Racers taking over."

His brow furrowed.

"Too soon?" She asked.

"Too soon to joke. But if you must have an answer, my master plan is to make you happy."

"Works for me."

Caleb grabbed her hand. And together, she meandered through the meadow with him. "I'm so happy you're better. I miss you every minute you're not by my side. And I was so scared. Actually, you had everyone worried."

He drew her into hug, and she found the closeness comforting. His warm lips fell to hers, and his hand traced the curve of her spine. His kiss was home, and she wanted more. Her arms encircled his neck, then twined in his hair.

An owl's hoot made Jenna jump.

Broad pine trees perched a few feet away. Dark foliage beckoned. One part of her worried she and Caleb shouldn't be alone in the woods. It was reckless and stupid without a weapon of any kind, and they should turn back.

But Caleb's gaze was ravenous, and she couldn't wait. She wanted to live for the crazy, wonderful moments that could be. And this moment could soon be one of the most memorable ones.

He drew her back into his arms and reclaimed her lips. She didn't stop him, enjoying the longing and intensity building. His hands caressed her curves.

"I love you so much. I need you now." He stroked her in the darkness. "Let's go back to the inn."

A grin spread across her lips. "Where's your sense of adventure? Where's the daredevil I know and love?"

"I've had enough adventure to last a lifetime."

"You have to admit, you're having fun. Just say it. Say—I like kissing you in the field. Say it, and we'll go back inside."

"I don't have to admit anything to you."

"I'll admit I like this moment. I appreciate the thrill of being outdoors on a cold night, warming each other up in the best of ways. Why can't you say it? Chicken?" Her smile spread at the same time her nails raked against his thigh.

Caleb grabbed her arm and attempted to usher them back toward the inn, but she planted her feet, drawing him back.

"You'll be the death of me." His hands traveled along her curves. When they reached her shoulders, he began to gently knead them.

Tension dropped from Jenna's body. She closed her eyes, inhaling the scent of grass and pine. "You'd be my masseuse in our alternative reality, and I'd get massages every day."

He didn't release her. "What's in it for me?"

"What do you want? Keep doing what you're doing."

"How about I do more?" His hands dropped to her midriff and slipped under her sweater. They were cold against her skin, but fire ignited elsewhere.

"I've got an idea." She murmured against his chest.

"What's this brilliant idea?" His fingers traced the line of her hipbone before exploring upward.

Her heart pounded. "Catch me, and you'll have your way with me." Jenna ran into the forest, ducking behind a tree, but making it easy for Caleb to find her.

He made it fun, letting her get away a few times, pretending to stumble around in the dark searching. Jenna staggered over roots and branches, not paying attention to the direction she headed. Light from the moon winked out.

She ran back the way she thought led to the meadow but staggered into a mossy thicket instead.

The smell of death assaulted her.

Jenna screamed. Caleb was by her side. The clouds moved

away, and they noticed the thing perched against a tree. The clouds released rain and hail with a force of gun blasts. The thing in the trees showed no reaction. Jenna mopped the bangs from her forehead.

Caleb crept close. "It's not moving. It's a corpse."

"They're all corpses," Jenna followed. The undead were a blur in the night, but she covered her nose with her sweater sleeve to limit the odor of decomposing flesh. The slumped, putrid dead sent a shiver through her.

A reminder that mere existence was never going to be normal. She'd never regain the life she lived prior to the pandemic. Her hope for starting a new one was stupid.

Caleb stepped forward and kicked the exposed flesh, boot making a soft thump. The two Streakers lacked any signs of animation. Returning to Jenna's side, he grabbed her hand, and she followed him back to the inn. Once inside, she led the way, informing the group. After setting up a meeting, Jenna returned to her room to change. She pulled on dry clothes and plopped in a chair, depressed by the evil that would never let her be.

The urge to cry overwhelmed her, but she forced the tears back.

This was not the time.

She didn't want to join the conversation, jaded as she was but would. Every voice counted.

A few minutes later, Caleb knocked on the door and stepped inside her room without waiting for an answer from her.

"Don't you wait for an invitation? I could have been naked."

"That would have been a pleasant surprise."

"What?"

"We're going to meet downstairs soon to discuss what we found."

"I'm not even sure what it was."

"Two dead Streakers close to the inn."

"Can you be certain? I couldn't see well in the dark."

"I'm sure."

"How'd they'd get so close."

He shrugged. "Don't know but something stopped it, and then left them for us to find. We need to figure out what's going on. The weather's stormy, and there's obviously no immediate danger, but we'll investigate. You'll have to show people the way in the morning."

"Okay." Jenna stared at the floor.

"What's wrong?"

"I believed my life would change. It'd be better now."

"Things are different. We're happy together."

"We're never going to live in peace." Her hand thumped the chair.

He lifted her from the chair and carried her to the bed, ignoring her squeals.

She landed on her back, and the springs groaned.

"Never doubt I'll make you happy." Caleb moved over her and claimed her lips.

She jerked her head to the side. "We should talk."

"About what?"

Planting her palms against his chest, Jenna pushed. "Our future."

He refused to budge. "What about it?"

She pushed again.

Caleb settled on his back in the bed, staring at the ceiling.

"I thought we were safe," she said.

"We can't go back. We'll never live in a world without Streakers." His brow furrowed. "You have to accept it and acknowledge this new world. I love you, and I want to be with you in the here and now and for forever."

"I love you, but what if I lose you? I wouldn't be able to go on."

"You're much stronger than you imagine. You survived

the last few years, and you'll keep surviving. It will just be more fun now that you have me along for the ride."

How could she explain the ominous premonition something bad was going to happen?

There was nothing she could do to change her situation or to make Caleb understand the dreams when she didn't. They could be nothing, but she was unable to dismiss them. Caleb was right about one thing, she needed to learn to enjoy the here and now, especially if something worse than Streakers and Tundra was on its way.

She loved Caleb. Loved him with her entire self, and she wanted to show him tonight in case there wasn't a future for them.

"We should go to the meeting in a few," Caleb said.

She yanked him on top of her. "Let them wait. You're not going anywhere. I need you more than ever." She wrapped her arms around his neck.

Caleb placed a kiss on her forehead. "Let's not waste any more time." His fingers traced the curve of her cheek, and his lips met hers.

She pressed herself into Caleb. Heat built between her body and his, and soon, it flared and became an inextinguishable wildfire.

Both she and Caleb wore smiles on their faces when they entered the meeting late. With little to do thanks to the stormy weather and the late hour, the group put off investigating until morning, but extra patrols were set up inside. Caleb took one of the first watches.

Jenna, exhausted, made it back to her room and quickly fell into a deep slumber.

When she woke, a remnant of a dream filtered through her mind but faded when she sat and stretched. She grabbed a T-shirt, threw it on, and watched the dust dancing through the air.

Was the room dirty? Had the dust in the air always been so visible and had such a strong smell?

She needed fresh air and opened the window, inhaling the scent of plants from the garden. She sneezed.

What was going on with her?

Needing an escape from both her thoughts and the confinement of the room, she decided to check on the horses. The animals calmed her, and she needed that now. Jerking on jeans and boots, she headed to the front door, ignoring whoever she encountered.

Outside, the breeze churned the loose leaves, littering the driveway while a drizzle splattered the walkway.

Jenna had not brought a coat, but her skin still burned. She sloshed through the mud the earlier storm had caused, not caring about the filth seeping into her boots and jeans. The outline of the barn was dim in the early light, but Jenna could see it clearly and arrived to find the barn door open and the horses taking refuge in the stalls. While they were free to spend the night either inside or out, they usually preferred the safety of the barn at night.

She checked on Moon and Star. Both horses were at ease, water buckets filled. Jenna laid a cheek against Moon's mane. Chills ran through her, and her head began to throb.

Dizzy, she left the stall shivering.

"Caleb." The words spilled from her lips, and she sank to the ground, weightless.

The world faded in and out of view, then went dark and when Jenna awoke, everything had changed.

SNEAK PEEK OF BOOK 2

Placeholder for book blurb.

1

SOMETIME IN OCTOBER . . .

Jenna's eyes flared open. She wheezed, sucking in large gulps of air. The dream receded, scratching and clawing as she forced it deep into her subconscious. Struggling to sit, the room flailed in a dizzying spiral around her. She fell back against the sheets and stared at the dull-streaked ceiling.

She scratched at aching eyes. More pain surfaced, making rolling into a fetal position the only option.

The squeak of a chair had her squinting at the moving figure. A guy dropped to the corner of the bed. Black hair escaped the edges of a hoodie.

How are the horses? She wondered, the last memories of leaving the High Point Inn to go check on the Clydesdales in the barn rushed back.

"Caleb?" she croaked like a frog.

"You were having another nightmare." He brushed dark brown, damp bangs off her forehead in a gentle caress.

"What happened? Where am I?" Trying to sit, nausea

erupted. Sinking back down, questions instantly forgotten, Jenna dry heaved over the side of the bed.

His hand caressed her back. "You had me so scared. Everyone here is worried about you. Are you okay?"

Her rumpled t-shirt was soaked with sweat. When her stomach stopped rebelling, she sputtered, "What happened?"

This feels anything but all right.

"Don't you remember?"

She curled in a ball and tried to think. Memories were slow to emerge. "Wait. I couldn't sleep and went to visit the horses in the barn.

The animals provide comfort in this awful world like nothing else, except maybe Caleb.

"Here." He handed her some water.

Sipping it, she waited for an explanation, but he said nothing. She bit her lower lip and continued to wait.

He wore his favorite hoodie and snug jeans. Although the hoodie was large, it did not hide the muscular physique and muscles underneath.

"Are you not telling me something?" she waved a hand in front of him. "I remember feeling sick and sleepless and going outside to check the horses. What else do I need to know?"

"Billy found you there in the morning, unresponsive. We don't fully understand what happened, but you've been out of consciousness for close to three days."

"Three days? Can't be." She shivered, tried to sit again, but fell back, muscles aching. "All I remember are my dreams."

"What dreams?" His eyes were a vibrant dark red—a trademark of the New Race. At this moment, those beautiful eyes regarded her with both love and concern.

"The one where Eric is alive and calling for help."

"You can't feel guilty about his death. He chose to fight."

"He was only a child."

"Childhood is a thing of the past. He was strong and able

and willing to help fight Streakers." Caleb moved closer and placed a cold cloth from the nightstand to her forehead, then grabbed her warm hand in his cool one.

She rested for a moment, disheveled bangs over her eyes, gulping a few deep breathes.

"Enough coddling me." She pushed his hand with the cloth away.

Normally self-confident to the point of being smug, the man next to her appeared nervous and unsure of what to do.

Too weak to laugh at this image of Caleb, perched like a mother bird protecting her young. Who knew he was such a nurturer?

His hair, straight and shoulder length, highlighted the worry in his face.

Jenna could never get enough of what she considered an art masterpiece: straight nose, angular cheeks, and most importantly, kissable lips. Lips, right now, set in a straight line.

"You're not a dream, right? I'm awake now?" She reached out to caress Caleb's cheek, her fallen angel sporting clothes Jenna was sure he hadn't changed for days. His midnight black hair was disheveled, and he was very much in need of a shower, maybe as much as she.

"Feel any better?"

"You're stalling. I can tell there's bad news and you're trying to sugarcoat it."

"Tell me more about the dreams. Was it only the one about Eric or were there more?" His hand grazed the overzealous stubble on his chin. "You've been having them often, sometimes crying out. Most nights, you call out for Eric, but you also called for Lilly, which is odd."

"The dreams are so life like. They're terrifying, but when I wake, sometimes they fade away too quickly to remember. Eric keeps calling out for me to save him. I can't forget that."

"Do you remember details?" His fingers stroked her arm, sticky with feverish sweat.

"I saw him in the dream. He seemed like his old self, but different. In the dream, he's stronger, grown. There were these things surrounding him. Not Streakers." Jenna paused, tilted her head thinking about how to describe it. "Some new evil. Shadow creatures. They circled him, then engulfed him. He's calling out for help. I yell, *I'm coming for you. I haven't forgotten. I didn't leave you!*"

"What do you do in the dream?"

"Nothing. I kept screaming at him, telling him not to move. But when I finally got close and peered into his eyes, well, he's dead. His eyes scared me more than anything." She shivered. "They held a world full of malevolence. Evil."

"It's only a dream."

"There's this stupid bird too. A crow or a raven." Her fingers twined together in a restless motion. "I think the dream meant something. Maybe Eric's alive."

"Don't go there." Caleb gathered her into his arms. His solid frame should have radiated heat, but it was cool. "You need to eat. That's priority number one. A few days in bed and you've dropped too much weight. You feel skeletal."

As one of the New Race, Caleb survived the pandemic that decimated the world. It hadn't killed him, or turned him, but had not left him unscathed.

"Way to cheer up a girl."

"I want to run and get you food right this moment." His eyes spiraled into crimson orbs. "Are you hungry?"

"Not hungry."

If only blood sustained me like it did Caleb.

Although most of the poor souls killed by the virus returned as Streakers, zombie-like creatures, a few humans had changed in other ways. They weren't quite human but tended not to gut and disembowel people. They survived off the blood of living, breathing creatures, the same as the Streakers. However, they didn't kill humans for their blood.

"Thirsty," she squeaked.

All this talking and thinking is too much. She really was sick. She never got sick.

"Take it slow." He handed her the glass of water again, and she gulped greedily.

A coughing fit ensured, wracking her frail frame.

"What happened to taking it slow?"

She shrugged her shoulders.

Caleb took a long, slow breath. "You have to get better. I'd bear the sun for you. I can't live in this world without you."

Stronger and faster, the New Race healed quicker, but there were many challenges for them. They were unable to venture out into the sun. They had skin blistering so bad, it might lead to their deaths if out in the bright light long enough.

Who could have guessed he'd turn into such a romantic?

"I'm fine," Jenna said. "Or I'll get there in a few days. You don't need to worry about me or baby me."

"There's something else I need to tell you. Something important. I'm not sure you're ready for it, but I don't want anyone else spilling the news."

"Tell me what?" A shiver ran through her.

His hand threading over her tangled, dark-brown hair. "You shouldn't have to find out this way. Lilly's gone." He paused long enough to draw in a breath. "So's Gunnar. The same day we found you with the horses, they disappeared." He rushed through the end of the story. "We believe Gunnar kidnapped her because there's no reason for Lilly to leave."

"Lilly's gone?" she echoed.

2

THREE DAYS PRIOR...

Nostrils flaring, Eric recoiled from the gore around him and the smell of death saturating the air. His heart pumped irregularly, the blood roaring in his ears like a truck accelerating under a bridge.

His glance was quick and furtive. Although the room was murky, blood stains the color of dirty, sunbaked bricks, decorated the floor and walls like abstract paintings.

What had happened here?

Naked, Eric sat covered in blood, somehow alive. He lifted himself. Everything hurt. He held back a scream, gagging as he stared at the carnage that was his body.

Loose chunks of chewed flesh covered muscle.

Someone or something had attempted to gnaw at an elbow. An arm was chewed like someone wanted the bone for dinner. His other hand went to cover the wound, but it was also decorated with missing flesh, half-healed scabs, and open sores.

A snippet of a prior conversation surged back to him. He

and the rest of the survivors had taken refuge in this old movie theater, but the undead he called Streakers had found them.

A fragment of the battle flitted through Eric's mind, making his head pounded. Memories cascaded like a tidal wave.

Dead eyes stared from outside the theater, not nearly as decayed as the rest of the creatures' bodies that, in many cases, lacked clothes. Even with ruined body parts exposed, the Streakers blurred into a mirage of rot and decomposition. The maggoty swarm had assembled along the large glass windows and doors. They were agitated, writhing and swaying against the barrier. His friends, Jenna and Caleb, had tried to herd him to safety in back, but Eric jostled them away. He was nearly sixteen and had to prove himself. One of the zombies focused its lifeless eyes on him.

The window in front of him had shattered. The battle began.

Where were his friend now? Had they all died? Had they abandoned him?

Broken glass crackled. Eric jumped. His heart once again pounded to an irregular surprise that flooded his aching limbs into action.

Frantic, he searched the ground for a weapon but found nothing. He crawled to the corner and waited. There was little else to do.

The thing moved toward him. An atrocity Eric easily smelled from a distance over his own unpleasant scent.

As the figure emerged from the shadows, he recognized a human face covered with tufts of matted hair.

A long, unkempt beard hid already thin lips. More hair, in knotted dread-like tangles ascended from the scalp and cascaded in all directions. Twigs had lodged in the mess and Eric had an absurd vision of a bird springing out of the tangled dreadlocks like an animated character in an old-fashioned Disney movie.

The beast pointed and spoke. "What happened to you?"

Eric's mouth dropped open, but words failed to emerge.

Not undead?

Before him stood a man, not a zombie. Despite being in much better condition than Eric, his appearance indicated life had not been kind, but that's the downside of the zombie apocalypse. Life had not been good to anyone as of late.

A shy teen again, he tried to find a place in the room to conceal his nakedness from the man's critical gaze. Finding nothing to shelter him other than darkness, he squeezed back into the shadows.

"I don't remember what happened or why I'm here alone." His voice was deep and scratchy, sounding a little like he remembered.

The crowbar the stranger brandished in front of him glinted. Eric slipped deeper into the recesses of the darkened, abandoned movie theater until he met a wall.

Not much protection but with these wounds I'll be dead soon anyway.

The stranger took a step closer. In addition to the crowbar, a lethal curved sword hung from the belted loops of torn, stained jeans encasing the man's long legs. A bandana hung loosely around his neck, but Eric noticed scars slithering from side to side. A grungy t-shirt with an ironic smiley face highlighted muscles underneath, corded and ready to deliver a deadly blow if needed.

Would this be how he died? *I'm not ready.*

Eric turned his head in a desperate search for an escape route.

"Wait, kid. Don't get scared. I haven't come across another human for months now, but you look worse than the undead. Shit, are you human?" The man scratched at the untamed beard.

Eric nodded. "Think so. I feel horrible and very human."

The stranger looked like a magician out of a fantasy

novel, but this man was no wizard. There was no magic or spells to ever make this world right again.

Long beats of silence followed, but the nameless man set the crowbar on the ground and slid his backpack off. A rifle was strapped to the top.

"I travel light kid, so don't expect a choice, but you need some clothes. Here's my spare t-shirt and jeans. I don't have extra shoes, but I'm sure you will find some if you live long enough."

"Who are you? What happened to my brother Billy? Where's Jenna and my friends?" Unanswered questions jumbled his frantic thoughts.

The man shrugged, handing over the clothes. They were nearly as disgusting as the articles he wore.

"My name's Abraham, but people used to call me Abe. We appear to be the only two idiots crashing this movie theater tonight. I didn't notice any other humans in my travels. There's definitely no one in this town unless you're a fan of the undead. They're everywhere, so keep your voice down."

"Yesterday?" He scratched at his face. "I think it was yesterday, we were all in this theater. But where's everyone?" He stood, awkward and shaky as he put on the clothes.

"What's your name?"

"Eric." He scowled as he tried to remember the recent days. He ran a hand through his blond hair, but half-way back it stuck to a matted clump of what he hoped was just blood. It was thick and chunky. He pulled the hand away in a quick motion, choking back a gag.

"Sit down, kid. You're in rough shape. I pray you're not changing into one of them. I'd have to put you down then."

"I'd want that."

"What do you remember?"

"There were sixteen of us traveling together." He halted, thought back, noting the details were foggy. "We were heading to this inn in Virginia. It was supposed to be safe, but we got stuck in this movie theater one day. Lots of undead."

"Sixteen. That's a large group these days."

"All good people." Eric felt heat in his cheeks from the unabashed praise, but conversing elevated his mood. "Humans and some of the New Race."

"New Race, huh?"

"Some of the people we travel with are different." He stuttered, stuck on exactly how to explain his former companions. "They don't like the light."

"Been doing this long enough that I've been introduced to them. Call themselves The Others or the New Race." Abe massaged his beard. "They have an allergy to the light. Tend to avoid the sun and are a lot stronger than the average human."

The boy nodded. "The front window shattered and a bunch of Streakers attacked. Me and my brother Billy had to save one of the New Race who ventured too far out and got caught in the sun. Jenna tried to get me to go in the back to safety, but I refused."

Eric's head swarmed with bees. The pain traveled to his spine.

"How'd you get left here?"

"I have no memory of it." He slapped the ground with his hand. "We moved Victor, he's the New Racer I mentioned, into the shadows. I remember being swarmed by the Streakers but after, well, my memory fails."

"I'm making camp here tonight. If you don't plan to eat me in my sleep, you're welcome to join me."

"I wouldn't." Eric mouth drew tight.

"A little humor. Relax, kid. We should move to one of the smaller theaters. I'll patch you up some. I got medical supplies and canned goods. I'm not usually willing to share, but you had a tough day, and it's nice to have company for once. The last interaction I had with humans didn't really end well."

"What happened?"

"I'll tell you more once we're all set in back. Let's hope for an uneventful evening."

Eric trudged after Abe through the ruined remains of the movie theater. The once grand cineplex was now a chaotic wreck. Bits of plaster mingled with the remains of Streakers.

Broken benches and glass covered the floor like the water flooding the beach at high tide. Eric watched his steps, avoiding the largest, sharp fragments, but they found him, pricking his soles.

He must be dead. He just didn't care. He didn't notice the pain.

The two made their way across the large lobby, listening for sounds of the undead. The door of the small, black theater squealed in rebellion when they opened it, noise trumpeting. The door squealed in rebellion when they opened it, noise trumpeting. Both Eric and the man waited anxiously for anything to reveal itself, but nothing ventured forth.

Abe grabbed the blade. "Here."

Eric accepted the offered crowbar and inched his way into the theater. Heavy in his hand, it hurt to lift the weapon. He was thankful when nothing greeted him.

Together, they stepped deeper into the darkness, Abe's flashlight leading the way. Silence. Abe stopped, stood motionless, and waved a hand at Eric.

What now? How much can I take?

A Streaker sashayed from the shadows as if performing *The Nutcracker* on stage. It limped to the front of the slashed screen,

"Not good," the older man whispered.

Eric moved closed to his new traveling companion.

The undead's gaze found him. Panic filled him, and he stepped back.

Dried blood etched a whimsical design on what remained of the zombie's clothing. It shambled forward, stumbling over the wrecked seats in its path, limping forward with unblinking, cataract-filled eyes.

Eric readied himself to fight. The boy's palms were sweaty. His body shook with fear. He glanced at Abe, who now clasped the large curved sword securely in his hands.

The creature charged the older man, ignoring anything blocking its way. Its teeth chomped, the noise loud in the otherwise empty space. Putrid ooze dripped from between its teeth and spots of mold devoured its already gangrenous skin.

Eric watched as Abe stepped in front of him, hoisted the blade, and hacked. The sword sunk into the creature's arm, but the monster did not stop.

The older man stepped away from the slow-moving Streaker and swung at its neck, strokes steady as if he had trained for this battle his whole life.

Bone-bare, hooked fingers reached Abe's face. The head of the creature flew off its decrepit shoulders and onto the carpet. The headless body swayed briefly, then pitched forward.

Greasy, dark blood decorated the stained carpet.

Eric sank to the ground, weak and nauseous.

"Dinner, anyone?" Abe asked.

"It's not funny."

"Sorry kid but being alone for such a long time warped my sense of humor a little bit. You okay?"

"I'll live." He gave the older man a small smile. "How'd you do that?" Even the brief exertion had left him short of breath and in need of a minute to regain his strength.

"Ex-military or rather I was in the military until the world collapsed around me."

The teen grunted, huffed in breath to steady himself and

rose to his feet. He swayed but moved deeper inside the small confines of the theater.

Abe collected body parts.

"Need help?" He wouldn't be able to do much.

"That's the spirit." Abe kicked the corpse. He appeared unfazed from the fight. "I'm good for now. You sit and rest for a couple of moments. That's an order."

"Thanks." He dropped into one of the remaining upright theater chairs.

"Once I rid us of the remains, I'll clean up those wounds and prepare dinner. You hungry?" He didn't wait for a reply. "I got beans or beans."

The teen observed as Abe sealed the door against any new invaders, sheltering the two. The closed door brought a small amount of security, but it wouldn't last long.

"What are you going to do with the body parts?" He rested his head against the seat back."

"I'll venture out into the lobby with them and leave the pieces for the vermin." The older man dropped his supplies and started to move pieces of the Streaker to the entrance. With the body parts assembled, he ventured into the main lobby, hauling the remains.

Eric rose from his seat even though every muscle protested.

"Might as well be useful." He lifted the corpse's head by the sandpapery hair and threw it into the corridor as Abe hauled the remainder of the body out of the room by its legs. The older man returned with additional supplies.

"I stashed my additional gear near the entrance in case I needed to make a quick escape. Always have a back-up plan, Kiddo."

"I don't have any plans. I don't have anything at all."

"Come here and let's see what we can do about that."

With a keen eye, Abe survey his wounds under the dim

light of a battery powered lantern before ripping the last of the shirts, turning them into bandages.

Abe poured clear liquid on his shoulder. The cold fluid burned like battery acid as it dripped down his arm. "Ouch."

"It's just alcohol, boy. I'd say you been through a lot worse. Hold this."

Eric held a strip of cloth as Abe bound another piece around the remaining bits of flesh clinging to Eric's muscle and bone.

"I can't believe you're alive with these wounds and scars everywhere. How'd this happen?" Once done with the bandages, Abe offered Eric the canteen.

"I still don't remember. I'm trying." He steadied his nerves by taking a gulp of water.

Wrapped like a mummy, Eric's stomach growled.

Abe opened a can of beans and split it between them.

"Sorry for the meager meal, but I wasn't expecting guests. I'm here because I was running low on supplies and needed to restock. Pittsfield was the closest town to the latest house I took shelter in, but it was time to move on. I was getting too much attention from the Streakers."

"My group was trying to find a safe place too." He gazed at the older man, trying to gauge a reaction. "There was an inn in rural Virginia someone suggested, and they were headed there. That was the plan."

"Sounds like a smart idea." He scratched at his bird's nest of a beard. "I was on active duty with the Army when the virus broke. My wife and family lived in New Jersey. I lost everyone quick. I didn't even get to tell them goodbye."

"I'm sorry."

"People who made it this long all share the same story these days. No one has any family left."

"I have a twin brother, Billy," he said. "At least I did."

The older man arched an eyebrow. "There weren't any

human remains around the theater. Maybe everyone escaped."

"It's just as likely the Streakers didn't leave anything to be identified."

"Undead don't usually eat bones."

"The other option is Billy, Jenna, and the rest of them left me here."

"Jenna?"

"A friend. They wouldn't leave me here to die?" His voice cracked.

"They're either all dead or left you here to die, Kiddo."

"I'm not sure." He covered his face with his hands to hold back the tears.

ABOUT THE AUTHOR

Lisa Acerbo is a short-story writer, novelist, and former journalist. Her work has been showcased in numerous anthologies such as Asylum, Carnival of Strange Things, and Scary Snippets. Her science fiction stories and story podcasts have appeared in Ripples in Space magazine. Her novels include Twelve Months of Awkward Moments, Wear White to Your Funeral, and Remote. She writes romance under her pen name Dakota Star.

Lisa enjoys teaching high school and is an adjunct at Norwalk Community College and Post University in Connecticut. She is a graduate of the University of Connecticut where she earned a BA in English Education before going on to earn her EdD from the University of Phoenix. When not reading, writing, hiking, drinking coffee or wine (depends on the hour), she spends her time with her husband and two rescue dogs.

Made in the USA
Middletown, DE
03 July 2021

43414205R00159